More Praise for
Ride the Jawbone

"When you read Jim Moore's *Ride the Jawbone*, you have to constantly remind yourself that it's fiction and you haven't slipped into Montana in 1902—One heck of a read." — Craig Johnson, author of *Cold Dish, Hell is Empty*, and other Walt Longmire mysteries.

"Brilliantly using his vast knowledge of law and Montana history, master storyteller Jim Moore plunges the reader into a world of mystery and moral dilemma. Realistic, intriguing, captivating." — Lauri Olsen, author, *Cold Moon Honor* and *Whispers on the Wind*

"The Jawbone railroad binds a community of small towns and ranches populated by quirky people, while a young man is torn between following his father's footsteps into ranching and starting his law practice, his mother's dream. A novel of memorable characters, among them the Jawbone railroad, in an odd corner of Montana history." — Carol Buchanan, author of *God's Lightning Bolt & Gold Under Ice*

"Rich in detail, Jim Moore's novel enlightens readers about the day-to-day labors, cowhands, horses, and equipment involved in ranching in 1902 and the habits and mores of people struggling to exist in the small towns strewn along the rails of the Jawbone. Interspersed in this history is the story of a fascinating murder trial and the young untried attorney who

defends a seemingly indefensible accused. We root for this young protagonist and smile a little at how easily he is distracted by attractive young ladies."
— Joan Bochmann, author of *Absaroka: Where the Anguish of a Soldier Meets the Land of the Crow.*

"A vicious murder. A reprehensible vagrant accused of the crime. A town ready to lynch. A new, untested lawyer trying to save the defendant. A sagacious country judge presiding at an extraordinary trial. Will the jury acquit? The depiction by Jim Moore of action in a one-hundred-year-ago courtroom grabs the reader and won't let go." —Judge Joseph B. Gary

"Jim Moore has brought us a vivid and historical story with Ride the Jawbone. His accurate portrayal of the people and the country bring back to life those interesting people and places along the Jawbone Railroad and the Upper Musselshell Valley in the early days of the last century. It is truly a contribution to the historic literature of the state. Well done!" —Lee Rostad, Montana author and historian

Ride the Jawbone

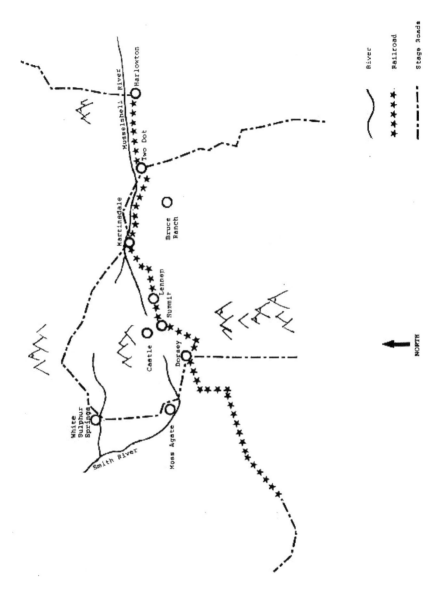

Harlowton
Musselshell River
Two Dot
Martinsdale
Bruce Ranch
Lennep
Summit
Castle
Dorsey
White Sulphur Springs
Smith River
Moss Agate

NORTH

River
Railroad
Stage Roads

Ride the Jawbone

by

Jim Moore

Raven Publishing, Inc. of Montana

Published by **Raven Publishing, Inc.**
P.O. Box 2866, Norris, MT 59745
Info@ravenpublishing.net   www.ravenpublishing.net

Cover art "Jawbone Railroad, Sixteen Mile Canyon"
by R. E. DeCamp (1858 - 1936) 1904, Oil on Canvas
Courtesy of the Montana Historical Society
John Reddy, Photographer 2/99

Jim Moore's photo (back cover) © 2011 Susan Moore
Discussion questions © 2011 Marcia Melton

This novel is a work of fiction. Names, characters, places, and events are the product of the author's imagination or are used fictitiously. Any similarity to any person, place, or event is coincidental. The author has used the real names of three of the ranchers of the area and era, including that of G. R. Wilson, for whom the town of Two Dot and its hotel were named. The stories involving the ranchers are fictitious.

978-0-9827377-3-6

Library of Congress Cataloging-in-Publication Data

Moore, Jim, 1927-
   Ride the Jawbone / by Jim Moore.
      p. cm.
   ISBN 978-0-9827377-3-6 (alk. paper)
   1. Lawyers--Montana--Fiction. 2. Attorney and client--Fiction.
3. Trials (Murder)--Fiction. 4. Women--Crimes against--Fiction.
5. Ranch life--Montana--Fiction. 6. Montana--Fiction. I. Title.
   PS3613.O5626R53 2011
   813'.6--dc22

                                        2011000109

For Kay
for all the years

April 20th, 1902

It was noseless Pete that found her.
The magpies had found her first.
They left her with only one eye.

May 2nd, Morning

T. C. Bruce cringed at the endless yammering of the man three seats behind him.

"He cut her guts out. That's the way I heard it." The drummer continued his harangue to the hung-over cowpuncher seated across the aisle, ignoring the competing noise made by the small child at the other end of the railcar.

The sodden man of the range shifted in the uncomfortable seat to face the window. He glanced over his shoulder at the garrulous peddler of trade goods before flopping his head back against the side of the car. Then he closed his eyes and mumbled, "What you heard and what's right probably ain't the same."

The drummer scooted the satchel of samples to make room for his feet and peered at the passing terrain. After a moment he turned back to look at the somnolent figure on the other side of the car and growled, "Well, he damn well killed her, we know that much for sure."

The hung-over one scowled and rubbed at his forehead as though to relieve pain before pulling his hat over his eyes. "The sheriff and the county attorney can sort that out. It ain't none of my business."

"They got him in jail waiting for a trial." The drummer cackled, "Maybe they'll get me on the jury. I'll sure as hell vote to hang him."

Without responding, the cowpoke slumped farther down in his seat. He groaned in apparent agony. Too much liquor the night before.

The drummer, who'd babbled almost continuously since the train left Harlowton, fell silent. Seeming resigned to the lack of audience, he turned to stare at the world passing by as the train traveled westward through the Musselshell River valley. The sound of the sodden man's sonorous snoring replaced the prattle of the drummer.

T. C. turned toward the front of the car where a more vexatious, sound continued unabated.

The boy's high-pitched scream, as he ran down the aisle, almost drowned the sound of the cars clattering over the track. The running and the screaming had persisted since T. C. boarded the train at Two Dot. The lad, about six years old, would not stay in a seat as his mother begged him to do. She sat five rows ahead of T. C., holding a baby that cried without stop. Nothing the young mother tried relieved the baby's agony. Fear that her children were bothering the other passengers seemed to cause her even more distress.

Two women passengers—one old and one young—were seated two rows in front of T. C. on the other side of the aisle. They might have been mother and daughter, although their facial appearance and mannerisms indicated otherwise. The older woman was short, plump and smiley. The younger, taller than her companion, had a straight, mannish body, an attractive face, but a severe countenance.

+++++++++++

T. C. had boarded the train, a funnel-stacked steamer pulling the coal car, two passenger cars, and a freight car, at Two Dot. The engine strained to pull its load, even though the grade was slight and the cars nearly empty. Heavy black smoke and burning cinders belched from the stack. The worn seats in the passenger cars were patterned with stains and tears. T. C. counted himself lucky to find an empty seat that didn't have a spring pushing up sharply against the fabric.

After a spell of cold, rainy weather, the day was very warm and the air inside the car was stuffy. T. C. guessed that the uncomfortable heat aggravated whatever was causing the crying baby's anguish. Shortly after the train had pulled out of Two Dot, the conductor entered the car to make his rounds. He was a talkative, rotund old fellow who seemed to enjoy visiting with people. He wandered along the aisle searching for conversation. Tipping his hat politely to the ladies he asked, "Is this your first ride on the Jawbone?" The younger of the two glanced at him briefly, looked straight ahead, and clutched her purse tightly in her lap.

The older one smiled. "Yes. It's our first chance to enjoy the pleasure of this railroad." She explained that they had ridden the stage from Lewistown to Harlowton, where they boarded the train. "We're going to visit my cousin, Willard Morton, at his ranch near Martinsdale." She added that her traveling companion, whom she called Sarah, was a schoolteacher, hoping to secure a position at one of the schools in the valley.

Sarah glanced at the conductor and asked, "Why do they call it the Jawbone? Isn't it really the Montana Railroad?"

"This railroad? Well, ma'am, old man Harlow had the idea to build this thing but he just didn't have the money. He wouldn't let that stop him, though." He chuckled. "It's amazing. Harlow just talked the landowners along the right of way into giving him the land for the tracks. He talked steel mills out of rails and lumber mills out of wood for ties. He talked storekeepers out of the goods that he needed. Old Harlow just talked this railroad into existence. He built it on jawbone, so no one calls this the Montana Railroad. Everyone just calls it the Jawbone." Lowering his voice he added wryly, "I was told I'd get a better wage than I had on the Northern Pacific," Shaking his head, he smiled at Sarah.

The conductor was a stranger to T. C. With a face bloated and red, it was obvious that the fellow liked his whiskey.

On all of the railroads, the conductors collected fares from the passengers. They were trusted to turn the receipts over to the station agent at the end of each run. When they felt that the pay they received was insufficient, they increased their salary by keeping some of the money for themselves. In deciding what was a fair split, it was said that they threw the gathered fares up in the air, reasoning that the amount that stuck to the ceiling belonged to the railroad, while the money that came back down belonged to the conductor. T. C. was willing to bet that he had lost his job on the N. P. by getting greedy with the fares.

While the conductor rambled on to the women, the small boy ran down the aisle with all the abandon of childhood and collided with the man's legs. The demeanor of the conductor changed from pleasant to rage in an instant. He leaned down and yelled, "Get back to your seat and stay there!"

The little boy backed away, looked up at the man in the uniform for a moment, and then stepped forward and kicked him in the shins.

The conductor immediately drew back his arm to retaliate. Before he could, Sarah reached out and pulled the boy close to her.

"He's only a child, sir. He didn't mean to cause any harm." Her voice was firm.

Ride the Jawbone

T. C., who'd been gazing with interest at Sarah's attractive face, felt his admiration grow. If she were to be teaching in a lonesome school some place along the river, there might come a time when she would welcome company.

The conductor scowled, red faced and angry, as he backed away. He turned and started toward the rear of the car, mumbling to T. C. as he went by, "That brat needs a good whipping."

The boy soon escaped from Sarah's arms and ran to his mother who continued the struggle to keep her baby quiet. She scolded him some more, then looked over her shoulder, and mouthed a "Thank you," to Sarah. The boy responded to her scolding by crossing the aisle. He looked in the direction the conductor had gone, and then jumped on the cushion of the seat.

"Jacob, please!" the mother begged, and immediately turned her attention back to the baby. She rocked her child in her arms, but the crying continued. She attempted to walk up and down the aisle but the swaying of the train made that task difficult. The mother's face was damp with perspiration, and a limp wisp of hair hung over her spectacles. As she walked past T. C., he smelled a sour odor from her clothing. The boy continued to run about the railroad car despite her pleading and scolding. The baby began to wail again. The mother returned to her seat to rock and coo to her infant. When the train slowed for the next station, the baby stopped its fierce cries and, for a while, merely choked out small sobs.

When the conductor announced the Martinsdale stop, the drummer grabbed his satchel and rushed to be first off the train. The two women also gathered their belongings to leave. T. C. recognized Mr. Morton waiting on the platform. When the women descended from the car, he greeted them with his hat in hand and a big smile and bowed slightly from the waist. His cousin chose a less formal approach. She gathered him up in a hug that left him gasping and flustered.

Sarah, on the other hand, remained distant. Mr. Morton lifted their baggage onto the buckboard and helped the ladies up to the seat. As they drove away, T. C. realized that Sarah had never changed her facial expression from the time he first saw her till the last. He wondered if she ever smiled.

Of the crowd of people gathered to watch the train come and go, only Silas Grant and his wife got on. Short, stooped, and old, both were dressed almost entirely in black.

Mr. Grant led the way down the aisle between the seats. As they passed T. C., the old gentleman nodded in recognition and asked, "How is your father, young man?" When T. C. replied that his father was in good health, the man nodded again then turned his attention to his wife. He offered her the seat next to the window, but she chose to sit on the aisle. Mrs. Grant had a face like a prune, and the creases deepened when she was displeased. She exhibited much displeasure despite the efforts of her husband to make her comfortable.

As soon as the train started to move again, the baby resumed its crying. The mother rocked and sang in an effort to quiet the child. Jacob ran by the Grants, hitting Mrs. Grant's purse that was lying on her lap but protruding slightly into the aisle. She gave him a wicked look as he scurried to the end of the car, only to turn and run back again. T. C. wondered how long Mrs. Grant could stand the baby's noise and boy's activity. They had not gone far when he found out.

The old woman rose from her seat and walked to where mother and baby were swaying back and forth with the motion of the train. The wrinkles in Mrs. Grant's face relaxed, and her voice was kind. "Let me hold the little one for a while so you can have some rest." She took the crying infant into her arms and sat next to the mother.

The mother sighed in relief, slumped down in the seat, and poured out her troubles to Mrs. Grant. "I've been staying with my mother-in-law while Jake finds us a place to live. He wrote that he has a job near Lennep and has been looking for a house. The baby's been sick, and Jacob's been naughty. Jake's mother has been just awful. I know the children bothered her, but I did my best to keep them quiet. She screamed at them constantly. And at me. I tried to help with the housework, but everything I did seemed to make her angry. I'm so glad to get away, but the baby's sick, and I don't know what to do."

Mrs. Grant looked at her, and a smile changed the wrinkles on her face. With one hand she patted the mother on the knee and then reached deep into her purse and took out a small silver spoon. She put the handle of the spoon into the baby's mouth and began to rub it gently along the bottom gum. There was resistance at first, and the cries grew louder but soon diminished and finally ceased.

Ride the Jawbone

In the near silence that followed, the mother relaxed against the side of the car and closed her eyes. But Jacob seemed determined to keep it from lasting. His screams grew louder as he ran along the aisle. Again, his exhausted mother attempted to control him by asking and then scolding. Weary and dejected, she got up from her seat to pull him down, but he kicked at her shin just as he had done to the conductor. Climbing into the seat across from the one in which Mrs. Grant was holding the baby, he managed to jerk the window open.

For a moment, the breeze that flowed into the car felt refreshing to the passengers. But then a gust of wind blew cinders from the smokestack directly into the face of old Mr. Grant. The poor man sputtered and brushed at his eyes as T. C. rushed forward to close the window.

The distraught mother hadn't moved since the boy kicked her. "Oh Jacob!" she wailed, fell back into her seat and burst into great racking sobs. The baby began to cry again.

It was all too much for T. C. He grabbed the boy by the hand and said, "Come on, Jacob. Let's go watch for deer."

Jacob looked wary, but T. C. gripped his hand firmly. He led him down the aisle toward the rear door and out onto the platform between the two passenger cars. He began pointing to things of interest as they passed by. "There's the Comb Butte. They call it that because it looks like the comb on a rooster. And back there are the Crazy Mountains."

Jacob looked up at T. C. "Why do they call them that?"

"Well, the Indians had a name for them that meant mad—meaning angry. They thought the mountains were angry because the clouds and wind were always swirling around them. The white men got it wrong and thought the Indian word meant crazy—like loco—and so they called the mountains Crazy." T. C. told him the names of the ranches they passed and showed him where buffalo had created depressions, called wallows, in the ground.

Jacob looked down at the creek when the tracks crossed a bridge. "Are there any fish in that creek?"

"The fishing's good in the North Fork and all the little streams that run into it. Your father can take you fishing, once you get settled."

The boy dropped his eyes and muttered, "He don't have time for that."

T. C. kept up the discussion until the train slowed for the next station. Then he took the boy back to a seat near his mother and sat with him keeping him quiet until the train stopped at the depot.

The young mother gathered her belongings and reached for the baby. Mrs. Grant gave it up gently and put the spoon back in her purse. The mother thanked her over and over again, then stood with the baby on one arm and reached for one of the bags resting on the seat behind her. T. C. waved her forward. He gathered the bags, a large one in each hand and a small one tucked under his arm. She walked down the aisle and out onto the station platform clutching the baby close to her breast and leading Jacob by the hand. T. C. put her bags on the ground and stepped back into the railcar. He waved to acknowledge her thanks.

T. C. and Mrs. Grant both watched to see if her husband was there to greet them. A dirty, unshaven man in rough clothing walked up to her, picked up her bags, and started down the street leaving her to trail behind. Once he looked back and snarled at the boy. Jacob grabbed his mother's skirt and walked as close to her as possible.

T. C. wondered if she would be any better off with her husband than she had been with her mother-in-law. He would probably take her to a filthy shack, deposit her bags on the floor, and demand that she cook a meal for him first thing—no matter that the baby was sick and that she was exhausted. T. C. turned to look at Mrs. Grant and found the wrinkles of displeasure that covered her face were deeper and more pronounced than ever. As she passed him on the way to her seat, she muttered, "God, be merciful."

Six more travelers got on the car, some carrying bundles. T. C. surmised that they had come down the creek from the town of Castle and were on their way out of the country. The hung-over cowpuncher roused from his slumber and staggered off the car just before it began to roll again.

When the new passengers were seated, the conductor walked the aisle from front to rear, collecting fares. He stopped between the Grants and T. C. "They found her body about a half mile west of Summit, you know. When we get to the place, I'll point it out to you. I suppose you've already heard they have old Loco in jail for the murder."

The look of disgust on Mrs. Grant's face indicated that she did not want to hear about a murderer. Wrinkles crowded together until it appeared that her eyes, nose and mouth were all in one place. She returned to the task of cleaning the cinders off her husband's face with a handkerchief she had wetted with spit. Mr. Grant moved his wife's hand and said, "Well, they'll hang Loco, and that'll be the end of it."

The engine worked harder, and the smoke and cinders from the stack became blacker and thicker as it struggled up the grade to Summit. T. C. listened to the clickety-clack of the wheels and thought about the creation of the Jawbone. It began because of the mines at Castle. The lead and silver ore had to be hauled by wagon to the Northern Pacific Railroad at Livingston, a trip of over fifty miles.

Richard Harlow concluded that there was money to be made through the construction of a railroad that would replace the wagons. The work that began at the town of Lombard on the Northern Pacific was eventually completed eastward to Leadboro, below the town of Castle. A year after the railroad reached Leadboro the price of lead and silver collapsed. Within another year most of the mines stopped producing ore. Harlow had a railroad, but nothing for it to haul.

Herds of cattle and sheep roamed the open ranges of a broad valley down the Mussellshell River from Castle. Harlow reasoned that the ranchers needed a way to bring supplies in and haul their livestock out. The decision made, Harlow extended the track from the town of Summit—using more jawbone to get it done—to Lennep, to Martinsdale, to Two Dot and, finally, to his namesake, Harlowton.

Even though the trains seldom ran on time, and the passenger cars were old and not very comfortable, it was better than traveling by horseback, wagon, or stage. T. C. rested against the seat back, thankful that Harlow had dreamed his dream.

Summit sat on top of a divide between the Smith and Musselshell rivers. Because it had existed longer than the towns farther east, it had an appearance of permanence. In addition to the depot, store, church, boarding house, blacksmith shop, and saloon, there were several dwelling houses. All were on the north and faced the roadway that ran parallel to the track.

The stop at Summit was short. None of the passengers got off. Three got on. Two of them appeared to be unemployed miners who had spent more time in the saloon than was wise. The aroma that engulfed them indicated that they were not devotees of the bath. The third new passenger was female, coarse, and fat. T. C. surmised that she was a lady of the evening heading for greener pastures.

The grade leading up to Summit from the east was relatively gradual, but it sloped steeply down the other side. For that reason, the track went west only a few hundred yards and then turned south on a long traverse cut into the side of the mountain. Fills of earth held the grade where it crossed coulees carved by rainwater and snow melt. When the train left Summit, T. C. rode on the platform between the cars where he found it cooler and more pleasant. The rear wall of the car sheltered him from the cinders that blew from the smokestack. The conductor found him as the train crossed the first of several coulees. He nudged T. C. and pointed. "Pete found her body down there. That's where they picked her up and hauled her back to Summit."

Where the track crossed the coulee there was no growth other than sagebrush. Farther down, however, was a stand of willows and two cottonwood trees. It was toward this foliage that the conductor pointed. The coulee had the appearance of a bowl partially surrounded by brush. T. C. figured there must be a water source where the willows and the trees grew.

The conductor was enjoying himself. "You live at Two Dot, don't you? What do you know about her?"

"I just know that she called herself Penelope Burke," T. C. said without looking at the other man. He was not inclined to get into a discussion with the old gent about the dead woman or anything else.

The conductor grunted, shot the young man a look of disgust and took his leave into the railcar.

T. C. rode the rest of the way to Dorsey on the platform, enjoying the panorama of the upper Smith River valley as it stretched toward the Big Belt Mountains in the distance.

May 2nd, Afternoon

Dorsey sat at a crossroads where the train depot also served as the stage station. The stage to The Springs, as most people called the county seat, began its run as soon as the train passengers could finish lunch, so that they could arrive in time for the evening repast.

Ride the Jawbone

T. C. found a stool at the counter and ordered his food. Tea made from cold spring water and available in large quantities made the hot, greasy food palatable. Out of the rumble of voices in the crowded room, a few clear words could be heard. The general conversation concerned the death of Penelope Burke.

The stage pulled up to the north side of the depot as T. C. finished his victuals. The stage driver, an old hand known to the locals as Hargo, poked his head through the door and hollered, "Stage out."

The stage itself was not the heavy, comfortable kind found on longer overland runs. Relatively light, it could be pulled by four horses rather than six. The cab's two seats faced each other and were just wide enough for three people to sit, side by side.

The two down-on-their-luck miners from Castle were the first to the stage and seemed intent on securing a seat in the cab. Hargo reached the door before they could open it and directed them to step aside. He ushered Silas and Mrs. Grant into the relative comfort of the cab. Next, he directed the coarse woman from Castle to join the Grants. She was careful to sit across and as far from Mrs. Grant as the structure would allow. Two older women, whom T. C. recognized as the wives of businessmen from The Springs, were the next to receive Hargo's help up the step into the stage. The first sat next to Mrs. Grant. The second had no choice but share a seat with the gross woman. She sat as far to the other end of the bench as she could. T. C. watched with some amusement until Hargo motioned him to load up.

T. C. eased by the merchant's wife and sat in the middle of the seat facing forward. The stench of cheap perfume wafting from his fleshy seat companion convinced him that the odor of the miners could not have been much worse. The miners crawled onto the top of the stage to sit with Hargo. The stagehand started the team slowly and then moved them into a brisk trot.

What little wind there was came through the window openings on the left side of the cab—the side on which the poor creature who reeked of perfume was sitting. That odor, together with the swaying of the cab, soon moved the lady on T. C.'s right to nausea. She clasped a handkerchief over her nose and mouth and rested one hand over her stomach. The stage rattled and bumped along with the passengers riding in stubborn silence. As time passed, T. C. became somewhat accustomed to the foul air, and the merchant's wife seemed less distressed. She did, however, hold her handkerchief to her face the entire trip to Moss Agate.

The stage stop at Moss Agate marked the halfway point in the twenty-mile trip from Dorsey to White Sulphur Springs. It consisted of a long, low log cabin that served as the attendant's home as well as a place where travelers could be fed. On one end there were two small rooms, each with one bed and nothing more. A traveler caught there at nightfall could rent sleeping space and console himself that it at least provided protection from the elements. There was a barn and an extensive set of corrals to handle the horses that made up the relief teams for the stages. The South Fork of the Smith River that flanked the stage stop was ordinarily no more than a small stream, but warm weather of the past few days had hastened the snowmelt in the mountains and water flooded the corrals and surrounded the stage station itself.

Hargo stopped the stage on high ground away from the buildings and invited the passengers to get out and stretch. The two merchants' wives scrambled to be first out the door, quickly followed by Mrs. Grant and her faithful Silas. T. C., although anxious to escape the rank odor that permeated the interior of the cab, moved across the aisle to the seat on the other side and motioned the problem passenger to go ahead.

The two women walked off a distance to speak privately. T. C. concluded from their gestures that at least one of them needed to get to the privy, located on the far side of the station and now standing in a considerable amount of water. When no one offered the ladies a solution, they seemed resigned to suffer the remainder of the ride into The Springs.

The attendant sloshed through the flood to exchange fresh horses for the ones that had trotted the ten miles from Dorsey. With Hargo's cry, "Stage out," his passengers loaded as before and the journey began anew.

The two-tracked road ran northward, parallel to the river on high ground above the floodwaters. Not far from Moss Agate, the river turned westward and the road crossed a bridge. Hargo halted the horses to survey the scene. The high water had not overtopped the bridge but was up to the log stringers that supported it. He asked the miners to check the bridge abutments to see if they were sound.

The two merchants' wives burst from the cab and hastened for a grove of trees that stood a short distance to the west. The miners tramped across the bridge, jumped up and down on it, crawled on their hands and knees to look under it at each end, and reported to Hargo that it was safe to cross. The ladies strolled back at a more leisurely pace. When all were loaded again, Hargo spoke to the horses and headed them toward the bridge. Each horse dropped an ear and looked carefully at the edge of the bridge and the water so close to their hooves. The four animals crowded together against the tongue but pulled the stage across without incident and trotted easily once more in the direction of town.

About the time the group seemed at ease, the coarse woman's head dropped against T. C.'s shoulder as she fell into a deep sleep. The scent of her hair so close to his nose was more than he could bear. He reached up and carefully leaned her head against the back of the cab and then wiped his hands along his trouser legs. The woman remained in the position she had been placed. The swaying of the cab caused her head to roll from side to side, as though loosely attached at the neck. Her jaw slackened and dropped open and she began to snore. The sound, a gentle sigh as she inhaled and a rhythmic rumble as she exhaled, interrupted the chattering of the ladies and Mrs. Grant's face reacquired its wrinkles. Silas patted her arm, and T. C. began to wish he had taken advantage of the trees back at the bridge.

So the little group rode into White Sulphur Springs, the finest city in central Montana—population seven hundred twenty four.

May 2nd, Evening

T. C. rapped on the doorjamb once, pulled the screen door open, and walked into the kitchen. His mother, facing the kitchen range, looked over her shoulder at him and smiled a very small smile.

"Am I in time for supper, Mother?" The aroma wafting from the stove reminded him how hungry he was for his mother's cooking.

"Of course you're in time for supper, Thad, but you might have let

13

us know you were coming." Her reply was brisk. "The food will be on the table in a few minutes. Go tell your father you're here."

As he watched his mother turn back to her work, T. C. felt the urge to walk around the table and hug her, but displays of affection did not come easily to her, so he let it pass. She had raised him, given him care and comfort when he was small, but had not attempted to hold him close since he was about ten years old.

It occurred to T. C. that he couldn't remember if he had ever called his mother "Mama." Nor could he remember hearing his father call her "Dear." Her name was Prudence, but his father referred to her as "Mrs. Bruce" when speaking of her outside their home. At home, he called her "Boss."

T. C. found his father seated in his usual chair; left leg propped up on a low stool, reading the latest edition of the weekly newspaper.

"Well, Thad, since you're here at suppertime, the train must have run on time today." His father's welcoming smile held more warmth than that of his wife.

"Yes, Papa. It arrived at Two Dot on schedule and made it all the way to Dorsey without breaking down. It even left Dorsey for Lombard on time."

"Maybe Harlow'll make that railroad reliable yet." The older man motioned to a chair and added, "Sit yourself down and tell me how things are at the ranch. With the rains and warm weather, the grass should be coming good. What about the hay? Has the creek been running enough water to irrigate?"

"Only enough to keep two ditches going until the last couple of days. This hot weather brought high water, and Seth had the boys spreading the water over the whole meadow bottom when I left. The grass is good the entire length of the Musselshell. The roundup wagon will leave about the first of June."

Mr. Bruce nodded. "Yes, Hank Freezer told me that. Seth has crew enough to send along so we carry our part of the load?"

"The same men as last year, with Chappy in charge." When his father shifted around in his chair obviously seeking comfort, T. C. asked, "How's your leg, Papa?"

His father wiggled the toes on his left foot and lifted his leg off the stool. He didn't bend the knee that had been wounded when he fought

14

with Confederate Army in the battle at Missionary Ridge. His leg had not been a problem for the first few years in Montana, where he settled immediately after the war. Hard work at a sawmill, cutting planks for the miners in Confederate Gulch, earned him enough money to acquire cattle to run on holdings along the Smith River. Later he moved them to the Musselshell valley where the wind blew the ranges bare of snow in the winter months

For a while, after the Musselshell Roundup was organized, he rode with the rest of the livestock owners, but as time went by, his leg stiffened, and the pain from riding and ranch work became unbearable. About ten years ago, resigned to the fact that he could no longer handle the ranch operation, he hired Seth Black as manager, built the house in White Sulphur Springs, and moved his family to town. T. C. remembered how frightening it was to leave a tiny log one-room school for the larger one in The Springs.

His father's voice jerked him back from his musings. "The leg isn't any better but it doesn't seem to be getting any worse, so I can't complain." He returned to the discussion of ranch matters. "Hank thinks the Mussellshell Roundup will only run for another year or two. Even the lower river is getting fenced up. We can probably run steers on the open range in the Lower Country for a few years before we have to keep them at home. We have keep expanding the irrigation to produce more feed. How's the ditch work coming?"

"The ditches have been extended about as far as they can go on the west side of the creek. Seth has men extending the lower ditch on the east side. They should have it far enough for use during the high water in June. Much farther, and we'll be getting onto land used by George O'Toole."

"Hate to do that, even though he hasn't filed on it." The older man chuckled. "George is a good Irishman and a good friend, but never too ambitious. We don't want to move in on his operation. When you go back, tell Seth not to go too far with the ditch."

Mrs. Bruce stood in the doorway and summoned the men to eat with a single word, "Come."

The table in the middle of the kitchen was set for three. Mr. Bruce took his accustomed chair facing the window that looked out onto the back yard. Mrs. Bruce sat directly across from him. T. C. sat in the chair facing the big coal range, still glowing with the heat needed to cook the evening repast. Even though the day had been hot and the kitchen almost insufferably warm, the men expected a full meal. Mrs. Bruce would not think of depriving them. The menu was the one Mr. Bruce always expected—beef steak fried to a crisp, boiled potatoes, canned beans, and dried peaches that had been stewed.

T. C. waited as his mother quietly recited the prayer he had heard as a child. His father was not particularly religious but always acknowledged his wife's need for spirituality by bowing his head as she prayed. They ate in silence until Mrs. Bruce carried a fresh chocolate cake to the table to supplement the dried peaches.

Mr. Bruce picked up the conversation where it had ended before the eating began. "We should be able to run at least seven hundred cows at home under fence, and we can probably continue to run their yearling and two-year-old offspring on the range east of the big bend of the Mussellshell until they're ready to ship. Keeping all of the cows at home will be more expensive than running them on the open range, but we should have a much better calving percentage. We can use better bulls and produce better calves. We've got to take every opportunity to acquire land close to home. It won't be long before there won't be any grass to use except the grass we own."

T. C. had heard all of this before, and he knew it was repeated for his edification. His father wanted him to assume the management of the ranch as soon as he was willing. Seth Black knew this and had asked T. C. when he intended to take over. T. C. just wasn't sure he was ready for the responsibility.

"You go and smoke your cigar, Papa," T. C. said. "I'll dry the dishes for Mother."

He carried the dishes from the table. His mother poured hot water from the teakettle into two large pans, carving soap flakes from a bar of homemade soap into one of them. She washed the dishes and put them into the rinse water. As T. C. dried with a towel made from a flour sack, his mother finally asked the question he knew was coming.

"What of your profession, Thad? There's a fine opportunity here in town. Or, if you'd rather, in one of the new towns on the Mussellshell. With the railroad, all of the towns will grow rapidly."

"I'm thinking about it, Mother," he replied. She merely looked down and said no more. The truth was he had been unable to reach any decision about what he wanted to do with his life. For the moment, escape lay in the hot springs that had given the town its name.

"If I can have a towel, Mother, I think I'll go down to the springs and bathe. The ride from Two Dot was hot and dirty."

"Take some clean underclothes and a clean shirt, and don't forget to wash your hair." He was her only child and would remain a child to her as long as she lived.

The springs hadn't changed since T. C.'s last visit. Hot water flowed into a large pool formed of rough concrete, with a stone bathhouse adjacent to it. A high board fence with a single gate for an entrance surrounded the pool. There were dressing rooms in the bathhouse, one for women and one for men. The proprietor of the springs and pool had an office in the front of the bathhouse, and those who wished to take the waters paid twenty-five cents for the privilege.

Saturday night was the busiest time. By custom, only men swam on Saturday night when cowboys, ranch hands and sheepherders came to town. They always stopped first at the springs. Their next stop was a saloon. Rumors existed of businessmen cavorting in the pool late at night with ladies of the evening. T. C. thought of his odoriferous seat mate on the ride from Dorsey and doubted anyone would find excitement by a swim in the nude with her.

On this Wednesday night, T. C. had the pool to himself except for two boys, about eight years of age. They paused in their play to stare as he locked the gate behind him. When he nodded a greeting, they went back to jumping into the water, arms wrapped around their knees, in an effort to make as big a splash as possible. T. C. took advantage of the absence of any women to bathe without a suit.

The secret when washing was to apply the soap near to the outlet and then move toward the inflow to rinse the soap off without polluting the whole pool. After the soaping and rinsing were complete, T. C. swam the length of the pool several times. Clean and refreshed, he dressed in the clean shirt and underclothes his mother had provided. He used a small wire carpet beater that hung on the wall to whip the dust out of his pants and coat.

Fully dressed, T. C. began a leisurely stroll back to his parents' home. Half a block along the boardwalk, two young women ambled toward him. He assumed from their approving glances that his attire made the proper impression. At twenty-three years of age, T. C. Bruce was six feet tall, spare of frame but broad in the shoulders. He had carefully selected the clothes he wore, and made sure they fit perfectly. His greatcoat was chocolate brown, rather than the usual black, and his trousers were fawn colored. The colors complemented his dark brown hair and hazel eyes. The cravat at his throat was the color of gold, and he wore his flat brimmed hat cocked slightly to the right. This sartorial splendor was more likely to be found in the large city where he had learned to enjoy fine clothing.

He doffed his hat to the young matrons and gave them his warmest smile. They smiled and spoke in unison, "Good evening, T. C."

Thaddeus Cassius Bruce II, son of one of Montana's prominent ranchers and a newly anointed lawyer, intended to enjoy his life to the fullest on this beautiful day, May 2, 1902 and every day of the year.

May 3rd

After breakfast and helping with the morning chores, T. C. changed out of his work clothes to others more suitable for a walk to the general store for shaving supplies. The real reason for his trip to town was Mr. Spencer's niece, a young lady who had recently arrived from the east. Miss Spencer was said to be clerking in the store.

As he shared some final words with his father and mother, a sharp knock came from the seldom-used front door. Before his parents could move, T. C. made his way down the hall to the front entry where he found Sheriff Archibald Shea standing on the step. The appearance of the sheriff—tall, muscular and gruff—gave T. C. something of a start. He still remembered when, as a small child, he had been caught throwing snowballs at the wall of the church rectory. It was fun to watch the snow splatter, and he didn't see any harm in it, but the parson inside didn't like the noise. The sheriff had dragged T. C. home by his ear and handed him over to his parents. His punishment was to clean the parson's stable each day for a month. It was hard, smelly work.

Shaking off the old memory, he invited the sheriff in for a cup of coffee. After a moment's hesitation, Shea followed T. C. to the kitchen.

Ride the Jawbone

Mrs. Bruce was already pouring black coffee into a large mug. Mr. Bruce made a half-hearted attempt to rise from his chair, then waved the sheriff to an empty seat at the end of the table.

"What're you here to arrest me for this time, Archie? You know I'm too old and crippled to cause much trouble."

The sheriff grinned as he took the proffered cup and nodded his thanks to Mrs. Bruce. "I haven't anything on you this time, Thad, but don't get too careless. This time, I'm after your son." He took a sip of coffee and looked sideways at T. C. "Judge Henry told me to bring you to his office right away. He said it was important."

Mr. Bruce snorted. "What's old Jonas want with T. C.? Does he need someone to teach him the law?" Jonas Henry and Thad Bruce played pitch at the Stockman Saloon whenever the Judge was in town. Neither of them touched any alcohol, but the loser was obligated to buy coffee. The friendly rivalry was well known in the community.

"I don't know what he wants. I was just told to come up here, get T. C., and take him to the courthouse."

T. C. nodded at the sheriff's remark. "Well, I'm on my way downtown anyway, so I can stop at the judge's office as I go by. Finish your coffee, Sheriff. I'll go find out what's up." But the sheriff climbed to his feet, thanked Mrs. Bruce, and followed T. C. out the door.

Judge Henry's chambers were on the second floor of the courthouse. T. C. had learned in his short period of clerkship in a big city law office that it was always best to talk to the clerk of court before approaching the judge. This clerk was a crotchety old fellow, generally liked in the community. His name was Horatio Albers, but the locals always called him Hakes. When T. C. inquired if the judge was available, Hakes gave a curt nod toward the door of the judge's office. At the door, T. C. looked back to see if the sheriff was still with him. The sheriff leaned upon the clerk's counter top and made no move to accompany the younger man. T. C. knocked, heard a muted "Come in," and entered.

The chamber was much smaller than the one T. C. had seen while clerking in St. Paul. It had a single window overlooking the street. Bookshelves along the side held the Montana Codes and the Legislative Session Laws. Judge Henry sat behind a desk that seemed too large for the room. It was covered with court files, loose legal briefs, and three open volumes of the Montana Reports.

19

The judge was also a veteran of the Great War. He had fought on the Union side. He was of medium height and weight with a rather slight frame and a growing paunch. His thick, snow white hair framed his kindly, round, slightly wrinkled face. He smiled warmly and invited T. C. to sit in the only other chair.

"Nice to see you again, T. C. The last time you were here, you were still in law school. I understand you clerked at one of the larger firms in Saint Paul. But now you're home. Will you practice here in town? Or in Two Dot?"

"I was only admitted to the bar a month ago. I haven't decided what to do. As you probably know, my father thinks I should concentrate on the ranch."

"Well, your father has his reasons. But you're a lawyer, and you've just told me that you're admitted to practice law in this state. You're about to begin your practice." T. C. wondered what the Judge meant.

"You must know about the murder of the Burke woman and that they have old Loco—I guess his real name is Lawrence Silverman—in jail." The judge shuffled some papers on the desk. "The reason I say I think his name is Lawrence Silverman is because he refused to talk when he was brought before me on arraignment." He stopped shuffling the papers and sat back in his chair again. "Here's the problem. Loco has no money and no friends. He won't talk to the sheriff or anyone else. He's charged with first-degree murder, and he doesn't have a lawyer to represent him."

T. C., beginning to feel uneasy, inhaled to make his response, but the judge continued before he could get a word in.

"There's nothing in the law that I know of that says a man must have a lawyer when he's charged with a crime. If he chooses not to, so be it. If he can't afford a lawyer, our society lets the poor devil suffer the consequences of his penury. Most of the time, it's not too much of a problem, because most of the time, the crime is small and so is the punishment. And most of the time, the guilt is clear. But when the punishment is hanging, it simply isn't proper, in my view, to lead such a man into the courtroom without any legal representation and subject him to the tender mercies of the county attorney. Of course, any county attorney can get a conviction under those circumstances. But will justice have been served? I think not."

Ride the Jawbone

T. C. got his chance to speak. "Well, this isn't the first time that someone charged with a crime has refused or couldn't afford a lawyer, is it? Surely the Supreme Court has given some guidance to trial judges when that happens."

"The Montana Supreme Court is like all the other appellate courts. It takes the position that the Constitution only says an accused person can't be prevented from having an attorney to represent him. It doesn't say having such an attorney is a matter of right. So, anyone charged with a crime who can't pay for a lawyer or find one who will represent him for free, will almost certainly be convicted. As I said, in most instances the one accused is clearly guilty. That may be the case with Loco. But if he's not, and if he's convicted only because he didn't have anyone to represent him, his hanging will be the worst kind of injustice."

"I take it he hasn't attempted to get someone to help him out?"

The judge shook his head. "He won't talk to anyone. Hasn't even asked to go to the privy. The deputy just takes him there from time to time."

"Well, there's an experienced lawyer in town besides the county attorney. What about Justin Potts? Have you asked him to take on the case? He handles most of the criminal cases in your court, doesn't he?"

"Justin Potts knows that everyone in the county thinks Loco killed that woman in cold blood and in a most brutal way. He's not about to risk losing a client by defending a man everyone thinks is guilty."

"How about the lawyer who set up shop in Harlowton? He's had experience with this kind of thing. Or so he's telling people."

"Horace P. Smith wants to be state senator, and maybe governor. He won't do anything that may tarnish an image he's busy polishing."

"What about the lawyers in Helena? Any one of them could handle Loco's case quite easily now that the railroad makes travel less of a problem."

"Son, there isn't a lawyer in this part of the world who wants to take on old Loco, no matter how nicely I ask. And I can't order anyone to do it. But you're in a different position than the others. I know your father thinks he needs you on the ranch, but his ranch is in good hands. You don't have to be there. You've had some experience in court while you were clerking. And, from what I hear, you have a sense of justice." The Honorable Jonas P. Henry leaned across the desk, pointed a hand at T. C., and looked him in the eye. "I can't order you to do it, but I'm asking you to represent Lawrence Silverman when he's tried for the crime of murder in the first degree."

T. C. leaned back in his chair to distance himself from the request. "But Judge, I only sat through one trial, and that was a civil matter. And as a clerk, I didn't do much. I have no idea how to defend anyone accused of murder. With me for a lawyer, Loco wouldn't be much better off than he would with no lawyer at all."

Judge Henry smiled. "I notice that you say Loco wouldn't be much better off. You're admitting that he would be some better off. T. C., visit with the sheriff about his investigation. Talk to the county attorney. He'll provide you with the Information and other documents. And go see Loco. He may talk to you. After you've done all that, come back to tell me your decision." He rose, extended his hand, and thanked T. C. for stopping by.

The clerk and the sheriff were leaning on the counter when T. C. came out the door. His first inclination was to pass them by and go on down the stairs. He had planned the trip to town so he could get acquainted with a newly arrived, attractive young lady, not to find himself entangled in a murder trial. But the judge had told him to discuss the matter with the sheriff, and the sheriff was right there.

Hakes was the first to speak. "You going to defend old Loco?" It was not so much a question as an accusation.

T. C.'s business was with the sheriff, not the clerk. He asked the law officer, "What has your prisoner told you so far? Has he confessed?"

Shea leaned back against the counter and let out a snort. "That crazy devil hasn't said a word since he was arrested. He just sits in his cell and stares at the floor or the ceiling. I can't even tell which way he's looking, much less what he's thinking."

"Where was he when you arrested him?"

"He was camped in the brush down by the river, on the north side of town. I picked him up after we got word of the murder."

"How did you find out the woman was dead?"

"The stationmaster at Summit sent a telegram that they'd put her body on the train and we should pick it up at Dorsey. He said Loco was the one who killed her."

"What made him so certain Loco did it?"

22

Ride the Jawbone

The sheriff straightened up and crossed his arms on his chest. "Loco and the murdered woman were both on the train from Two Dot that day. Near Lennep, she got up to change seats when Loco came down the aisle. Evidently, he said something to her that she didn't like because she called him a stinking old man. Then she swung her purse and hit him on the side of his head. He raised his fist like he was going to hit her, but the conductor got between them. Then, according to the conductor, Loco threatened to kill her." The sheriff paused for a moment. "They had a run-in at Two Dot before that. She was walking along by the store when he crossed the street and spoke to her. I guess no one heard what he said, but the whole town heard her yell at him. She told him to get away from her and never speak to her again. They tell me he swore and shook his fist at her back as she walked away. But since he didn't hurt her, nobody did anything about the way he behaved. I wish someone had realized just how crazy he really is."

"But what's the evidence that he actually killed her? The fact that he'd been unpleasant isn't evidence of murder."

The clerk grunted. "Yup. You sure sound like they taught you good at that law school. The old coot swears at a lady and tries to hit her, and you say he was unpleasant. Is that what you plan to tell the jury?"

T. C. ignored him and waited for the sheriff to answer.

"She was stuck with a large knife, once in the stomach and once in the throat. Loco had the same kind of knife on him, and it was covered with blood. He had blood all over his clothes too, although, he's so dirty it was hard to tell. And, when we got him, he had a brooch that belonged to her. It was in his sack. That should be enough to convince a jury."

"How do you know the brooch belonged to her? It could have belonged to anyone. Maybe it was a remembrance of his mother."

Hakes laughed derisively.

The sheriff glanced at Hakes, and then looked back at T. C. "Mrs. Hopkins, who runs the hotel in Two Dot, described a brooch that the Burke woman wore. It fits the one we found on Loco."

"Has Mrs. Hopkins actually seen the brooch you found?"

"No. But she'll identify it at the trial, if need be. I'm not worried about that. It's the same brooch—and the jury'll believe her. If you plan to defend that rascal you'll have your work cut out for you."

"I haven't said I'd defend him." T. C. scowled. "The judge said I should try to talk to him. When can I do it?"

"Whenever you want. But you may want to talk to the county attorney first as long as you're here in the courthouse."

Of course, T. C. thought. I'd better find out what Gallahan has to offer. He thanked the sheriff and said goodbye to Hakes. As he walked down the hall, he wondered how the clerk and the sheriff knew he'd been asked to help Loco. In a small town there were no secrets.

When T. C. walked into the county attorney's outer office, the clerk looked up from his work without saying a word. T. C. introduced himself and asked to see the county attorney. The clerk arose from his desk, more slowly than T. C. had ever seen anyone move, walked to the inner office door, and said, "There's someone to see you." The speed of his movement did not increase as he went back to his desk.

T. C. stepped to the door. Conrad Gallahan half rose from his place behind the desk and pointed to a chair that faced him. T. C. glanced around the room as he took the chair. There were files piled everywhere—on the desk, on the shelves behind the desk and covering most of the floor space. All but those on the desk had collected dust.

The man T. C. faced was about forty-five years of age. His body was short and rectangular like a large brick; his head, square-sided, to match his body. His hair was coal black and combed straight back from his brow. Fidgeting hands belied his appearance of solid calm.

"I understand you're going to defend Loco." Gallahan's dark brown eyes mocked him.

"I haven't decided if I want to or not. I'd hardly know how to begin." T. C. didn't like to appear incompetent, but Conrad knew he was a brand new lawyer, and it seemed best to admit the obvious. "The judge said I should look at your file on the case."

"The court file has everything in it that I have. The charging Information is there together with my Affidavit in its support. The matters set forth in the Affidavit were provided to me by the sheriff. He did the investigating. You can look at the court file on your way out."

"The sheriff seemed pretty sure that Loco killed her, but I would hardly expect him to tell me otherwise."

"Well, my young friend, the evidence does seem to be overwhelming. But you might try the insanity defense. The State of Montana has not adopted the M'Naughton Rule, but it hasn't rejected it either. You do know the M'Naughton Rule, regarding a plea of insanity, don't you?"

The patronizing tone irritated T. C., but he maintained his composure. "Yes. They taught us criminal law in school and that rule was part of it." He paused for a moment, then asked, "Is Loco really crazy, or do people just think so?"

"If you can convince the jury he's insane, it makes no difference what the rest of us think. His appearance will help. But the townsfolk are pretty upset about the brutality of the murder. Most want to hang him without waiting for a trial. We won't do that, of course. We can hang him after the trial."

T. C. rose to leave. As he reached the door, Gallahan said, "It will be good experience for you, though, if you intend to practice law."

T. C. politely thanked the older man, but for the first time since the judge had asked him to take on the case, he began to feel inclined to do it. Gallahan had aroused his competitive instinct.

Back in the clerk of court's office, Hakes handed T. C. the court file. Inside the file, he found the Information with the heading, "State of Montana vs. Lawrence Silverman." The Information alleged that the defendant was guilty of murder in the first degree because he "killed one Penelope Burke in a manner that was willful, deliberate, and premeditated by stabbing her once in the abdomen and once in the throat and then casting her body from the Montana Railroad train in violation of Sections 8290, 8291 and 8292 of the Codes of Montana, all of which occurred in Meagher County, Montana." The supporting Affidavit simply elaborated upon the details of the killing. It listed as witnesses the sheriff, the conductor on the train at the time of the killing, the stationmaster from Summit, Dr. Eldon Granby, and Mrs. Charity Watson. The file also disclosed that the defendant was to be held without bond until trial. No date for the trial was shown.

When T. C. left the Clerk's office he intended to go to the jail, located back of the courthouse, to interview the defendant. Descending the stairs, however, he decided he needed to discuss the recent events with his father. As soon as he entered the house, he saw that his parent's already knew of the judge's request.

"Jonas thinks you can save Loco's bacon, is that it?" His father asked before T. C. could open his mouth.

"That filthy old man deserves to hang!" The words rushed out of his mother's mouth on the heels of his father's question.

"Now, Boss," his father said with a smile, "we won't decide if the old devil is guilty until after the trial. He may not be, you know."

"I walked by him on the street one day about a year ago, and the stench was almost more than I could stand." Mrs. Bruce wrinkled her nose. "And from what I hear, there isn't much question about his guilt." She glared at her husband. "That should not have anything to do with it." Looking at her son she went on. "Besides, your father wants you to be with Seth this summer, learning about the ranch business. If you don't go out with the roundup, Chappy will be short one rider."

T.C. was taken aback by the emotion in his mother's voice and her insistence that he devote his time to the ranch. From his childhood, she had told him he should be a lawyer. Now, without warning, she was objecting to the application of his legal training. His father's response, too, was puzzling. An education for his son had never seemed important to him. While he didn't object to providing money for his son's schooling, at times he had expressed his impatience with the amount of time that it required. He had always wanted T. C. on the ranch, carrying out his plans for its growth and improvement. Now, he seemed to be of a different mind.

"Well, it's a certainty that the old scoundrel will hang if you don't help him, son. And I suppose the evidence will support a hanging whether you help him or not. But it isn't fair for a man accused of a crime to go into a trial all by himself, without any legal training or experience. That's the same as no trial at all. We may as well go out and hang him today and save the county the expense of the show."

"Papa, I know very little about the things a lawyer should do in a criminal trial," T. C. said. "Most of what we were taught in school was theory. The county attorney mentioned an insanity defense, but I don't know how to go about the proof of such a defense. All I can remember is that the defendant must prove he had a mental defect, and, because of that, he could not form the necessary intent to commit the crime. How can that be done? The only doctor in town will be one of the witnesses for the prosecution. There isn't one person with any professional skills who would testify that Loco is really crazy."

"Son, there are law books at the courthouse. And, if I recall correctly, you brought a bunch of them with you when you returned from Saint Paul. They're on shelves in your room at the ranch. Somewhere in those books, you can find the things you need to know to do the job."

His mother turned on her husband. "Thaddeus, what about the ranch? It will take nearly all of Thad's time to prepare for this, just when the roundup and the haying are going on. What will everyone think if our son tries to get that filthy man off? Let someone else do it. There are other lawyers in the county. Why not one of them?"

"Mother, the judge said that no other lawyer would take the job without pay—or at least Justin Potts wouldn't. The new lawyer in Harlowton is afraid it will ruin his chances of election to the state senate. The judge thinks I'm the only one who might consider it. He didn't say that I have to do it, but he was pretty insistent." T. C. paused and frowned. "The county attorney seemed downright amused that I might go up against him in the courtroom. I guess he doesn't think I would present much of a challenge."

His father snorted, "Conrad Gallahan has an exaggerated opinion of his abilities. He brags about how many criminals he's sent to prison, but most of them just pled guilty. It's not often that he actually has to try a case. He'll buffalo you if he can. Don't let him do it."

Mrs. Bruce rose from her chair, her indignation evident in her every movement, and offered one final remark before leaving the room. "You men! Let that disgusting, filthy old man hang! No one ever deserved it more. Let perdition have him."

As his mother marched off into the kitchen, his father reached into the drawer in the table by his chair and pulled out his cribbage board. "Son, we haven't had a game since you got home. Cut the cards."

A game of cribbage was the farthest thing from T. C.'s mind, but he did as he was told and reached for the deck. His father cut low card and got the first deal.

While shuffling, his father began a monologue that T. C. had never heard before. "The history books printed in the North say that we in the South were fighting to retain slavery. That is simply not correct. My family didn't have any slaves. The war began because South Carolina believed that it had a right to leave the Union voluntarily, just as it had joined voluntarily. The war was fought to answer the question, could a state that voluntarily joined others to form a union be compelled to remain in the union when it no longer wished to do so?"

Mr. Bruce tossed his two cards into the crib. "We in the South were right in principle but we lost the war anyway." T. C. played a six. His father put down a nine, said, "Fifteen two," and moved his peg two holes. While T. C. thought about his next play, his father added, "The slavery question did one thing for fellows like me. It made us think about the way we treat one another. Slavery was an abominable institution. But slavery has not been the only way that we treat each other unfairly. We do it every day in lots of ways."

T. C. laid down a seven. His father immediately put down a nine and said, "Thirty-one for two," and pegged some more. As the game went along, Mr. Bruce continued his explanation. "One of the ways we treat people unfairly is in the court system. We like to tell ourselves that it works for all. That isn't true. It works for those who have money and doesn't work for those who don't have money. Loco is just another example. No one will help him unless there's money involved, and Loco probably doesn't have a cent."

T. C. watched his father count the crib and move the peg the proper number of holes. "Papa, having me for a lawyer won't give Loco fair treatment. No matter what you think of Conrad Gallahan's legal skills, he's had experience in the courtroom, and I haven't. He'll have that advantage, and Loco will suffer because of it."

"That may be true, but it's a certainty that he'll be better off if you help him. I can't order you to help him, but I hope you will. Call it charity if you want, but do it. You'll not regret it."

"What of mother? I can't ignore her feelings."

"Of course not. I wouldn't want you to. But I'll visit with your mother, and she won't stand in your way. She's proud of the things you've done, and, once she's thought about it, she'll be proud of you for taking on an unpopular task."

At that moment, Mrs. Bruce called from the kitchen doorway, "Come." Dinner was on the table.

Ride the Jawbone

The courthouse was up the hill and south of Main Street. T. C. left the house after dinner and started in that direction with the words of his father on his mind. The war was never mentioned in their home, so it was a surprise to hear his father offer a justification for the struggle of the South. It was an even greater surprise to hear his father speak of fairness in relation to the Negroes. By the time he arrived at the courthouse, T. C. had made up his mind to tell the judge that he would defend Loco. He stuck his head into the office of the clerk of court only to have Hakes nod toward the judge's office. When T. C. entered, Judge Henry slid his chair back, crossed his legs and clasped his hands in his lap.

"Well, son, what's your decision?" His face remained expressionless as he looked across the desk at T. C., still standing, hat in hand.

"I've no clerk or scrivener, so how can I arrange for the preparation of the required documents?" That concern occurred to T. C. at the moment he spoke the words.

The judge nodded. "T. C., there's not much in the way of paperwork in a criminal case. You can make any motions that you feel are appropriate orally, if you wish. While it's the duty of the county attorney to prepare standard jury instructions, you will almost certainly want to offer some of your own. They must be in writing and must be in proper form. I'm told there's a fellow at the store in Two Dot who used to clerk for a lawyer in Helena. Ask him to act as your scrivener. If the storekeeper objects, let me know, and I'll speak with him personally." The judge looked up out of the corner of his eye and gave the young man a sly smile. "Your father gave you his fairness lecture, didn't he?"

"His fairness lecture? Does he go around giving fairness lectures?"

"Only when we discuss the war. I may be the only one who has heard it—except you. And I'm certain that you heard it today."

"Yes, sir. I discussed all of this with my parents. My mother's feelings are very strong. She doesn't want me to have anything to do with a criminal." T. C. paused and corrected himself by saying, "alleged criminal. And my father did talk to me about the need to treat everyone fairly. So I guess I'll try to help Loco."

29

He was about to say more when the judge raised his hand to stop him. "Open the door and yell at Hakes to bring Conrad to my office. We may as well discuss a trial date right now."

The county attorney strode into the office with Hakes following. While Judge Henry told Conrad Gallahan that he had an adversary for the Silverman trial, Hakes dragged chairs in from the courtroom. When all were seated, the judge began. "Gentlemen, there's little likelihood that the defendant will plead guilty, so we may as well schedule a date for the trial right now. I suggest that we look at the last week of June. That way, the ranchers in the jury pool should be done with their irrigating, and they won't have started haying, so we shouldn't have to put up with too many excuses. Mr. Gallahan, how long do you think the trial will take?" Before Conrad could answer, the judge answered his own question. "It should take two days, but we'll schedule it for three. We'll start on Monday, the twenty-seventh. Mr. Albers, please plan to get out the notices to the jury panel on time. And you'd better call at least forty potential jurors. With the notoriety of this matter, it's likely that many of them will have opinions and be excused for cause. Mr. Gallahan, will that fit your schedule?"

"Yes, Your Honor. I can be ready for trial by that time. I will, of course, have to subpoena some witnesses who don't live in town, but we'll get them here."

"Mr. Bruce, I suppose you will need subpoenas also. Mr. Albers will help you get them issued. The sheriff will see that they are served."

The only person that T. C. could think of who might be a witness was someone to testify that Loco was as crazy as his name indicated. The judge continued. "If either of you wish to make any pretrial motions, I'll hear them when I am here on my usual rounds in the first part of June. Are we all agreed?" Since no one was going to argue with the judge, the conference came to an end.

Outside in the hallway, Conrad Gallahan said to T. C. "I'll help you to the extent that I can, but I can't help you if it will jeopardize my case in any way. As a practical matter, you're on your own."

T. C. offered the thanks that professional courtesy required, nodded to Hakes, and headed for the jail. Sheriff Shea was reading a book when T. C. walked in. After marking his place in the book, he motioned for T. C. to follow him.

Ride the Jawbone

One cell was empty, the other held a solitary figure, seated on the bunk. Without a word, the sheriff left T. C. alone. T. C. stood for a minute or two, expecting the figure on the bunk to give some acknowledgment of his presence. When nothing happened, he stepped to the cell and grasped the bars with his hands.

"I'm T. C. Bruce. The judge has appointed me to represent you at your trial."

Before he finished, the figure leaped its feet and reached for the cell bars. T. C. lurched backward and looked up at Lawrence Silverman. The man was at least six feet, four inches tall. The hands on the cell bars were huge. His filthy clothes smelled like a scavenging animal. But it was the face that held T C.'s stare. The hair that grew out of that face was as black as coal, as coarse as wire, and as dirty as a beard could be. His nose was wide and long, with flaring nostrils that were covered with grime. The eyes seemed wider from top to bottom than from side to side. Only the left eye looked at him. The right eye was cocked to its outside corner and seemed to be looking at the side of the cell. The eyes were black and the whites were bloodshot. The man's lips were drawn back in a silent snarl that exposed large, straight teeth as white as the rest of him was black.

T. C. felt a tinge of embarrassment at his reaction and stepped forward again toward the cell bars. "The judge has scheduled your trial for the last week in June. You and I will need to discuss your situation and plan a defense."

Before he could say more, the mouth of the figure behind the bars opened wide and poured out a howl unlike anything that T. C. had ever heard from a human. Despite his intention not to react again, T. C. jumped back. The sight and the sound of the wild and strange creature were terrifying. Before T. C. could recover, Lawrence Silverman returned to the bed where he sat with his head turned away. Staring at the unmoving, filthy figure, the young lawyer realized that any further attempt to communicate with his first client would be futile.

As he stopped in the front office, T. C. demanded, "Sheriff, why haven't you cleaned that man up?" His disgust over his reaction to the the creature called Loco colored his voice.

"Son, we've tried to work with that old devil, and he won't cooperate at all. We took a tub full of water into the cell and left it for him to bathe. He dumped it out on the floor. If you have any suggestions, we'd welcome them. I don't like his stink any more than you do." When T. C. didn't respond, the sheriff returned to his reading.

T. C., at a loss for words, stomped out of the office and onto the street. He paused for a long time with his hands in his pockets, wondering if he should tell the judge he'd changed his mind. The thought of going into the courtroom and sitting next to that huge, stinking man during a trial was revolting. Instead, he strode back down the hill to the general store. At the men's clothing section, he began to sort through the shirts. Immediately, a young woman appeared at his side and asked if she could be of help. T. C. raised his eyes and realized that he was looking at the lady he had come to town to meet.

All of the single men, T. C. among them, kept track of the young women in the area who were not spoken for. When word of the arrival of this lady drifted down to Two Dot, he quickly planned a trip to White Sulphur Springs. He formed a mental picture of the woman based on his knowledge of her uncle.

Mr. Spencer was tall, slim, and dignified, with graying hair and a silvery mustache. T. C. supposed his niece would be tall, slender, blue eyed and blonde. Quite naturally he pictured her as beautiful. Reality didn't match his mental image. She was five feet, two inches tall, with caramel colored hair and warm brown eyes. Her round face was attractive, but not strikingly beautiful. She had a radiant smile.

The events of the day so fogged his mind that he could think of none of the witty remarks with which he planned to impress her. All he said was, "I need clothes for a big man."

"I'm Felicity Spencer and you are, I believe, Thad Bruce. My aunt and uncle spoke of you at dinner today. They said you're the lawyer who will defend the murderer."

"He's not a murderer unless the jury says so, and that hasn't happened. And I don't intend to let it happen." The last part of the statement was pure bravado, intended to create an impression.

Her smile remained.

"Of course, you'll try to prevent a conviction. That's what you are trained to do." She didn't seem impressed, and he found that annoying.

"Well, for now I need a large shirt, a large pair of pants—and some men's underwear." He added the last in an attempt to embarrass her.

Ride the Jawbone

The smile disappeared, but her face and voice remained pleasant as she explained that they had many kinds of shirts and pants. "Do you want dress clothes?"

T. C. was tempted to tell her he knew they had a large stock of goods, and that he had purchased clothing before. But he realized she was only trying to be helpful. "No, I need work clothes, size large. The colors don't matter." He examined a blue shirt from a pile on a counter. "This will do. Let's look at some pants."

She led the way to a display of work pants. As T. C. sorted through the pile, Miss Spencer walked down the aisle and selected some long underwear of a size to match the shirt. T. C. was clutching a pair of pants of about the right dimensions when she returned.

Holding the underwear by the top for everyone in the store to see, she asked, "Are these the kind you had in mind? They are quite large and durable." There was no hint of embarrassment in her manner.

T. C. glanced around to see if any others were looking at them. Two older women took in the whole performance and smiled at his discomfort. He quickly growled, "The underwear will be just fine." After she had bundled the clothing in brown wrapping paper, he grumbled again, "Put the cost on my father's charge account."

As he turned to leave the store she smiled once more and said, "I know you'll do your best for that man. Considering how angry the whole town is about the murder, not many would be willing to help him. I wish you well."

T. C. mumbled his thanks. Back outside, he shook his head in self-disgust. Instead of impressing her, he'd only made himself look foolish.

His thoughts didn't linger long on Felicity, however, but returned to the matter in which he had become entangled. At the sheriff's office, he put the bundle of clothing on the desk, and said, "I don't know how you're going to do it, but get that man cleaned up." He left without waiting for a reply.

The sheriff watched him walk out the door and then looked down at the clothing. He had spent much time during his years in law enforcement dealing with the youth of the community. Some were sneak thieves. Some were vandals. Some were brawlers. Some seemed to be in trouble all of the time. T. C. Bruce had been none of those.

The sheriff remembered the snowball incident as the only time that T. C. had done anything wrong—and that the parson's stable was cleaner while T. C. was serving his punishment than it had been before or since. To the sheriff, he had always seemed nice enough but much too mild mannered. If he were to be a lawyer—especially a lawyer defending a killer—he would have to be aggressive. The orders he had just given seemed to indicate that T. C. had that potential.

Contemplating it all, Sheriff Shea broke into a smile. "Maybe that young fellow has some fire after all."

++++++++++

The courtroom took up the entire upper floor of the courthouse. All the books that comprised the county law library were housed in that room. T. C. stood back from the shelves to size up the collection while he attempted to devise a trial strategy. In light of the defendant's appearance and considering the manner in which he had behaved since his arrest, it seemed reasonable to try to convince the jury that the man they called Loco really was crazy.

The first step would be to learn what the Montana courts had to say about such a defense. He looked through the Montana Penal Code to learn if, by statute, the State had recognized insanity as a defense to the charge of homicide. The Code defined homicide and also defined the defenses of excusable homicide and of justifiable homicide. Nowhere in the Code could he find any statutory reference to insanity as a defense. He then checked the annotations under the statutes defining homicide. In none of the Montana cases that were cited was insanity asserted as a defense. He went on to read through the cases relating to homicides which were cited in the reference system that covered the courts in the western states. His attention was focused on the State of California, because the Montana courts frequently followed California court decisions. The California courts had adopted the principle that a man could not be convicted of homicide if he was totally incapable of understanding the nature of his act. Any lesser degree of mental impairment was insufficient to excuse the act and provide the basis for an acquittal.

Having gathered that information, T. C. sat in one of the jurors' chairs and tried to think of a way to show that his client was incapable of understanding the concept of murder when the client wouldn't even talk. Nothing came to mind. Furthermore, he had no real idea how to present evidence of insanity in court. His knowledge of courtroom procedure was frightfully scanty, and he could very well appear to be a blundering idiot at the trial. It would be bad enough to have to bear that burden himself, but the thought of the embarrassment to his mother was an even greater concern. He decided to review the treatises he'd brought to Montana from law school for some guidance, and this time he would really pay attention to their content.

+++++++++

It was nearly five o'clock in the afternoon when he got back to his parent's house. His mother was obviously displeased, and she was taking out the displeasure on the cooking utensils as she prepared supper. She didn't respond when he offered his greeting, but went about her work with even more ferocity. Escaping the kitchen, T. C. joined his father who sat in his accustomed position, foot up on the stool.

"We have time to finish the cribbage game we started this morning. It's my deal." His father pulled the board from a shelf near his chair.

T. C. pulled up a chair as his father dealt the cards. "Something's bothering Mother. I suppose it's because I agreed to defend Loco."

"No, that's not it. Your mother went to the store for groceries this afternoon and met Mrs. Barnaby. That old girl really insulted her. She's about as angry as she ever gets."

"What about? It isn't like mother to make a fuss about anything."

"Mrs. Barnaby asked her how she could live with herself, having a son who's trying to save the life of a brutal murderer. It was a mistake to pick on your mother's only child. From what I can gather, that lady was put in her place." His father laughed softly as he laid down his two cards for the crib.

The thought that he had caused his mother to get into a quarrel with another lady of the town made T. C. forget the card game for the moment. "Mother didn't want me to get involved with Loco. I suppose I can ask the judge to allow me to withdraw as counsel."

"Son, you need to listen to your mother before you do anything different. She'll tell you her thoughts while we're eating. Now, pay attention to your cards because I'm about to skunk you."

Skunk T. C. he did, just as Mrs. Bruce called, "Come!"

Mrs. Bruce ate in silence, and her husband and son were not inclined to make small talk, considering her mood. When they finished eating, she spoke in firm, even tones. "Thad, that woman said you agreed to defend Lawrence Silverman for publicity. She said Conrad Gallahan would make a fool of you, and we would be the laughingstock of the town." She leaned across the table to look her son straight in the eye. "It's not important that you persuade the jury to acquit that man, as long as you to do your very best. Your father and I will help. Just tell us how we can. I want you to put that woman in her place!"

The anger in her voice and the vehemence with which she spoke were new to T. C. Her manner was so out of character that he didn't know how to respond. His father softened her remarks by adding, "Of course, we'll provide whatever help we can. We understand the difficulty of the task and know that you'll do a fine job."

As his mother rose briskly from the table to carry plates to the sink, T. C. wondered what she would do when it was all over, if he didn't do well. He was terribly unsure of his ability.

When the meal and the cleanup were finished, the family adjourned to the sitting room where father and son returned to the cribbage board. T. C. had difficulty concentrating on the game and was soundly beaten by his father in two games. When the last was finished, he excused himself and went upstairs to his room. Once in bed, his mind kept returning to the events of the day. Before sleep overcame him, he resolved to dig more seriously into the books at the courthouse on the morrow.

May 4th

The following morning, T. C. did chores for his mother and then returned to the empty courtroom. He began a more orderly search through the legal digests for any court decisions that might give guidance or assist him in preparing for the trial. In the process, he got a better feel for the thinking of the justices of the Montana Supreme

Ride the Jawbone

Court. Such knowledge would help him adapt his courtroom manner to the High Court's standard. By midday, however, it was apparent that the library available to him in White Sulphur Springs was not adequate to allow him to prepare a defense for Lawrence Silverman. His books from law school contained information on trial techniques and the practical activities that a lawyer performed at a trial. Those volumes were at the ranch. After supper, he told his parents he planned to head for Two Dot in the morning.

Mr. Bruce said, "Son, what's your hurry? You know the train runs east on Tuesday, Thursday and Saturday. You'll miss it tomorrow."

His mother added, "I hoped you would stay for a few days. I plan to invite the Spencers to supper one evening soon. Mr. Spencer's niece is visiting, you know."

T. C. knew the niece was visiting. The opportunity to get better acquainted with the friendly Miss Spencer gave him pause. But the need to deal with the task the judge had imposed upon him prevailed. "The rains and snowmelt have washed out portions of the track in Sixteen Mile Canyon. And the train isn't reliable even in good weather. If I take the stage, I can be in Two Dot tomorrow evening and at the ranch the next morning."

"Well," his father said, "Bill Webster and his stage will get you there. You can meet the Spencer girl another time." His mother nodded in reluctant agreement.

During the evening T. C. attempted to divert his thoughts from the trial by reading one of his father's novels, but concern about the trial kept returning to his mind. Finally, he gave up and lay in bed, trying to envision the trial He thought of asking Justin Potts for help, but that would be admitting he lacked confidence in his own ability. His ego would not allow such an admission. When sleep finally came, it was not restful.

May 5th

Morning arrived, and with it a bitter cold wind from the west. T. C. donned long underwear and work clothes. He didn't have a heavy coat and warm gloves. Those were at the ranch on the Musselshell. Only

37

his flat-topped hat covered his head, not the warm cap he would have liked.

The stage left the hotel at eight o'clock in the morning with T. C. as the only passenger. He offered to ride up on the driver's bench with Bill Webster, but the gruff old man said, "You'll be better off inside. If you want to keep the wind out, lash the window coverings." He pointed to a buffalo robe for use as a covering. The thought of the robe to keep out the cold drove further thoughts of sociability from the young man's mind. He climbed in and heard the driver tell his horses, "Git, ponies, git."

The stage that Bill drove was not the kind that carried T. C. from Dorsey to White Sulphur Springs. It was more of an oversized surrey. The facing seats in the passenger area could hold only two people each. The leather roof was held in place by metal supports. The sides of removable leather now sheltered the passenger from the wind. Openings in the sidewalls for ventilation in pleasant weather were now screened with canvas, held in place by tie-downs. The wind seeped in around the many holes and cracks in the structure.

T. C. found that the place in the cab where the wind bothered him the least was in the middle of the seat facing forward. With the buffalo robe pulled over his body and tucked about his feet, he was comfortable even though the air grew colder the stage went along.

While the coach thumped and swayed, T. C. let his mind formulate an outline for his activities at the trial of his client. The first matter would be jury selection. His research told him that the defendant in a capital case was entitled to ten peremptory challenges, each of which allowed him to exclude a potential juror without giving a reason. The State of Montana, represented by the county attorney, was entitled to half as many. The jury would consist of twelve men—no women—and the judge would probably want to seat an alternate juror.

The State had the burden of proving, beyond a reasonable doubt, that the defendant committed the crime and committed it as charged. For that reason, the State is allowed beginning and ending arguments. The attorney for the defense only has one opportunity to be persuasive, that coming between the opening and closing arguments made by the prosecuting attorney. The final arguments usually attract the largest crowd in the courtroom.

Ride the Jawbone

The jury, having heard the evidence and the arguments and having been instructed in the law, would be sent to the jury room to deliberate. From his one experience in the courtroom, T. C. knew that the wait for the return of the jury was a time of agony for a lawyer. T. C. decided he should put an outline on paper so he could check off each task as he prepared for that part of the trial.

The stage first stopped at the mining camp of Copperopolis. When T. C. pulled back the flap on the side of the cab that served as a door, a heavy snow was falling. He went into the stage station to keep warm while Webster changed horses. When the stage rolled out again, he huddled under the buffalo robe, glad to have it to himself.

The next stop was the Hall Ranch. Mrs. Hall kept rooms for travelers and provided meals to those riding the stage. T. C. descended stiffly from the cab, ducked his head against the blowing snow, and ran to the door of the building that housed the dining room. In his hurry to get out of the weather, he almost ran into Sarah, the lovely schoolteacher he had seen on the train. The lady who didn't smile.

He backed away in embarrassment and doffed his hat, apologizing for being rude. She nodded acknowledgement and stepped aside to allow him into the dining area. Mrs. Hall had prepared the noon meal with enough food for as many passengers as might arrive. Since he was the only one, T. C. would not go away hungry. When the stage driver and the proprietors came to the table, Mrs. Hall directed him to a seat. As Mr. Hall was about to bow his head to say grace, Sarah entered the room and sat in a chair one seat away from any other person. Mr. Hall asked for a blessing upon the food and reached for the potatoes. T. C. thought it odd that the operator of a public house would introduce prayer into a gathering of strangers, but they were entitled to any activity of their choosing in their home, so long as it was not unlawful.

Mr. Hall and the stage driver, men who had known each other for over thirty years, discussed the weather and the condition of the ranges in both the Smith River and the Musselshell Valleys. Their conversation then turned to the topic most dear to old men, memories of the past. Some of the tales were new to T.C., and the ones he'd heard before had a twist that was personal to the teller. Mrs. Hall only spoke to see that each one at the table was getting a fill of food. Sarah said nothing at all.

39

The meal ended with freshly baked mincemeat pie for the dessert.

While Mr. Hall and the driver went out to hook the new team to the stage, T. C. paid Mrs. Hall for the meal and complimented her on its quality. Sarah tendered her payment in silence. When T. C. saw the young woman prepare for the out of doors, he reached for her coat. She snatched it so as to avoid his assistance, put it on, tied a scarf tightly around her head, and pulled gloves on her hands. Her clothing was woolen and warm. T. C. was pleased with the thought of sharing the cab with her.

T. C. stood aside while the driver helped Sarah into the cab. He followed and found her sitting on the seat facing the rear. His first thought was to tell her that she would be more comfortable on the other seat and that he would trade with her, but her demeanor dissuaded him. She was seated in the middle of the seat and her feet were set firmly, side by side, directly in front of her. The space between the seats was narrow, so T. C. sat with his feet to the right side, against the leather wall of the cab.

He eyed the buffalo robe, folded on the seat. The warmth of the house was already seeping away in the cold of the cab.

As the stage lurched forward, he said, "The wind blows in through the cracks and makes it pretty uncomfortable. I suggest that you cover yourself with the robe." When he unfolded the robe and passed it to her, she accepted it without a word.

After some experimentation, she pulled the robe up under her chin and tucked it in around her body to keep out any drafts. While she stayed warm, T. C. grew ever colder. He crossed his arms to hold the heat next to his body. He tried different positions for his legs and feet. He even tried sitting on his hands to warm them. But his efforts did not keep him from growing so cold that he began to shiver. The shivering embarrassed him, but he could not control his body. Sarah seemed lost in her own thoughts and oblivious to it all. It was only after the cab had swayed violently that she awakened from her reverie, saw the condition of her traveling companion and spoke.

"It's foolish, sir, for you to be cold when we can both be warm. You may sit on this side with me, and we will share the robe." With that, she moved to her right, indicating that T. C. could sit on the left end of the bench. He moved to the other side of the cab and sat as far away from her body as the space would allow. At the moment he was seated, a gust of wind blew snow into Sarah's face. T. C. suggested that the other bench offered more protection. Without a word, she moved to the forward-facing seat. It was left to T. C. to drag the robe across and spread it over them. He did so with great care not to touch her in any way. As they sat, T. C. against the cab on one side and Sarah against the cab on the other, they found that the robe would not stretch enough to cover them so that both could be warm. When T. C. relinquished enough of the robe so she would be covered entirely, she looked directly at him for the first time and said, "Sir, you may sit next to me. I said that we both should be warm." She moved toward the middle of the seat and raised the robe so that T. C. could scoot toward her. He did so, but hesitated to get so close that his clothing touched hers. Sarah made the move that left them touching, shoulder to thigh; both fully covered by the precious robe.

T. C.'s thoughts were no longer on his legal challenge. When he dared, he glanced at the profile of his seat mate. Her features were regular and beautifully carved with unblemished, light olive skin. The hair that surrounded her face was a shade less than black. Her brows gently curved and slanted downward to the outside. Her nose was narrow and straight above a mouth that was properly proportioned, giving balance to the rest of her features. In all, T. C. thought her as attractive as any woman he had ever seen. He guessed that she was probably about his age or somewhat younger.

After they had ridden in silence for a long time, T. C. gathered the courage to speak. "I was on the train from Two Dot to Martinsdale on Wednesday past and couldn't help but hear that you are seeking a teaching position."

She glanced at him, and then returned her gaze straight ahead. "I've been offered the position at the Flagstaff school and may accept it. Mrs. Hall told me that I may live with them during the school year."

Now that there was conversation, T. C. wanted to keep it going. "Will you stay there during the coming summer months?"

"I'll be at the home of Mr. and Mrs. Morton." The finality of her reply discouraged further questions. Although she spoke not another word, her closeness consumed his attention. There was a scent about her that was subtle and feminine. It contrasted sharply with that of his seat mate on the stage from Dorsey. He could feel the warmth of her body, even through the heavy clothing. The swaying of the stage caused them to constantly rub against each other. The ride from the Hall Ranch to Martinsdale was both too long and too short for T. C. Too long because of a need to escape a situation in which he felt awkward. Too short because of the excitement of feeling her body close to his.

When the stage rolled into Martinsdale and stopped at the hotel, T. C. removed the robe from both of them and placed it on the other seat. He exited the cab and turned to offer his hand to the descending lady. She took it for support, but quickly withdrew it when she was firmly on the ground. A man whose identity was unknown to T. C. was standing nearby, obviously waiting for her. She turned to T. C. as she left. "Thank you, sir, for being a gentleman." She looked away, then back at him and continued. "Mr. and Mrs. Morton would not mind if you were to call on them one day." And with that she was gone.

As he watched her go, T. C. realized that she hadn't smiled the entire time, nor had she frowned or shown any other change in her facial expression. He wondered if that indicated she was without strong feelings, but he put that thought from his mind. A creature so lovely must be warm and affectionate. He hoped to find out. She had given him the opening he needed.

It was not snowing in Martinsdale, but the wind was blowing, steady and cold. T. C. warmed himself in the hotel as he waited for the stage to roll again. When it did, he was once more the only passenger, with the robe to himself on the final leg of the journey to Two Dot. It was nice to be comfortable with the covering tightly wrapped about him, but he would rather be sharing it with Sarah.

May 6th

At 5:30 in the morning T. C. awoke in the Wilson Hotel in Two Dot. He dressed quickly in the chilly air and hurried across the street to the cafe, choosing a seat near the rear of the room against the wall. A quick breakfast consisted of fried potatoes, eggs, and ham, with lots of bitter coffee.

Ride the Jawbone

T. C. strode to the livery stable to retrieve his horse. After saddling up, he rode south out of Two Dot toward the Bruce Ranch.

The wind of the day before had died away, but the temperature remained cold. He stopped and put on the long oilcloth slicker that was tied to his saddle. Thus sheltered from the elements, he followed the trail southwest toward the foot of the high ridge that was simply called the "Butte" by those who lived near it.

As T. C. rode, his attention was on the world around him. The events of the past few days began to seem remote and dreamlike. He had not ridden far before the clouds started to break away. The sun smiled down and the air warmed, compelling him to remove the slicker. Enjoying the warmth and beginning to feel the closeness of home, he rounded the toe of the Butte and headed up the Little Elk Creek valley toward the ranch headquarters. About two miles from his destination, he came upon two of the Bruce ranch hands plowing the ditch extension he had described to his father. This extension would carry water from the creek to irrigate the natural hay that sprang up on the bottom lands when watered. The results of this activity were very important to his father.

Building a ditch was the hardest kind of work. Two horses pulled a walking plow that rolled sod to the downhill side to create a furrow. Another furrow was then plowed beside the first. Finally, the sod from the second furrow was lifted by hand and placed on top of the sod from the first furrow to make a bank to hold the water.

As T. C. approached, one man plowed a stretch of the second furrow. The other lifted the sod onto the ditch bank. Both men had stripped off their shirts and had draped their long underwear tops down from their waists. Sweat streamed from their armpits and faces. The horses, too, were dripping sweat, and their sides heaved as they gasped for air while dragging the plow through the hard sod.

"Hot work?" T. C. asked, his hands resting on the saddle horn.

The younger man, the one moving the sod, said. "Yup, T. C. Damn hot work." They watched the teamster plow out the end of the furrow and throw the implement over on its side. He tied the lines to the plow handle, left the horses to blow, and walked back to join the conversation. He was a burly fellow, about thirty years of age. When he took off his hat, he exposed a head that was nearly bald. Both men sat down on the sod bank to rest. As T. C. stepped down from his horse, the older of the two pulled a sack of Bull Durham tobacco from his pocket to roll a cigarette. The other wiped his dirty head and neck with the sleeve of his equally dirty underwear. T. C. declined when offered the cigarette makings. He had never been able to tolerate the bitter smoke.

After some preliminary discussion of the weather, the conversation turned to the problems the men had encountered in cutting the ditch through a rocky area not far from where they were now working. "The damned plow jerked out of the ground every time we hit one of them rocks. Then we had to dig it out with a pick. It took a hell of a lot of work to hold the grade." Smoke from the teamster's cigarette came out of his mouth and nose as he talked. "We're through the rocks now and should be able to work this ditch out the rest of the way in a few more days."

T. C. knew his father would approve of how Seth had laid out the ditch. When finished it would allow irrigation of another eighty acres.

The men ground their cigarettes into the dirt, and the bald headed fellow gathered the lines and spoke to the team. The horses responded by again pulling the plow into the hard ground. As T. C. rode away, he considered the agonies the horses suffered in doing the work that men asked of them. Their reward was only a gallon of oats twice a day, yet they did it without understanding the purpose. He patted his pony on the neck and swore to treat that horse—and all other horses—with consideration.

As he traveled to the ranch buildings, the Coffin Butte stood tall before him. A flat-topped geological structure, its sides were covered with a dense growth of evergreen trees. It appeared as a coffin draped in a huge black pall. T. C. gazed at the Crazy Mountains that towered beyond the Coffin. Little Elk Creek flowed from canyons in those craggy peaks. Snow banks on the downwind sides of the canyons promised that the creek would carry enough water for irrigation well into midsummer.

From the mountains, the creek traveled northward for several miles to its confluence with the Musselshell River. Diverted through irrigation ditches on the Bruce property, it created hay meadows where once there had only been sagebrush flats. Young Mr. Bruce smiled at a world splashed with varied hues of green and the lush, blue textured native wheatgrass hay on the irrigated lands.

At the ranch headquarters, T. C. rode up to the hitching rack. He dismounted, pulled the saddle and blanket from his horse and placed them on a rack in a small shed next to the barn. He hung the bridle on the peg above the saddle. He rubbed the animal down with a gunnysack before turning him into the small pasture near at hand.

Thaddeus Bruce had chosen the site for his first cabin carefully. A reliable source of water for the horses and other livestock was essential. Little Elk Creek, like many of its kind, did not flow throughout its course the entire year. During the hot months of summer, long stretches of the stream were devoid of water. At other locations, the water would spring from the ground and then flow onward for considerable distances before disappearing once again. Thaddeus Bruce constructed the first building at one of the constant flows. Built on high ground, it faced away from the prevailing southwest winds that could pound the walls during the winter months. Another small spring creek flowed behind the cabin on the south and met the main stream a short distance below.

The original structure had grown with log additions until it was quite spacious. In the center of the building were a sizable living room and a bedroom for Seth and his wife. The original cabin, now the far north end, was reserved for T. C. At the other end, a large open area served as the kitchen and eating space for the crew.

T. C. cleaned his boot before entering the kitchen. Seth's wife was a pleasant woman, but she had little patience for those who caused additional work by their carelessness. Despite her good nature, T. C. wasn't comfortable calling her by her first name, and Mrs. Black seemed too formal, so he called her Mrs. B. She was churning cream into butter, and she smiled hello without removing her hand from the crank that turned the barrel on its spindle.

Seth and his wife were about forty years old and childless. It seemed a tragedy to T. C. that they had no children. They were both kind and gentle. He felt certain that a child would have been given all of their love. They seemed to have compensated for the lack of children by lavishing affection upon one another.

With a smile and wave to Mrs. B., T. C. traipsed through the kitchen to his room. He threw his hat on the bed and pulled a chair from the front of a small desk. Once seated, he leaned back and surveyed his library. Books he brought from law school lined the shelves above the bed and desk. He'd come to spend time with those books, but now, away from town, they were not so inviting. T. C.'s interest was in the ranching activities. He felt at home here. His parents' house in town felt more like a place to visit.

To pass the time until the meal hour, when he could speak with Seth, he brought hot water from the kitchen, lathered his face, and scraped away his whiskers with a straight razor. After shaving, T. C. pulled a book from the shelf and began to review defenses to a murder charge. Try as he may, he could not keep his attention focused upon his reading. When he heard the clang of the dinner bell, he closed the book with relief.

A washbasin and pail of hot water sat on a wooden bench outside the kitchen door. Each ranch hand washed as he went by. Each hung his hat on a peg on the outside wall. Seth stood by his chair at the head of the long table while the men gathered, each in his usual place. Their behavior reminded T. C. of the milk cows that always went to the same stanchion in the barn at milking time.

Oilcloth covered the table. The stoneware plates and metal utensils were plain but serviceable. Salt, pepper, sugar, and toothpicks were there for all to use. Food, in huge, steaming amounts, filled bowls and platters, ready to eat.

The table would seat eighteen, but only nine of the usual crew were on hand. They carried the odor of their sweat into the room and it mixed with the aroma of Mrs. B's food. The familiar scent made T. C. feel even more at home.

As they began the meal, Seth told T. C. that Chappy, the ranch foreman, and six others were helping neighbors with the early branding of calves on the Big Elk side of the Butte. Talk subsided into silence, broken only by requests to "Pass the bread," or "Pass the spuds." When each had finished his meal, he placed his utensils and drinking glass on the plate and carried it to the long counter against the wall.

While T. C. and Seth drank a final cup of coffee, Mrs. Black prepared to wash the dishes. Moving to help, T. C. dried, and Seth put the dishes away and set the table again for the next meal with the plates and glasses upside down. The many pots and pans were hidden out of sight until they would be needed again in a few hours.

T. C. told Seth of the happenings in White Sulphur Springs. Though intrigued by T. C.'s new responsibility, Seth expressed concern over losing a roundup hand. Seth agreed with Mr. Bruce's request to move the ditch building and cleaning along as rapidly as possible until the haying began. "I guess it won't be much trouble to hire another rider for the roundup" he added.

"I don't have to be in court until early in June, and then only for a conference. I can help until then." It stung a bit to hear how easily he could be so replaced.

"The neighbors along Big Elk Creek and American Fork have started the early calf roundup. It'll keep Chappy and our boys busy for a couple of weeks to finish working those ranges from the river to the mountains. The outfits north of the river are about to start, too. With the fences that've been built along the river, it's not often that any of our cattle get across. Nonetheless, they'd like to have a rep from this outfit ride with them, just in case. Would you be interested in doing that? It may take two weeks, if the weather doesn't get 'em. They're going to work the range from Daisy Dean east. You shouldn't need to ride with them much beyond Haymaker Creek."

"You bet," T. C. said quickly. He hadn't ridden with the men from the north ranches except during the main roundup on the lower river. This operation would be smaller. The mention of the outfits north of the river brought to mind the Morton ranch—and a mental picture of Sarah. Maybe an opportunity to get to know her might yet arise.

Seth said, "You could help this afternoon by riding to the head of the upper ditch and shutting off the water and turning it into the next ditch down. There's straw and manure stockpiled at each place, so all you need is a pitchfork and maybe a shovel."

"I'll do it." T. C. headed for his room to change into the woolen work shirt and denim pants that were the ordinary uniform of any ranch hand. He pulled on gumboots, rather than the customary riding boots, caught and saddled the horse that was generally used for tasks such as irrigation. Before mounting, he stuck a pitchfork and a shovel in the ground so their handles were near to each other. Once in the saddle, he rode by them, pulled them from the ground and balanced them over his shoulder. He headed up the valley toward the ditch, about two and a half miles above the ranch buildings.

As T. C. rode along his thoughts ran to the stage ride from the Hall ranch to Martinsdale and the warmth of Sarah's body next to his. If he didn't get an opportunity to visit the Morton ranch during the roundup he might at least find out about Sarah from Mr. Morton or one of the men who was riding for him. Another face intruded into his thoughts as well. The face of Felicity Spencer was not as beautiful as the face of Sarah, but her smile was warm and lovely and she surely smiled easily and often.

So as he rode along on the gentle old pony humming to himself, thoughts of Lawrence Silverman just faded away.

May 7th

T. C. headed north after breakfast, riding a bay walker and leading three horses, tied head to tail. The second horse carried a pack consisting of a bedroll and spare clothing. He planned to use both the walker he was riding and the pack animal for circle horses. Both were good travelers. The other two would be used to drag calves to the branding fire.

As T. C. rode away, Seth called out some final instructions. "You should find the wagon at the head of Willie's Coulee. They plan to start from there Monday morning."

Thaddeus Bruce was one of the few ranchers who had fenced his entire ranch. However, he only owned about half of the land enclosed within his boundary fences. When the United States government decided to encourage the construction of transcontinental railroads, it granted sections of land to the railroads in square mile checker-boarded blocks. The land grant comprised a fifty mile wide strip along the entire course of the roadbed. The railroad then sold much of the land in order to pay the debts incurred in building the line. The property that comprised the Bruce ranch was under the Northern Pacific Railroad land grant. Bruce purchased as many of the checker-boarded sections as he could afford, supplementing the small acreage that he had homesteaded. It was that land, and the public land interspersed with it, that he had enclosed within the fences. He recognized that he could not stop any person from homesteading the public land within the fenced area. He had, however, the foresight to control all of the critical water sources within the fenced area by assuring that the land around such sources had been homesteaded by others at his request. Then he purchased the homesteads. The likelihood of further homesteading activity within his ranch boundaries was thus minimized.

T. C. remembered how some of the neighbors grumbled when his father first began fencing his ranch. Other ranchers complained that Bruce was depriving them of the use of public range that had always been available. He agreed that their complaint had some merit, but since he would keep his livestock within the fenced area, the rest of the open range would be available to others without any use by him. They accepted his explanation in good grace, and many of them began doing the same thing. As a consequence, much of the river and creek bottomland in the upper Musselshell valley was now enclosed. Large areas away from the watercourses were still open and used by all.

The first cattle brought into the Smith River and Musselshell River drainages were Durham, a breed more often called Shorthorn. Thaddeus Bruce and other progressive ranchers were now buying purebred Hereford bulls with which to breed their cows. In an open range operation, it was difficult to get the full benefit of high-quality bulls because not all of the ranchers shared the same philosophy. Some simply turned out any bull that appeared capable of breeding, regardless of its heritage or appearance. With the Bruce Ranch fenced, the Bruce cows could be kept separate from others at breeding time. Not only did this give him the opportunity to use quality bulls and thus produce animals with more value, but he could determine the time of year when the calves would be born. In short, he was no longer at the mercy of his fellow cattle ranchers.

T. C. opened a gate and led his horses through the fence marking the north boundary of the Bruce holdings. Before remounting, he scanned the terrain around him. Upstream the valley of Little Elk Creek was narrow, but downstream it widened out to the east. Looking at the lay of the land, he pictured in his mind a large ditch taken out of the creek upstream a short distance from where he stood. A ditch around the bottom of the butte would allow irrigation of several hundred acres of land. Water was almost always available during the month of June when the creek flooded from the snowmelt in the mountains to the south. But George O'Toole claimed the land north of the fence. If the Bruce ranch were to prosper, the land T. C. was viewing should be acquired. As he mounted his horse, he vowed to discuss the matter with his father.

The day was clear and the sun bright. The Little Belt and the Snowy Mountain ranges stretched across the horizon from west to east ahead of him. Cottonwood trees traced the course of the Musselshell River through the middle of the valley as it worked its way toward its confluence with the Missouri far to the east. T. C. thought of the two attractive young ladies who had recently and briefly entered his life. He thought of the coming gathering of men and cattle. He thought of the Bruce ranching operation and its future. But he thought of Judge Henry, of Conrad Gallahan, and of Lawrence Silverman, not at all.

T. C. crossed the Jawbone railroad tracks and the Musselshell River just below the place where Little Elk Creek and the river came together. From there, he rode across the GL Ranch meadow and onto the bench lands beyond. Traveling north-westward, he reached the eastern edge of Willie's Coulee and followed it toward its head. In due course, he mounted a rise in the ground and saw, in the distance, the GL wagon pulling into the campground.

When T. C. rode up to the wagon, Greasy, the cook, was setting up camp so that he could prepare a meal for the men who would soon arrive. Greasy's name did not speak properly of his abilities. An excellent cook, men who rode where he provided the grub never had reason to complain.

T. C. hobbled his horses, helped level the wagon, and spread the fly. Arriving alone or in groups of two or three, riders from various ranches came into view, bringing he horses they would need for the roundup and branding activities. The wrangler came with the Haymaker crew. He soon had the horses gathered in a rope corral, allowing them to get acquainted before taking them out to graze. While the horses were renewing acquaintance, so were the men who would ride them. Most had ridden together in the past, but some were new. They drank coffee and told stories that fit the occasion.

Late in the day, the last of the ranch hands rode in about the same time that George Lyons, owner of the GL ranch, and G. R. Wilson, owner of the Two Dot spread, arrived in a buggy. Too old to ride with the crew, they liked to visit the wagon before the roundup began. Willard Morton usually acted as the wagon boss, but, as T. C. learned to his dismay, Mr. Morton was down with the gout. Paul Kramer, foreman for the GL, would take his place. T. C. paid his respects to the two older gentlemen. They in turn asked about his father. The small talk continued until Greasy hollered the customary, "Come and get it." When the evening meal was finished, Mr. Lyons and Mr. Wilson left in their buggy while the men sought comfortable places to roll out their beds for the night. The work would begin at daybreak, which came early this time of year.

May 8th

Paul Kramer sent them off to work the range east of Daisy Dean Creek, beginning at the river area and continuing north to the mountains. T. C. was paired with a rider from the Morton outfit, and that suited him just fine. As they headed out, T. C. started the conversation. "I rode the stage with an attractive young lady who said she was staying with the Mortons."

When his companion merely nodded, Bull Durham cigarette hanging from his lip, T. C. asked, "What can you tell me about her?"

The Morton rider threw the cigarette on the ground. "Yup. She's good looking. We seldom see her."

"I know she's called Sarah. Do you know her last name?"

"I don't know her name or anything about her." The abrupt answer told T. C. that the conversation about the lady was at an end. He hoped he might learn something later from one of the other Morton riders.

T. C. and his companion made their circle and hazed the cattle they found to the gathering place near a small stream where they would be held for the branding. Soon all of the men had ridden in, herding their find before them. They'd gathered about two hundred cows, most of which had calves following them. Some were yet to calve, some had borne calves that had died, and some had simply not conceived. The tired cattle were content to lie down or stand quietly, chewing their cuds. Three riders held them on the flat, while the others rode to the wagon for the noon meal.

Each of the north side ranches had sent five riders, and each rider had brought four to six horses. About a hundred horses were held near the wagon in a rope corral. After eating, one by one, the cowpokes caught the horse he would use to rope calves and drag them to the branding fires. Branding irons for each ranch were placed to heat in three fires near the cattle.

T. C. watched with interest as Paul organized the branding activity. Three men riding through the cattle would locate a calf that was with its mother, rope it by a hind leg, and drag it to the nearest branding fire. The rider dragging a calf called out the brand to be placed upon it. Pairs of calf wrestlers waited at each fire. As a horseman dragged a calf toward the fire, two of the wrestlers would step forward. One would grasp the rope that stretched between the saddle horn of the rider and the leg of the calf, while the other would reach down and grab the calf's front leg. As the second man lifted the front leg of the calf into the air, the other lifted up sharply on the rope. By doing so they flopped the calf onto its side on the ground. The man in front placed his knee on the neck of the calf while holding its front leg doubled up tightly against its body. The man on the rear removed the rope from the calf's leg, sat down on the ground behind the calf, and pulled the top leg toward him. He braced his foot against the bottom leg of the calf above the hock. The calf, thus immobilized, was ready to be branded.

One man at each fire handled the branding irons. The Wilson brand was two dots, each about two inches in size, on the rib. The brand gave G. R. Wilson the name, "Two Dot" by which he was known. The town bearing that name was established on land that he owned.

In addition to a brand, most ranchers used another identifying mark on their cattle. Most often it was a notch of some kind cut from the animal's ear. The mark made it easier to tell the cattle of one owner from those of another without the necessity of reading the brand. That could be difficult once the brand healed and the long winter hair grew over it.

The Bruce brand was a lazy T, placed on the right rib. The Bruce mark was a "waddle" on each jaw. The waddle was created by cutting a flap of skin partially away from the calf's jawbone and giving it a twist. As time passed and the skin healed it left a lump on the jaw. The Bruce cattle were easy to locate among others. All that a rider had to do was approach a bunch and yell. The cattle would look toward the noise. Those with the waddles belonged to Bruce.

T. C. took his turn at the various tasks. He wrestled calves. He ran the branding iron. He did the earmarking. He used his pocketknife to castrate the bulls, and when it was his turn, he mounted his horse and roped. As representative of the Bruce outfit, he was to assure that any calf following a Bruce cow was branded with the Bruce brand. Among the cattle gathered the first day not one belonged to his father.

Branding was completed late in the afternoon and the cattle were allowed to spread out over the range. The riders then moved northward to the place where Greasy had set the wagon for the night. Men turned their horses over to the wrangler and ate their supper. Before long, they all retreated to their blankets for the short night's rest.

May 9th – May 18th

In the early light of the next morning, circle riders rode out again. This day they gathered only about seventy cows at the branding location. Only one belonged to Thaddeus Bruce. When its calf was properly branded and marked, T. C. noted the fact in a small booklet carried in his breast pocket for that purpose. The wagon moved in the afternoon to a new location. The activity continued in the same manner, day after day.

The days were cool and dry and often the wind blew from the west. There was talk that the new grass would burn up if rain didn't come soon. This kind of talk never ceased in ranching country. Either it was too dry or too wet or too hot or too cold, or if it was just right, it wouldn't stay that way. But for now, the weather was good for the branding activity.

Calves born in the winter months were sometimes too large for the cowboys to wrestle. A rider would rope a big one by the hind leg and another rider would throw a rope around its neck. The horses, one on each end, would stretch it out and hold it for branding. A certain feeling that any man worth his salt should be able to wrestle any calf, no matter how big, prevailed. For that reason, the second rider didn't rope the neck until the team of wrestlers indicated that they couldn't handle the animal in the usual way. Out of a sense of pride, some men would grab onto a huge calf rather than admit that they could not throw it to the ground and hold it there.

Such an occasion came on the fourth day. The wrestling team consisted of two men from the GL ranch. One was an older experienced ranch hand. The other was about eighteen years of age and working his first roundup. It was Art, the younger man, who grasped the rope on the rear leg of a monstrous calf dragged to them. The two men managed to get the calf to the ground and were prepared to hold him for castrating and branding. Art had the top hind leg gripped firmly with both hands, his foot braced against the lower leg of the calf. When the red-hot branding iron touched the calf, the reaction of the animal was instantaneous and disastrous. He jerked his leg forward and out of Art's hands then kicked back with the same leg and with all of its strength. Its hoof hit the young man squarely in the mouth. The force of the blow knocked him over backward and left him lying unconscious. The calf jerked free from the front man, turned, and ran over Art.

All operations stopped while the crew hovered over the prone cowboy. Someone brought water and splashed it onto his face. Art rolled his head to the side and started to sputter. As consciousness returned, he put his hand to his mouth and brought it away, covered with blood. Next, he put his tongue to his teeth, and found one front tooth missing and the other broken in half. Paul Kramer arrived on the scene and directed a couple of men to help Art to the wagon. T. C. and Art's wrestling partner hoisted him to his feet and walked him slowly away from the branding fire. At the wagon, they left him sitting with his back against a wheel, holding his hand to his jaw. T. C. and the rest of the crew returned to their tasks.

An hour later, Art came walking back and attempted to take his place as a wrestler. His lips were swollen to a grotesque size and his face was chalky white. Paul Kramer found him there and suggested he ride into Two Dot to have the doctor take a look at his injuries. The youth shook his head and started forward to grab the next calf that came to the branding fire. Paul stopped him with a word and sent him back to the wagon. He crawled under his blankets and slept through the remainder of the day and through the night. The next morning, he rode out with the rest of the crew and continued to carry his share of load, his otherwise handsome smile forever marred by the gaping hole that once had been his front teeth.

The work continued from morning to night. Some days the gather would be large, on one occasion about three hundred cows. On other days it would be small, although never again as small as seventy. After seven days they had covered the range east of Daisy Dean Creek. They then began to work the area west of Haymaker Creek from the base of the mountains downstream toward the river. In all of this time they came across only seven cows with calves that belonged to Bruce.

T. C. liked this work. He had been doing it since he was in his teens. He was confident of his ability, and the camaraderie associated with the roundup was unequaled in his experience. As time went by, however, thoughts of his other and newer responsibility began to creep into his mind with increasing frequency. And his conscience began to nag at him. While T. C. enjoyed the roundup, Lawrence Silverman languished in jail, facing death.

Days remained warm and pleasant and the nights cool and dry. But one evening, just as the day's branding was finished, clouds began to build up in the west. Before the evening meal was finished, it started to rain. The crew set up a large tent that was carried in the wagon and spread their beds inside. There wasn't room in the tent for all of them, so some sought shelter under the fly of the chuck wagon. One was T. C.

Heavy rain continued during the night, and it wasn't long until water seeped through the canvas tarp into T. C.'s bedroll. He tolerated it for a time, but finally the blankets got so soggy that he couldn't find any comfort lying in them. He got up, pulled the blankets away from the sodden tarp and hung them next to the cook stove. He stoked the fire, spread his blankets and clothes to dry, and stood near the stove. It wasn't long until others, whose beds had suffered the same fate, huddled with him. Time passed slowly until the sun made its appearance. Shortly after sunrise the rain stopped. But the good nature of the gathering was missing that morning. Grousing and exchanges of cuss words began before breakfast was over.

The horses, as well as the men, were affected by the cool and damp.

One Haymaker rider saddled his horse and climbed aboard for the day's ride. The old pony dropped his head and bucked easily through the gathering, splashing water and mud on men and horses as he went. A GL hand, having trouble with his own mount, caught most of the grime on his slicker and chaps. He growled, "Keep that damn jughead where he belongs."

"Its wide open country. I'll ride where I want," the rider snapped.

In a moment, the second man had his saddle cinched down and was ready to mount. His horse had ideas, too. He dropped one ear and humped his back up so far that the saddle seemed to stand on end. The GL hand pulled the horse's head around and swung quickly into the saddle, only to have the horse jerk his head away and go to it. Whereas the first horse had only pretended to buck, this one was serious. Even though he was slipping and sliding in the mud, he forced his rider to hang onto the saddle horn. The man's head flopped, and his hat flew off behind him, landing in one of the deepest puddles of soupy mud. The bucking stopped soon enough, with the rider still aboard, winded from his effort. The horse stood spraddle-legged and blew. The Haymaker rider snickered and said, "Don't forget your hat."

The GL hand jumped down, picked his hat out of the mud, and started for his tormenter with clinched fists. His voice was a growl. "Climb down off that nag, if you've got the guts."

It might have ended in a bout of fisticuffs, but the foreman interfered. He sent the pair off together for the day's work, concluding they might as well sort out their differences away from the rest of the crew. The two were still jawing at one another as they headed north toward the timberline.

The two erstwhile combatants were last to arrive at the branding ground with their gather. They ran their horses from there to the wagon with a whoop. The Haymaker hand was yelling as he stepped down. "You should have seen it. We jumped a yearling bear up next to the timber and Hiram made a run to try to rope it. He might have done it too, but the bear got into the timber." He could hardly stand still to talk. "Whooey! You should have seen his horse take to that bear. He just put his head down and stuck his nose out and ran right to it."

His companion, just as excited, carried on with the story. "Well, Jake helped. He tried to haze the bear away from the timber but his horse got scared and started to buck again." He giggled. "We damned near got him anyway." They harangued the rest of the crew with their tale throughout the meal. By the time branding began, all ill will created by the wet beds had disappeared. The operation was back to normal.

++++++++++

They finished the morning gather on the tenth day and were eating the noonday meal when Paul Kramer approached T. C. He removed his hat and wiped sweat from his forehead, "We're not finding enough Bruce cattle to make it worth your while. If you want to head on back, we'll keep track of any others that we find and let you know. It's up to you. We've appreciated your help but it seems a waste of your time to continue riding with us."

T. C. didn't hesitate. "If you don't need me, I'll be on my way. There are things I need to do." Paul nodded and they shook hands. T. C. gathered his horses and belongings and headed toward Two Dot.

His responsibility to Lawrence Silverman had become a burden on his mind. A person has lots of time to think while riding circle. At first, his thoughts had mostly been of the two young women—the one with the cool good looks and the one with the lovely smile—but ever more frequently, he found himself thinking about the upcoming trial and how he might save the life of his client.

It occurred to him a few days before, that he might attempt to work out an agreement with the county attorney. Perhaps the charge would be reduced to second degree murder in exchange for a plea of guilty from the defendant. The more he thought of the idea, however, the more unlikely it seemed. First of all, Conrad Gallahan was convinced that he would get a conviction to the charge of first-degree murder. Second, the feelings of the local citizenry were such that the county attorney would risk defeat in the next election if he agreed to a lesser charge. Finally, T. C. didn't believe he could even get his client to respond to such a suggestion.

He began, for the first time, to think seriously about the trial testimony and the people he would call as witnesses. If he were to present Loco as insane, he needed to give the jury some evidence of insanity. The sheriff would be called to testify by the county attorney.

On cross-examination, T. C. could ask him about the bizarre behavior his prisoner demonstrated while in jail. Then, when the doctor testified, he could ask if the behavior described by the sheriff was that of a normal man. Finally, he could ask Loco to take the witness stand and hope that he refused to do so or, upon doing so, behaved in a manner that would show he was completely crazy. T. C. might then argue insanity to the jury. If successful, he would save Loco from the gallows, but Loco would spend the rest of his life in the hospital for the insane.

T. C. needed the exact language of the M'Naughton rule, stating that a person could not be held accountable for his act if he were not capable of knowing the nature of the act and that it was wrong. He must also put an instruction to that effect into proper written legal form to present to the judge. The end of his duties at the roundup came as a relief. It allowed him to ride to Two Dot to see if he could hire the clerk, the man the judge had recommended as a scrivener.

He wondered who would be called as jurors and how he should question each one in an attempt to show prejudice. The jury pool was drawn from the freeholders of the county. That meant that each one of them would be a landowner. Most of them would be ranchers. None of them would be women, and he was thankful for that. Any woman would likely vote to convict Loco just because of the nature of the crime. His father knew nearly all of the ranchers in the county. If he got a list of those in the jury pool, he could discuss each one with his parents to decide who would be most inclined to listen to the evidence without bias.

It was late in the afternoon when he rode into Two Dot. After leaving his horses at the livery stable for the night, he went to the hotel to rent a room and then to the barbershop for a bath and a shave. As he left the barbershop, he looked up the street just in time to see Chappy going into the saloon. T. C. had intended to go to the cafe and get some supper, but seeing the foreman in town changed his mind. He walked up the street and into the dark recesses of the drinking parlor.

The Flynn Brothers Saloon consisted of one long room. Smoke clouded the air, and the place was filled with loud conversation. It surprised T C. to find a crowd in the drinking spot so early in the evening. He saw riders from the Big Elk and American Fork ranches lining the bar and realized that the Big Elk roundup had concluded.

Ride the Jawbone

He spotted Chappy in the throng and started in that direction. He didn't get far before a man with whom he had attended the Little Elk School stopped him. T. C. noticed that his erstwhile schoolmate had the beginnings of a paunch and his face had the first florid hue that came from too much liquor. Chris—the name that finally came to T. C.—was pleasant enough and wanted to reminisce about their school days. While T. C. attempted to extricate himself from the conversation, he sized up the Bruce ranch foreman.

Chappy stood with his back to T. C., engaged in conversation with a man leaning on the bar. The foreman was about five foot ten inches tall and muscular, with narrow hips and broad shoulders. His garb was typical of any cowboy—flat brimmed hat, cotton shirt covered by a vest, denim pants, and high-heeled riding boots.

T. C. knew that Chappy's mother was a religious woman and that she had given her son a saintly name at his birth—Ignatius Paul Chapman. His father, knowing that the boy would be the butt of schoolboy taunts if he were called Ignatius, started calling him by his initials when he was a baby. When the child got to school, the initials led to taunts that were even worse than his real name might have created. As a consequence, he had adopted the name of Chappy as soon as he was able, and had made it known that he was to be called that and nothing else.

The men in the saloon had apparently been there for a while and had not ignored the spirits that the bartender had to offer. One of them, huge in size and ugly in disposition, somehow found out about the initials that caused Chappy's grief as a child. After another belt of liquor, he wandered out into the middle of the floor where everyone could see him, pointed his finger at Chappy and called out in a raucous voice, "I. P., you pee, we all pee!" He burst into drunken laughter. Anticipating a reaction from the object of the remark, he doubled up his fists and started for the Bruce foreman.

Chappy turned, took one step toward the larger man, then paused. The quarrelsome one stepped close and pulled his right arm back to swing, but Chappy didn't wait for the blow. He kicked the huge man squarely between the legs as hard as he could. The man gasped, "Umph!" doubled over, and clasped his arms around his lower waist. Chappy's knee then hit him in the face, straightening him up again.

No sooner had that happened than Chappy delivered a terrific blow to the man's stomach with his left fist. When he doubled over again, Chappy clubbed him behind the ear with his doubled up right hand. The pugnacious man went down and didn't move. It had all happened so fast that everyone else, including T. C., was frozen in place. Chappy, breathing hard, stepped back and looked around the room. "People call me Chappy. Does everyone understand that?"

The thing that struck T. C. was the absolute silence in the barroom. Where a moment before there had been the steady sound of more than twenty voices, now there was nothing. The silence continued while Chappy turned to the man with whom he had been conversing and said, "Have your saddle at the livery stable at seven in the morning, and be ready to ride out."

With that, he turned and stomped out the door of the bar. T. C. waited only a moment and then scurried after him.

Outside, he found Chappy waiting for him on the boardwalk. The foreman was no more conversational with T. C. than with the man in the bar. "I'm sleeping at the livery stable and I plan to eat breakfast at six in the morning." Without waiting for a reply, he turned and walked up the street.

T. C. knew the man well enough to leave him alone. The commotion in the bar had been unexpected and left him with unsettled feelings. He had been involved in fights in the schoolyard as a child, but never since he had reached adulthood. As he crossed the street to the café, T. C. wondered what he would do if he found himself in a situation similar to the one he had just witnessed. He really didn't know.

May 19th

T. C. rose early in order to be at the cafe when Chappy arrived. He found a table and ordered coffee while he waited. As he drank the black, muddy liquid the waitress poured, he wondered how he should handle the incident of the night before. He liked and admired Chappy, but always felt somewhat uncomfortable in his presence. Chappy was short of speech and could be critical of those he thought were frivolous in their acts or in their talk. An excellent cattleman, he always rode the rank horses, not to show off, but to work them to the point that others could handle them. The foreman demanded a lot from the men in his crew, but never allowed any to out-work him.

Most of what T. C. knew about Chappy's early life he had heard from Seth. Chappy's education had ended with the death of his father when he was ten years old and he was sent to work for a neighboring farmer in his native Illinois. The work was brutally hard, and his pay went to his mother at the end of each month. When his mother died a year later, the farmer declared himself Chappy's guardian and continued to work him just as hard without paying for the work at all. Chappy labored for the farmer one more year, and then early one morning, he just walked away. He had heard men talk of "riding the rails" and at the nearest town he climbed into an empty freight car and left the world of his childhood without a backward look. He was now thirty-five years old, single, and as tough and hard as a man could be.

For some reason that T. C. didn't understand, Chappy seemed to enjoy his company. When T. C. was at the ranch, Chappy sat or stood near him during times of rest. Their conversations were sporadic because of Chappy's brusque manner. He tended to make fun of the education that T. C. had received but was always interested, nonetheless, in matters beyond the ranch world in which he lived. T. C. concluded early on that Chappy was intelligent, and he thought it sad that the man had not been able to go further with his education. He offered the foreman books to read, but the offers were always rejected. T. C. wondered whether he could not read easily, or if he just didn't want others in the bunkhouse to see him do it.

Chappy strode directly to the corner of the room where T. C. sat. He took a chair without a word and motioned the waitress to bring coffee. When the coffee arrived he ordered ham and eggs without looking at a menu or waiting for T. C., who held out his cup for a refill. T. C. ordered hotcakes and bacon. And there they sat, Chappy who seldom spoke and T. C. who did not know how to begin the conversation. At last, T. C. asked how things had gone with the calf roundup on Big Elk.

Chappy looked over his coffee cup and replied, "Pretty good." He directed his attention to his coffee and added nothing to that one quiet remark.

After eating in silence, Chappy finally looked T. C. in the eye and said, "I got a man to ride in your place." There was a long pause, and then he went on, "I guess you'll be lawyering."

"Yes, I agreed to represent Lawrence Silverman in the murder trial."

"So, that's his name. I never knew he had a name other than Loco." Silence again, and then, "How does a lawyer do that job?"

T. C. noted again the curiosity that emerged from Chappy at the oddest times. He explained that the evidence seemed to indicate that Loco had done the deed, but there was a question of his sanity. He went on to tell Chappy of his plans for the defense. Chappy listened without interrupting. T. C. had expected Chappy to ask, "How can you defend a man who is obviously guilty?" But that question didn't come.

Instead, Chappy said, "I don't know nothing about lawyering. But it seems to me that the first thing a lawyer should do is find out what happened. I'd talk to the sheepherder that found her. I'd talk to everyone else that knows anything that might help. Maybe Loco didn't do it." He rose from the table. "If you're going to the ranch, let's ride."

Chappy was right, T. C. realized as they rode toward the ranch. He should conduct an investigation and talk to every possible witness. He had been so engrossed in his thoughts of law and procedure that he had forgotten the most elemental activity of a lawyer—finding the facts. Before they reached the ranch buildings he decided what he would do. For the first time since he had allowed himself to be drawn to the man accused of murder, he felt as though he had a plan.

In his bed that night, T. C. remembered with chagrin that he hadn't inquired about the scrivener who worked at the store in Two Dot.

May 21st

"If you're going to The Springs, why don't you ride the Jawbone?" Seth posed the question as T. C. finished putting the pack on the horse.

"I intend to hunt up the sheepherder who found the body. I'm not sure who he herds for. It could be Albert Einerson or maybe Olaf Bakken. And he'll probably be out in a camp and not at the ranch buildings. Anyway, I'll need a horse to track him down."

Ride the Jawbone

"Well, tell your Dad that things are going well here. When the weather is more certain, we hope that he and your mother can come to size things up. We'll meet them at Two Dot in the good buggy and make them comfortable here at the ranch."

T. C. caught up the lead rope to the pack horse, climbed into the saddle, and headed out over the ridge that lay just to the west of the ranch buildings. The direct route to the ranches where he might find the sheepherder was due west. He didn't head that way, but instead rode more to the northwest. He hadn't told Seth the whole truth about the reason for his means of travel.

Since he arrived back at the ranch from The Springs, he had been trying to concoct an excuse to go to the Morton ranch. He finally decided that he would ride there on the pretext of visiting Mr. Morton. Thad Bruce and Willard Morton had long been close friends. It would be reasonable for T. C. to ride by on his way to town, ask about Mr. Morton's health, and then report on the visit to his father. He hoped, of course, that Sarah would be there. Perhaps she would answer the door and ask him to join them for a meal. That would give him the opportunity to find out more about her and perhaps arrange future visits. Such musings occupied his time during the eight-mile trip to the ford in the Musselshell River. The thoughts continued as he rode up the north side of the river to the Morton buildings.

Dogs barked as he rode into the yard but no one came to see what was causing the commotion. He tied his horses to the rail at the back entrance to the main house and walked up the path to the door. T. C. heard the noises of someone's slow progress in response to his knock. When it finally opened, Mr. Morton, leaning on a crutch, greeted the son of his old friend warmly. "Come on in."

T. C. followed him into the large kitchen, where Mr. Morton waved him to a straight-backed chair as he settled into a rocker. It was obvious the rocker was the place where he now spent his waking hours.

"So, you're on your way to The Springs. Well, it was kind of you to stop by to ask about my foot. Tell your father that the gout is no fun. Now I understand how frustrating it's been for him to put up with his game leg all of these years. But getting old is something we all have to suffer, unless we're lucky enough to die." The last was said with a smile and a laugh. "But son," he continued, "You don't fool me. Every young buck in the valley and some from across the mountains have come to this house since Sarah arrived. At least you have a leg up on the rest. You were kind to her on a stage ride. When she got home that night, she described you and it wasn't hard to figure out who she was talking about. You made a good impression. You're out of luck right now, though. Sarah went with my wife to help Mrs. Larson, who is sickly. You know where the Larson's live, don't you? It's down the river near Two Dot. They'll probably be gone for a few days."

T. C. shifted in his chair and hoped his embarrassment didn't show. His pretense for the visit was indeed transparent. The old gentleman didn't make the situation any more awkward. "I'd ask you to stay for dinner, but that's two hours away. You have a long way to travel. Besides, I need to lie down. That may stop the throbbing in this foot." He rubbed his leg. The pain showed on his face.

Before he could speak further, T. C. was on his feet, hat in hand, ready to bolt to the door. "You're right, sir. I plan to get to Castle tonight. I'd better get on my way if I'm going to make it. I'll tell my father about your gout. I can find my way out. You needn't get up." He shook Mr. Morton's hand and walked from the house as fast as decency would allow.

T. C. rode toward Martinsdale with his head hanging down, mumbling to himself about his stupidity. Every worthless cowpuncher in the country had done the exact same thing that he had just done in an attempt to make acquaintance with Sarah. Most of them had no knowledge of the social graces so their actions were excusable. His were not. He should have arranged a time to call at the Morton house with their approval. Instead, he had acted like an imbecile. Sarah would learn of it as soon as she returned and would laugh to herself. Any chance that he had of impressing her had disappeared. He realized, his hope was for something more than an acquaintance with the schoolteacher.

As he approached town, T. C. mused that he had recently crossed paths with two interesting women, and both had made a fool of him. After more thought, he admitted that he had twice made a fool of himself.

It was past noon when he reached Martinsdale, so he put his horses up at the livery stable and went to the cafe for dinner. The food was

Ride the Jawbone

like the food in the cafe at Two Dot and the atmosphere was much the same as well. He ate alone, left a tip for the waitress, and paid the bill. Back at the stable, he saddled and packed his horses again and headed west to the mining community of Castle. It was approaching seven o'clock in the evening when he rode into the decaying town that had been so busy a few short years before.

T. C. found a livery stable, paid for his horses' care, and then sought out the one hotel that remained in business. He checked in, took his belongings to his room, and then ventured into the hotel dining room. The place had once been rather elegant, but hard times had taken their toll. One of the windows was cracked and covered over with muslin to keep out the flies and some of the wind. The dishes and eating utensils still showed their past glory. T. C. ordered from a menu that had all of the extraordinary offerings crossed off. Those that remained were the standard fare in any eating place in the west. When his meal arrived, the beef was cooked to leather, the boiled potatoes were mushy, and the coffee tasted like iodine. He ate every bite.

++++++++++

Sarah arrived back at the Morton Ranch that same evening. Mrs. Morton believed she could be of more help if she cared for the man with the gout. Mr. Morton growled that he could care for himself, but was secretly pleased to have the company of such a charming companion. During supper he told her that young T. C. Bruce had come calling. The quiet woman nodded an acknowledgment and focused her eyes on her plate.

After the supper dishes were washed and put away, Sarah retired to her room and reflected upon the course of her life and the things that had brought her to Montana. She was born to an Iowa farmer and his wife and spent a lonely childhood. Her father was one who demanded work from others. He was neither mean nor abusive, but he never let his wife or child rest from the labors that he laid out for them each day. She had been allowed to go to school for only two years before he decided that her time would be better spent working on the farm. But the two years had been enough for her to learn to read. From that time on, she read anything that she could find, squinting at the

65

print by candlelight after a hard day's labor. She read her mother's Bible from cover to cover. She read the catalogues that sometimes came in the mail. On occasion one of the neighbor ladies would bring a book for her to read. Among them were novels, books of poetry, books of history, and even books that taught mathematics. When she was fifteen years old, Oliver, the neighbor boy, came calling. It was apparent that Sarah's parents approved of him. He was an only son and would someday inherit a large farm. Oliver was tall and powerful. He could work in the fields all day without rest. But his shoulders were narrow and hips were broad. He was neither good looking nor ugly. He was dull. As Sarah contemplated the future in her room at night, she could see herself with Oliver, living a life identical to one she had lived up to that point. The thought that there could be nothing more, nothing like the adventures she read about in the books left her with a feeling of hopelessness. The more frequent Oliver's visits became, the more she became distressed. One day, while she was hoeing potatoes, she realized that there was nothing that said that she had to stay in that small community for the rest of her life. The books had told her that there were other places and other ways of making a living. That evening, after the work was done, she went to her room and packed her few belongings in a cloth sack. At the age of seventeen, Sarah crawled out a window and walked down the road and away from the place of her birth.

She asked for work at the cafe in the small town closest to the farm. The woman who operated the cafe recognized her, knew that she would work hard, and put her to washing dishes. She allowed Sarah to sleep that night on a blanket under the stair. Sarah washed dishes after the morning breakfast was served, and then she told her employer she would leave. The woman was unhappy to have her go, but did not argue. She gave Sarah a fifty-cent piece for her wages and wished her well. Outside the building, Sarah looked at the coin in her hand with some wonder. It was the first time in all of her life that she had held money of any kind. It was the first time that she had ever had anything that belonged to her alone. She had always understood that everything, even the clothes she wore, belonged to her father. The young lady put the coin in her bag and began the walk down the road to the next town. She knew she must put as much distance between herself and her father's farm as possible before he came looking for her. She was certain that he would not let her get away if he could prevent it. To him she represented free labor. He would drag her home, if he found her.

Upon reaching the next town late in the evening, she walked down the main street, wondering what she should do to get something to eat and secure a place to sleep. A two-story hotel gave the appearance of prosperity. The burly wife of the proprietor said the chambermaid had just quit in a huff. Sarah promptly found herself making beds and cleaning rooms, all the while listening to her employer scold her because she didn't work faster. When she finished cleaning, she washed bedclothes. At eleven o'clock that night, food was placed in front of her on a bench in the washroom. The proprietress pointed to a table and said, "Sleep there." For all the washing there was not a dry blanket to be found. Being so weary from her labors, she needed none to sleep.

At five o'clock in the morning, breakfast consisted of cornmeal mush and black coffee. In less than fifteen minutes she was cleaning the lobby of the hotel. Before long, the proprietor himself appeared at the desk. He was bald with a huge belly and a foul odor of alcohol. As she worked, she noticed that he watched her constantly. Sarah worried that her efforts were not sufficient and the man would report to his wife that she was lazy. So her cleaning activities became even more frenetic. When she finished doing all she had been directed to do in the lobby, she was sent again to the washhouse to wash the bedding. Not long after she began, the proprietor walked in and, without a word, put both arms around her waist, pulled her close, and tried to kiss her.

Strong from a life of hard work, Sarah simply pulled away. She looked him in the eye and said, "I shall tell the Mrs."

A look of panic appeared on the old rogue's face and, in a half whisper, he ordered her not to do so. He reached into his pocket, pulled out a five-dollar gold piece, handed it to her, and told her to leave town immediately. He dashed out of the washhouse without looking back.

Sarah stood for a moment, thinking about the thing that had just happened. For the first time, she understood that she had some control over the way she was treated by men. Up to that time, she had assumed that a man, any man, had to be obeyed. It was certain, however, that she must leave. She went to the wife, told her that the wash was finished, and asked for her pay, not knowing whether the woman would compensate her. Having received money from the woman at the cafe, she understood that laborers expected payment. The woman scolded her roundly, handed her a silver dollar, pointed toward the door, and told her to, "Get the hell out."

Down the street she walked past the store, past two saloons, and past the livery stable to the stage station. Inside, people were buying tickets from a man behind a counter. She waited until they had all completed their business and left before she approached the ticket agent. When she walked up to the counter he smiled and asked, "Where to, Missy?" His teeth were yellow and crooked.

Sarah had not really thought about a destination. She was at first at a loss for a reply. "Centerville," she said. It was a name she had heard one of the neighbor ladies mention some years ago.

"That will be one dollar." The stationmaster continued to smile at her. The thought of giving up money that she had just acquired filled her, momentarily, with a sense of terror. That feeling must have shown on her face as she fumbled in her bag, because the stationmaster stopped smiling to ask, "What's wrong, Missy? Don't you have the money?" Before she could reply, he glanced around to assure that no one else would hear and then continued, "Such a pretty lady shouldn't look so sad." His voice dropped to a whisper. "Missy, I can let you on the stage, but you have to promise that you won't tell anyone. It could cost me my job." He handed her a ticket, smiled his broken tooth smile, and told her that the stage would leave in about an hour.

Sarah spent the hour sitting in the shade on the porch of the stage station, thinking about men. Certainly they were not very intelligent. Her father never thought about anything but work. Oliver was just plain dull. The man at the hotel obviously depended upon his wife to make the living. The stationmaster was taken in by her appearance as a woman in distress. If men were stupid, then that fact could be used to her advantage. In the short time since running away from home, Sarah had learned a great deal, and with it came confidence that she could care for herself.

At Centerville, she asked for work at the hotel. The man who ran the place told her that he had no need for another employee. As she was leaving, he told her that the minister's wife was ailing, and the man might need someone to help with the housework and the children.

Ride the Jawbone

Sarah wasted no time following his directions. They led her to a small house on a side street. A girl about ten years of age answered her knock on the door. She said her father was at the church, but her mother was home. The child led Sarah into a large room where a woman, reclining on a couch, introduced herself as Mrs. Dorman.

"What can I do for you," she asked Sarah.

"I was told you might need someone to help care for the house and the children," Sarah explained.

Mrs. Dorman scowled and finally said, "My husband must be consulted about such matters. Please come back in the afternoon."

Sarah sat on a log in a small park until she was certain that enough time had passed. Upon her return to the Dorman house, she found herself alone in the presence of the minister himself. He was tall, nice looking, and younger than the preacher who once called at the home of her parents. After some preliminary small talk, he told her that his wife had an ailment that had not responded to any kind of treatment.

"She's growing weaker as the days go by. Indeed, I need help. I can pay fifteen dollars a month and a bedroom in exchange for cooking and all the other household tasks. My wife must do nothing but rest."

Sarah, astonished that she would receive fifteen dollars each month and have a place of her own, accepted the terms immediately. The Reverend Dorman took her to the little room that would be hers and, as he left her to settle in, suggested that boiling beef would be good for supper. He told her the meat was in the meat house out back and the other supplies were in the pantry. He also gently suggested that she bathe before beginning the evening meal. He told her there was a room with a lock on the door and a tub into which she could pour warm water from the stove.

Sarah was not accustomed to such privacy. She had hated to bathe at home because the kitchen was the only place to do it. She looked forward to the opportunity to bathe in solitude, but decided to first acquaint herself with the pantry and kitchen. On her way to find the pantry, she saw the library. She didn't know so many books existed.

The Dormans proved to be kind and friendly people. Of their three children the girl who met Sarah at the door was the oldest. The two younger children were rambunctious boys. All were lovable. Mrs. Dorman, sick though she might be, was considerate of Sarah and constantly apologized because she could not help. At first, she tried to care for herself, but in time she came to trust Sarah's capabilities and began to spend more and more time at rest.

Though she was too ill to do much in a physical sense, Mrs. Dorman instructed Sarah in the manners expected of a woman in polite society. Sarah's upbringing had been harsh, and she knew little about how a proper person should act toward others. Sarah learned such things as the proper way to set a table, when to say "please" and "thank you," and how to sit, stand, and walk like a lady. Much to Sarah's delight, Mrs. Dorman asked her to make over clothing that she could no longer wear for Sarah to use. Soon, she not only exhibited all the social graces but was able to dress as a lady. No one ever again had to suggest to her that she should bathe.

The Reverend, too, was considerate of her. He involved her in discussions that he carried on with his wife and children at mealtime. Those discussions often had to do with events that occurred outside their small community. From them, Sarah began to understand much more of the world around her. Before long, she found herself not only learning, but helping to educate the children. The Reverend understood her desire to read and encouraged her to sample any of the books in the library at any time. He suggested that she read to the children, and she did so each evening before putting them to bed, sharing fantasies about the world beyond Centerville.

While the Reverend was kind to Sarah, he doted upon his wife. His love for her was obvious, and Sarah marveled at it. Nothing like it had ever been displayed in her home. For the first time, she began to think of the possibility of marriage to someone who would be kind rather than brutish, as was her father, and who would be intelligent rather than dull, as was Oliver.

She also began to realize that the Dormans received money for which they didn't have to work. The notion of investments that earned interest was, at first, beyond her comprehension. One day the Reverend told her that both he and his wife had inherited money from their parents, which they invested in such a way as to provide income. It was because of the investment income that he was able to pursue his calling to the ministry and still maintain a reasonable living standard. Sarah thought about the money she had earned since leaving home, money that she now kept in a belt she had made of canvas, worn about her hips. She was not going to give it to someone else on the promise that she would receive income. It was hers. But, if someday she met a man who also had investments and who would take an interest in her, maybe she would marry and live as the Dormans did.

There were men, lots of men, who were interested in her. She had come to realize that she was attractive and that her improved bearing, flattered by the clothes she had received from Mrs. Dorman, made her stand out from the other young women of the town. Men, young and old, came to call at the Dorman house, asking to see the preacher, but more likely hoping to visit with her and perhaps invite her to a social. She did nothing to encourage any of them because none of them met her requirements. Mrs. Dorman was her ally. The sickly woman told Sarah that she did not have to hurry into marriage just because she was at a marriageable age. She kept assuring Sarah that in time the right man would come along. After all, it had happened to her when she had found the Reverend.

It took Mrs. Dorman almost a year to die. After her death, the Reverend became withdrawn and introspective. He was still attentive to his children and kind to Sarah, but the loss of his wife left him sad and lonely. About six months later, however, his attitude began to revert to that which had existed before his wife died. One day, he brought another woman to the house, introduced her to the children and to Sarah, and told them that he and the lady planned to marry. She was a childless widow from his congregation who seemed to be genuinely interested in the Dorman children. That evening, after the little ones were in bed, the Reverend told Sarah that her services would no longer be required after the wedding. He told her that the school was in need of a teacher, and that he had arranged for her to fill the position, if she was interested. She could live in the teacherage. It was comfortable and stood close to the schoolhouse so she would not have to walk far during the winter cold. The salary would be thirty dollars a month.

The idea of payment of thirty dollars a month gave Sarah visions of savings large enough to assure her well being in the event she became sick or disabled. She had enjoyed reading to the Dorman children. Reading to other children should be just as enjoyable.

After she agreed to take the position, the Reverend reminded her that she would be required to teach, not only reading, but also mathematics, penmanship, geography, history, grammar, and music. Seeing the look of confusion on her face, he explained that she could simply read the textbooks ahead of her students and, in effect, teach herself to teach as she went along. She did just that. She taught the children of the town for the next two years.

Toward the end of the second year, the mother of one of her students spoke to her about the states in the west. The woman had an aunt living in Montana who frequently wrote in glowing terms of life in that far away place. Opportunities there were unlimited and young men of talent and ambition arrived daily. Sarah began to think about moving on. While she enjoyed the teaching and the children, there seemed little likelihood that she would find the future of which she dreamed in Centerville. The men who paid court to her were all too much like Oliver. But the men who ventured to Montana should not be dull. Apparently, it took courage and self-confidence to go there. If the opportunities were as plentiful as reported, some of those men should have accumulated wealth. Sarah's period of deliberation was short. She decided she would go to Lewistown, in central Montana, where the letter writer lived. There she would seek a teaching position.

Sarah arrived by train at Billings, on the Yellowstone River. From there, she rode the stage to Lewistown. The letter writer greeted her warmly and almost immediately arranged for them to visit Willard Morton. There was certain to be a need for a teacher in the Musselshell valley, now that the Jawbone Railroad had come and the population was exploding.

++++++++++

In her room at the Morton ranch in the evening. Sarah thought that it had been wise to leave Iowa. Young T. C. Bruce was obviously interested in her. He seemed to have all of the characteristics that she desired. Her task was to get to know him. "He's a lawyer. If I'm to teach, there will be a contract. That will provide me with the opportunity."

Later in the evening, thoughts of her mother crossed her mind. Not once since Sarah left home had she contacted her parents, fearing her father would somehow drag her back to the farm. But now, long miles from that place, it was only right to let her mother know where she was. Gathering the writing material, she said to the empty room, "I wonder what mother has thought of me all of these years? And what will she think of the things that I've done?"

May 22nd

T. C. encountered Olaf Bakken at breakfast the next morning. A Norwegian immigrant, he had accumulated thousands of sheep and the large land holdings needed to graze them. T. C. who had never met the man in person, recognized him by his imposing stature and the accent with which he spoke.

Mr. Bakken graciously invited T. C. to join him for breakfast, and when he realized that his table companion was the son of Thad Bruce, he warmed to the conversation. T. C. began by asking him about his experiences when he came to the United States, and Mr. Bakken, who reveled in telling of his hard work and financial prowess, entertained him throughout the meal. Not until the final cup of coffee, did T. C. ask about the sheepherder who had found the murdered woman.

"Ah, yes. He works for me." Mr. Bakken said. "He's camped on Allebaugh Creek below Castle Lake. He'll be bringing his band down to the ranch in a month or so for shearing."

T. C. told of his obligation to defend Loco, and asked if he could ride to the herder's camp to talk with him about the matter.

Mr. Bakken frowned. "I never thought the son of Thad Bruce would try to save the hide of a killer, but I won't try to stop you from visiting my herder." He gave T. C. directions to the sheep camp, paid the bill for both of their meals, and wished T. C. well before leaving the hotel. His well wishes seemed a bit half-hearted, however.

T. C. headed west from Castle until he reached Allebaugh Creek, and then followed the creek upstream. The morning was bright and cool, but not uncomfortable. The foul mood that had plagued him after his visit to the Morton ranch drained away. Enveloped in the beauty that surrounded him, he sang Scottish songs, learned from his mother, as he rode.

The sheep camp was on a flat bench not more than a hundred yards from the creek. T. C. noted the herder's wagon, typical in appearance. Large hoops topped the wagon box with heavy canvas covering them. Dutch doors provided entry and the top door was latched open. A woodpile flanked by a huge chopping block with an ax stuck in it was close at hand. A round of ham could be seen hanging from the branch of one of the trees that grew nearby. The ham was enclosed in a flour sack, suspended out of reach of bears and other varmints.

Arriving before noon, T. C.'s first inclination was to look for the band of sheep and the sheepherder. Then he reasoned that the sheep would bed down during the middle of the day, and the herder would probably return to the wagon to eat. It would be easier to let the herder find him than it would be for him to find the herder. To make himself useful and to pass the time, he chopped some wood. With the approach of the noon hour, he decided to prepare the noon meal while he waited. The inside of the wagon was as neat and tidy as a house kept by the most fastidious of women. The bed across the back was made up, with a tarp stretched over the blankets in the same way that a bedspread might be arranged in a fine hotel. The eating utensils were clean and in the cupboard. A flour sack dish towel, snowy white in its cleanliness, was folded over its hanger. Not the typical sheep camp.

T. C. started a fire in the stove. While it heated, he lowered the ham from its place in the tree and cut slabs from it for two men. He put the ham slices into a pan filled with water in order to boil out some of the salt with which the meat had been cured. After draining off the hot water, he dropped the ham back into the same pan for frying, then sliced potatoes into another pan and added chunks of onion for seasoning. In one of the cupboards, he found a can of stewed tomatoes, good when eaten cold. Whistling as he worked and concentrating on cooking, T. C. didn't see the herder top a rise to the rear of the wagon.

++++++++++

Leading his teepee horse over a small hill, Pete saw smoke rising from the chimney of his wagon. He stopped, wary, and watched to see who was there. When the intruder exited for more firewood, Pete could see that it wasn't the usual camp tender. He hesitated. Should he go back to the sheep or face his visitor? He pulled a large kerchief from his pocket and tied it around his face so that only his eyes were visible above the cloth. He picked up the halter rope, called to his dog, and walked briskly down to the camp.

T. C. stepped out just as the herder came round the front of the wagon. The two men met face to face, not ten feet apart.

The man staring at T. C. over the bandanna was about his size and appeared to be about his age. His dress was that of any man of the range, but much more neat and clean than one would expect on a sheepherder. When the man finally spoke his voice was soft and melodious. "Howdy."

T. C. stepped forward and extended his hand to introduce himself. "I took the liberty of cooking some dinner for both of us. It's ready—if you can stand my cooking."

The herder hesitated for a moment before he answered. "Your cooking will be fine. Let me put up my horse." He led his horse to the nearby trees where he removed the saddle and tied the animal to a picket rope.

T. C. got two tin plates out of the cupboard and forks and knives from one of the drawers, poured coffee from the pot into two tin cups. He watched the herder pull off his coat and hat and hang them over the tongue of the wagon as he prepared to wash. The cloth remained over his face.

At last the herder stepped up to the crude bench that served for a table. He looked T. C. in the eye and asked, "You don't know who I am?" Before T. C. could reply, he continued, "I'm called Noseless Pete by most people." Saying nothing more, he stood for a moment, waiting for a reaction from his visitor.

T. C. was at a loss for a reply. He remembered the story that the murdered woman had been found by a herder called Noseless Pete. He had put the name out of his mind as being of no consequence, since most herders had some kind of nickname. The tone of the man's voice made him realize the name was important. In an attempt at a proper response he said, "Well, Pete, as I said, I'm T. C. Shall we eat?"

Again, there was hesitation by the herder. Finally, he said in the softest of tones, "You may not be able to eat with me." He pulled the cloth down from his face and continued to look squarely at his visitor.

T. C. gasped. A sudden involuntary inhalation of air. He just stared at the face. After a long moment, he realized that he was staring and tried to look away, but couldn't. He opened his mouth to speak, but not a word came out.

The man had no nose!

The herder's mouth, above a firm jaw, was wide and perfectly shaped. But above the upper lip, instead of a nose, there were two large holes that allowed T. C. to look directly into the nasal cavities. The skin had adhered to the bone around the place where the nose should have been. The edges near the sinus openings were covered with scar tissue. Above the openings there was a long vertical scar that ran through the skin between his eyebrows and about an inch beyond toward his hairline. The word that came silently into T. C.'s mind was *hideous*.

After several heartbeats, while the two men stood immobile without a sound following T. C.'s gasp, Pete asked, "Do you still want to eat?" The question held no rancor or cynicism. It was just a question.

T. C. felt himself pull back a step. He then gathered his wits and looked away toward the food on the table. "I want to eat, but are you sure that you can stomach the grub?"

The lips below the nonexistent nose smiled. "Let's both try it," he replied with a soft laugh.

They sat cross-legged on the ground to eat the sheep-camp fare. Neither of them said a word until the plates were empty and they were holding a second cup of coffee. Then T. C. began his explanation. "I'm told that you're the one who found the dead woman near the railroad tracks below Summit. I'm a lawyer, and the judge has asked me to defend the man accused of killing her. If I'm to do that, I need to find out as much as I can about the case. The best place to start seemed to be with the one who found her."

"I found her. What else do you want to know?"

"Anything that you can tell me. Why not start by telling me what you saw when you happened upon the body."

Pete thought a moment before answering. "I was camped at a spring on the mountain just north of Summit. When the sheep pulled out in the morning, I pushed them down from the camp and across the divide just west of town. From there, they went up along the mountainside below the railroad tracks. The grass on the west slope was better than elsewhere. When the sheep crossed a coulee, I could see them shy around something down in the bottom. As the they moved beyond that place, the dog ran ahead of me. He stood absolutely still at the spot where the sheep had spooked. Looking down from the north side, I could see that it was a body before I even got near it."

The herder got up from the ground and stretched his legs. He continued his story while leaning against the front of the wagon. "I called the dog so that he wouldn't disturb whoever or whatever it was until I could get there." He paused, shaking his head slightly. "She was lying on her back with one arm stretched out on the ground and with the other across her body. She had a hat with a large brim that covered most of her face, but not all it. The magpies had been working on the one eye that wasn't covered. That eye was gone."

T. C. watched the face of the narrator while he talked. The movement of the lips below the place where a nose should have been was as normal as could be, but without any protrusion above them, their movement seemed grotesque. He was so absorbed by the strange appearance of his companion that he was not aware for a moment that Pete had stopped speaking. T. C. finally asked, "What did you do?"

"I didn't know what to do. But I couldn't just leave her lying there, and I had no way to move her. So, I hiked up the hill to the depot at Summit—it wasn't very far—and told the stationmaster what I'd found. Then I got out of there as fast as I could, so I didn't have to talk to anyone else."

"Where did you go?"

"I followed my sheep. They'd crossed the track and gone up the side of the mountain south of town. As I looked back from the mountainside, I could see people stringing out toward the coulee where she was lying. After a while, they got a buggy near enough so they could carry her back to town. I don't know what they did with her after that."

Pete turned away to look off in the direction of his sheep. From that position the facial distortion could not be seen, and for a moment he appeared to T. C. as an ordinary looking young man. But when he turned again to face T. C., the image vanished. The visitor saw only the horrible apparition that should have been a handsome countenance.

T. C. had difficulty in concentrating on his mission. The face filled both his vision and his mind. At last he asked, "How was she dressed?"

"I can't recall anything specific about her clothes. She wore a dress, and her skirt was kind of twisted about her legs. She wore no gloves, and I didn't see a purse. But then I didn't look for one. I didn't touch her at all, not even to move the hat to see what she looked like. It seemed almost sacrilegious to do so."

As the herder spoke, T. C. began to concentrate more upon the things that he said and less upon his appearance. He noticed that the man did not speak the course vernacular of an ordinary sheepherder. He spoke like an educated man. T. C. wanted to ask about his background, but didn't think he should. To keep the conversation going, he asked, "Could you tell how she got to where you found her?"

"The sheep trailed all around the body and would've tramped out any tracks there might have been. I saw nothing else that showed how she got there. I made a sketch. Would you like to see it?"

Without waiting for an answer, he stepped up on the wagon tongue and into the wagon. T. C. stood and watched. Pete went to the bed and reached under the coverings. He pulled out several large sheets of composition paper, shuffled them around until he found the one he wanted, and carried it to the door of the wagon. T. C. took the sketch, held it out at arm's length and gazed at it in amazement. It was an extremely detailed ink drawing of the location of the body, just as Pete had described it.

Pete stepped back out of the wagon as T. C. asked, "Did you do this?" Without waiting for the answer, he added, "Do you have one that shows the condition of the body?"

"No. I just made that sketch the day after I found her because it was so strange to see a dead woman lying where she was."

"Could you draw a picture of the body as you found it?"

"I'm sure I could. My memory is good. It's a sight that I'm not likely to forget."

T. C., now focused on the purpose of his visit, realized that pictures could be valuable evidence. He would need the artist in court to testify as to their origin.

"I pass the time by drawing pictures," Pete said. "Would you like to see any more of them? None of the others have anything to do with the murdered woman."

Ride the Jawbone

T. C. nodded.

Pete climbed back into the wagon, rolled his bedroll back, and picked up more stiff sheets that rested on the base of the bed. He carried them out into the light and leaned them, one by one, against the wheels of the wagon, against the chopping block and against a tree. T. C. walked along behind him, looking at each one in turn.

During his years in law school, T. C. had often visited the Minnesota State Gallery. These pictures may not have equalled the works of the masters, but they were as good as most of those that he had admired. Each picture differed from the others. There were landscapes, sketches of several different dogs, and some wildlife. Only one was of a person, probably the camp tender who brought the groceries and moved Pete's wagon. Each and every one was beautifully lifelike. He walked from one to the next and back again as Pete stood and watched his guest.

"None of them are in color. Have you tried watercolor or oil paint?"

Pete sat down on the wagon tongue, chewed the inside of his cheek, and, instead of answering, said, "Perhaps you would like to know more about me. My name is Pierre Bouteron. I was raised in St. Louis, where my father was a merchant. Well, actually, he was in the import-export business. He purchased goods abroad and brought them up the river from New Orleans. His agents bought goods for export in the Midwest, and these were sent down the river and to countries all around the world. Our family is well to do and I had a genteel upbringing." T. C. raised his eyebrows at the use of the word genteel, but Pete continued. "My parents sent me to private schools when I was small and to St. Louis University when I grew up. At the university I began to apply the artistic talent that I've had since childhood."

Pierre Bouteron shifted his weight on the wagon tongue, paused, and then renewed his tale. "Everyone who sees me wonders what happened to my face. You're no different from the rest." The herder stared into the distance as he continued. "We have a large farm outside of St. Louis where wild game abounds. My father taught me to hunt at an early age, and I really enjoyed tramping the woods and occasionally shooting at a wild animal that crossed my path. One day, in the fall of the year, I was out hiking. On the far side of a creek were some plants that I'd never noticed before. The leaves had turned and were the brightest hue of red that you can imagine. I leaned to my right to get a better look at the plants, and the rifle that I was carrying slipped in my hand and dropped to the ground. The jar as the butt hit the earth caused it to discharge. The bullet struck me squarely on the bottom of my nose and creased my forehead." Pete rubbed the scar above his eyes.

"The force of it knocked me flat. At first, there wasn't much pain and the blood didn't start to flow for a moment or two. I just lay there, kind of stunned. Then the pain came, and I realized what had happened. I got up and ran toward the house holding my hand to my face."

The herder stopped, his gaze still focused on the far distance. T. C., fascinated by the story, joined the herder on the wagon tongue.

Pete continued. "The wife of the farm manager was in the yard. I screamed that I was hurt and took my hand away, revealing my injury. The look of horror that appeared on her face was one that I've now seen over and over again. I asked for help, but she just stood there without moving. I reached out to her, but she jerked back away from me. I couldn't understand. I didn't know how I looked. Finally, she called for my father. He took me to a hospital where the doctors did all that they could for me, but there was no way to save my nose." He swallowed hard and looked at the ground. "The healing was slow, and I stayed in the hospital for a long time. The people there grew accustomed to my looks. It was after I left the hospital that my torment really began."

Of course, T. C. thought, no one could look at the man without being repelled. The reaction of others must have been almost impossible to bear.

"My parents tried to help. They had an artificial nose created from wood and painted flesh color. I tied it to my head, but it was painful to wear and only emphasized my disfigurement. Eventually, I decided that my only recourse was to avoid people."

Pete walked toward his horse and stood for a moment before facing T. C. again. "There was a girl. We had talked of marriage. At first, she tried to be kind and led me to believe that it would make no difference. But, of course, that could not be true. It was a difficult day for her when she told me that she simply couldn't cope with my appearance. The greatest hurt was that she wasn't able to look at my face while she told me." The anguish in his eyes told T. C. the pain had not lessened over time. "But, I couldn't blame her. Who would want to spend a life with someone who looks like this?

"For a while, I just stayed in my room in my parents' house. The servants brought meals to me so that no one would have to eat in my presence. I read a lot to pass the time, and from one of the magazines I learned of sheepherders who spent their days alone with the flocks. It was an occupation that suited my circumstances to perfection. So I came west, found Olaf Bakken, and began herding sheep." A smile moved his lips again. "I was right. This way of life is the only one I can follow. No one has to look at me but the camp tender, and I cover my face when he's here." He smiled again. "At least the sheep and my dog don't care how I look." Pete rubbed his jaw.

"Do you know how hard it is to keep clean in a sheep camp? I shave every day, but bathing is difficult. When it's too cold to bathe in the creek, I heat water on the stove to wash." Pulling off his hat, he looked at T. C. and said with a laugh that was close to a giggle, "Try cutting your own hair sometime." His hair was long and combed back over his head. He had simply cut it in a ragged line above his shoulders. His face turned sober again, and he went on, "I'm twenty eight years old. I'll herd sheep for forty more years or so, and then I'll die. When they lay me in the ground the rest of my flesh will fall off. But so will the flesh of all the others in the graveyard around me. Then, once again, I'll be like all the rest."

T. C. listened without interrupting. When the tale was ended, he didn't know what to say. To offer sympathy seemed hollow. To attempt to downplay the condition of the storyteller would be cruel. So he asked the same question again. "Have you done any work in watercolor or oil?"

The question was so far removed from the confession given by Pete that the herder burst into a loud laugh. "In the winter. In the winter I stay at a cabin not far from the Bakken ranch for about four months steady. While I'm there, I do some painting. It's too hard to keep the materials for painting in a sheep wagon that moves every couple of weeks."

The trial was on T. C.'s mind again. "Could you reproduce the picture of the place where you found the body but on a larger scale? And could you do a picture that would portray the body as you found it? I'd like to have them to show to the jury. If you could do that, I'll come back and pick them up before the trial begins."

Pete didn't answer right away, but stood off looking into the distance, as seemed to be his habit. At last, he turned to T. C. "I'll do the pictures as best I can, but I'll need larger paper to do it. I'll ask the camptender to bring some, but it will take at least two weeks to get here. And it will take some time after that to do the drawings. When is your trial?"

"The trial date hasn't been set, but I will know by the end of the month. The judge indicated it will be late in June."

"The shearing crew comes early in June. I'll be moving down to a camp near the home ranch. You can find me there." Pete looked at the sun. "It's time for the sheep to move again. I have to get back to them. You're welcome to stay as long as you wish."

"I'll clean things up and then be on my way. I plan to ride into White Sulphur tonight by way of Four-Mile Creek. But I'll hunt you up again before the middle of June."

After a handshake, Pete struck out for the sheep with his dog and horse in tow. T. C. washed the dishes and returned them to the places where he had found them. He saddled his horses and headed north across the mountain on his way into town. As he rode, he chastised himself. He hadn't told the herder that he would need him to testify in person at the trial. He feared the man would quit the country rather than face the crowd of people that was bound to be in the courtroom to hear his testimony.

++++++++++

Pete reached the band of sheep just as they were pulling out from their noon bed ground. He continued on to the top of a small hill where he could keep them in sight and sat down beside a large boulder that provided a backrest. The dog stretched out next to him with his head resting on Pete's leg. Pete stroked the dog's head and said, "That lawyer will want me to testify at his trial." Without realizing what he was doing, he reached up and pulled the cloth over his face.

Ride the Jawbone

T. C. crossed the top of the mountain and followed Four-Mile Creek down to the North Fork of the Smith River. From there, he followed the stage road to town. He knew he must soon visit Loco to learn if the man had changed his habits. Thoughts of Loco, and his filthy appearance brought to mind his trip to the store to purchase clothing for the man. And that, of course, led to thoughts of the lady that had waited upon him. He hoped she had forgotten his foolish behavior.

He went directly to his parents home, put his horses up in the barn, gathered his belongings, and walked in the kitchen door after giving one knock. His mother was busy with a mop in her continuing attempt to make a clean floor cleaner.

"Hello, Thad. Don't track the floor." She half smiled as she added, "Your father's in his chair. He'll be glad to see you."

The urge to hug her returned, but he only gave a pleasant nod as on his way into the sitting room. His father looked up from the book he was reading and, much to the surprise of his son, struggled up from his chair, and reached out to clasp T. C.'s hand. "It's good to have you home, son. Your mother and I have been anxious." Retreating to his chair, he directed T. C. to sit nearby. "What do you have to report?"

T. C. began to tell of the ranch activities, only to be interrupted by his father. "What are your plans for the trial? The trial is all the talk of the town." The question was unexpected. His father usually wanted to hear about the ranch before anything else.

"I've done some research about the insanity defense, and on my way here, I went to see the sheepherder who found the dead woman. He will help—if he will testify. I plan to visit with the doctor to learn more of the manner in which she died. I should probably talk to the stationmaster at Summit, since he was one of the people who picked up the body." T. C. stopped and looked intently at his father. "What are people saying?"

"Well, they're all wondering when the judge will set the trial. And, of course, they're all wondering how you'll try to convince a jury that Loco is innocent when everyone knows that he's guilty."

"And how do they know that?"

83

"They don't need any reason to believe he's guilty, they just know that he is. But as a practical matter, they've been listening to the sheriff. Archie tells anyone who will listen that there is no question that Loco killed her and that no reasonable jury will turn him loose."

"That will make it even more difficult to pick a jury. I wonder if I should move the court for a change of venue?" Almost without stopping, he answered his own question. "It wouldn't do any good. The judge isn't going to impose the cost of a venue change on the county and have the county commissioners mad at him. Besides, the newspapers around the state have all reported the murder, so it would be hard to find a jury anywhere that wouldn't know about it. I suppose I should make the motion anyway."

Mrs. Bruce entered the room and brushed a wisp of hair from her forehead as she took her accustomed chair facing her husband. "We know just about everyone who might be called to serve on that jury, and we can help you select the ones who will listen to the evidence in court and then make their decision. You'll be far better off here than in a strange town." She spoke in a tone of voice that T. C. had not heard since he was a small child. As a child he had heard it only when she had made a final, unappealable decision that he must accept.

He glanced at his father to see him smiling broadly. "You'd better listen to your mother. I've learned that she's right most of the time."

"What of this sheepherder that you said could help, but might not testify? You can make him do it, can't you?" Mrs. Bruce asked.

"Yes, Mother, I can serve him with a subpoena, and he'll have to come to court. But it may not be that simple." T. C. wondered how much he should tell his parents about the lonesome artist. Somehow, it seemed wrong to share the things Pete had told him. But, if the herder were to testify, T. C.'s parents would learn of the man's deformities. "The sheepherder's name is Pierre Bouteron, but they call him Noseless Pete. The name is given for a good reason—he hasn't any nose." T. C. watched for a reaction, but both of their faces remained impassive. "As you can understand, he doesn't like to be seen by others. That's why he's a sheepherder. But the man is a gifted artist and has made drawings of the murder scene that could be helpful at the trial."

Mrs. Bruce seemed to be having difficulty imagining noselessness and said, "Describe him to me."

"He lost his nose in a hunting accident. Where his nose should be there's nothing but two holes in his face. His appearance is grotesque."

"What kind of a person is he?" Mrs. Bruce asked.

"He's educated. He's neat and clean. He's tall, and, except for his deformity, would be very good looking. What happened to him is tragic, and I don't want to add to his hurt by forcing him to appear in court in front of all the people that will be there."

"Well, couldn't you just show the pictures to the jury without bringing him along?

"That's not the way it works, Mother. I'll have to lay a foundation for the introduction of the pictures into evidence. To do that, I must have the artist there to testify. He would have to say, under oath, that he produced them." T. C. thought for a moment. "I suppose I'll have to force him to appear. His testimony will be important." T. C. pictured the man again. "It will be terribly difficult for him."

"If his appearance is that troublesome, he won't want to stay at the hotel. We will put him up here."

"Mother, you don't know how difficult it is to look at the man—particularly at meal time. I'm not sure that you could tolerate his appearance. And he probably wouldn't stay here anyway. He just wants to avoid people."

"Well, when you see him, you can tell him that I insist he be our guest during the trial." With that order, his mother marched back into the kitchen to clean more things that had been cleaned at least once already that day.

Mr. Bruce smiled. "She has her mind set. You'd better invite the herder to stay here. It seems to me that he'll only be needed for a short time, so his stay shouldn't be intolerable for him or for us."

They ate supper in silence. Only after the dessert of fresh chocolate cake did Mr. Bruce allow his son to tell him of things on the ranch. When T. C. finished, he asked to be excused. Tomorrow he would begin in earnest to get ready to try his first case.

May 23rd

He planned to make his first stop at the sheriff's office to look in on his client, but the urge to call upon Miss Spencer at the store overcame his intention. He arrived at that emporium at eight thirty to find Mr. Spencer sweeping the front sidewalk. The older man greeted T. C. warmly. "You are all the talk of the town, T. C. Folks have wondered when you'd get back here and start trying to save old Loco. Not that they want him saved. They just wonder how you intend to do it."

"Maybe Loco wonders too." T. C. didn't know if Loco really understood what was going on, but he added, "Well, I'm here now and the judge hasn't set a date for the trial, so there'll be time to get ready." T. C. took a deep breath and asked, "Is Miss Spencer here this morning? I owe her an apology. When I was last in the store, I acted like a stuffed shirt."

Mr. Spencer smiled again. "Felicity mentioned that." The smile took some of the sting out of the older man's acknowledgment of his foolishness. "You'll find her in the office in back. She helps with the books and writes up the bills each month. Go on back and make your apology." He turned away and then looked back over his shoulder with a twinkle in his eye. "She may even accept it."

T. C. found his way to the office in the back of the store, knocked quietly, and stepped into the room when she said, "Come in." Felicity sat at a huge desk with papers spread across its expanse. She wore paper cuffs over the lower sleeves of her dress to keep from soiling the cloth.

Her look of mild surprise instantly turned to a warm smile. "Why hello, Mr. Bruce. What brings you to this part of the store? The men's underwear is in the front."

T. C. felt himself blushing, momentarily at a loss for a response. Then he did what he had been planning since their last encounter. "Miss Spencer, I owe you an apology. When we last met, I behaved in an abominable manner. I won't do it again." When the words were out, he wished he could take them back. He had been rehearsing a light, humorous way of saying the same thing, one that would accomplish its purpose and perhaps make her smile. He had forgotten the whole thing. He smiled weakly and began to turn to leave the room.

Ride the Jawbone

"What a nice thing to do, sir! It wasn't necessary, because I didn't think you behaved badly. But you are kind to come to see me. Now, let's go on as though we're meeting for the first time." She brushed her hands over her skirt, seemingly to remove any wrinkles. "And, if I may be bold, tell me how you plan to defend the man accused of murder. I'm just as curious as everyone else is this town." Her smile glowed, and he grasped the opportunity to keep the conversation going.

"Well, the burden is on the prosecution to prove that Mr. Silverman is guilty. It isn't Mr. Silverman's burden to prove that he's not." He wasn't sure how much she really wanted to know of his plans, but he kept on talking. "I must interview the witnesses to learn what each will say. After that's done, I'll have a better idea of how to present a defense. Then I must prepare any motions and briefs that are needed. I'll have to present jury instructions and a verdict to the judge for his consideration. But before I can do anything else, I have to find a scrivener who can put the documents in an acceptable form. My handwriting is not very good, and everything I submit must be readable. That's one of my tasks for the day—to see if there is anyone in town, other than Conrad Gallahan's clerk, who can do it." As he paused, he saw that he had been turning his hat around and around with his hands while he was talking. It was hardly the behavior of a sophisticated man.

Miss Spencer didn't seem to notice. Her brow furrowed as she looked up at T. C. "I don't know anything about the law, but I can write reasonably well. Maybe I can help. Here, take a look at these accounts." She started to slide some of the sheets of paper toward him, but then stopped. "I guess I can't let you see the accounts of our customers. Those are private. I'll bring some writing from home for you to see. Can you come back this afternoon?"

T. C. couldn't believe his good fortune. Whether her writing would be adequate for his purpose was not important to him at the moment. Her offer gave him an opportunity to spend more time with her. "I'll be back at 1:30." With a slight bow of his head he added, "I'm sure that your writing will do for legal purposes." With that, he took his leave.

As he walked toward the courthouse, the warmth of her smile remained with him. It didn't give him the same tingle of excitement that he found in the closeness of Sarah while riding in the stagecoach, but it was a smile that he couldn't ignore.

At the courthouse, he went first to the sheriff's office. Sheriff Shea wasn't at his desk, but the deputy, who was sitting in the sheriff's chair, simply jerked a thumb toward the cell block when T. C. asked to see his client. The thought of facing the man caused T. C. some concern. He remembered the pure violence that had seemed to emanate from the accused when they last met. But, he was trying to help Lawrence Silverman and Lawrence Silverman was locked safely behind bars.

As T. C. entered the cell block, the first sight of the prisoner sitting on his bunk was reassuring. He wore the clothes that T.C. had bought. His hair and beard were trimmed and clean. Loco didn't move or look up at the sound of T. C.'s entrance. T. C. stood for a moment near the barred door to the cell, unacknowledged by the man on the bunk.

"I'm the lawyer who is going to defend you. Do you remember me?" The man in the cell did not move or speak. "The judge is to be in town soon and will set a date for the trial. If I'm to provide any defense at all, I need your help. I can't do it if you won't cooperate and at least answer my questions." Still no movement by Loco. "Did you kill that woman?"

Loco turned his head. One eye looked at T. C. while the other looked off in a different direction. His lips curled into a crooked smile more fearsome than friendly, but no sound came from his mouth. After a moment, he looked down again at the floor in a way that convinced T. C. that any further attempt to communicate would be useless.

Back at the office, he found the sheriff seated at his desk. T. C. leaned against the doorjamb as he spoke. "Mr. Silverman is clean and wearing the clothes that I brought. Thank you for taking care of him."

The sheriff looked at T. C. "We didn't clean him up for you. We did it because we couldn't stand the stink. It took six men to hold him down while I scrubbed him with soap and a good stiff brush. My God, did he yell! But we got it done. Since then, he's been willing to bathe for himself, and we provide a tub and hot water in the cell once a week. We got more clothes so that we could wash one outfit while he's wearing the other. Your father paid for them."

T. C. was glad to hear that his client had become somewhat more manageable. "What does Loco do for a living?"

"Not much of anything that I can find out about. He hasn't a horse, as far as we know. Whenever he travels, he just walks. That makes his train ride on the day when he killed her seem odd. I guess he does some trapping and cuts some wood to get money. When you live the way he does, you don't need much."

"What has he told you since I was here before?"

"He hasn't said a word that anyone can understand. If he makes any noise at all, it's just to yell."

"Do you know if he can talk?"

"My deputy has wondered that too. He's tried to listen without being seen to find out if Loco talks to himself. So far he hasn't heard the old devil say one word that he could understand. He's been heard to talk before we brought him in, though. I just think he's crazy."

T. C. concluded that his client had not said anything that would implicate him in the murder. Whatever he could do to persuade a jury of Loco's innocence, he would have to do alone. The first thing was to get more information from the sheriff. "Did you pick up the body?"

"Of Penelope Burke? No. They sent a telegram from the depot in Summit saying they'd found a murdered woman and were sending her body to Dorsey on the train. I went out to meet them. They'd loaded her on a buckboard at Dorsey and were headed this way. I took charge after that and rode beside the buckboard the rest of the way into town. There was quite a crowd following along on horseback, and the whole gang was right on the fight. If they'd found Loco that day, you wouldn't have a client. They would've lynched him then and there."

"Where did you take the body?"

"To Doc Granby's office. I wanted him to be able to testify as to the cause of death, although it was obvious. Her throat was cut."

"What became of her after that?" T. C. thought the exchange of questions and answers sounded like a cross-examination.

"She was buried in the cemetery. We gave her a good burial with a preacher and all. The town took up a collection for a headstone, but it isn't in place yet. Your mother made a large donation."

"What about her family? She must have relatives, and they may have wanted her buried somewhere else."

"We tried to find out about that. No one seems to know anything about her. Mrs. Hopkins said she came to Two Dot on the stage from Big Timber and checked into the hotel a couple of weeks before the murder. She didn't give an address, and she pretty much kept to herself. Did you ever see her when you were in town?"

T. C. didn't think that he should be the one answering questions, but he answered anyway. "I'm not in town very much, but I did see her once or twice on the street. She was an attractive woman." Before the sheriff could ask any more questions, T. C. posed his own. "What else do you know about the murder?"

"Nothing that I haven't already told you. Loco killed her. The jury will find him guilty, and we'll hang him. I've already bought the lumber for the gallows."

"Well, don't spend any money on labor to build those gallows just yet." With that last admonition, T. C. turned to leave, grim faced. Before he got away from the door, the sheriff stopped him in his tracks.

"One more thing you should know. We had another prisoner in the cell next to Loco on a drunk charge. He got too close to the bars between the cells and Loco grabbed him by the neck. Nearly choked the poor devil to death before the deputy happened into the cell block and put a stop to it. That old man is truly crazy."

T. C. stood in the doorway for a moment, not knowing what to say. Then he wheeled and stalked away. He wondered how this latest development would affect his trial strategy. He hadn't reached any conclusion before he arrived at the county attorney's office. Conrad Gallahan didn't invite T. C. to sit down, but merely nodded as the young man entered. His broad body filled the chair while his hands fluttered about the papers that covered the desk. T. C. asked, "When will the Judge be in town? I'm anxious to know the trial date."

The county attorney sighed, as if to indicate that he was exercising patience before answering a foolish question. "So am I anxious to know the trial date, and so is everyone else in this town. The judge will be here next week, and he should set the date then. He'll want to know how long we think it will take to try the case. You should be prepared to answer that question."

T. C. thought for a moment and then asked, "How long will it take you to present your case in chief? When I know that, I can have some idea of the length of time that the trial will last."

Ride the Jawbone

Conrad's second sigh was even deeper than the first. "It will take a half a day to pick a jury, unless you take far longer on voir dire than most lawyers. The questions that I intend to ask of my witnesses are few. This is really a simple case. So the length of time for the trial really depends upon the length of time that you take on cross-examination and the length of time you take with your own witnesses."

T. C. didn't like the fact that the county attorney had not answered his question, but implied that the length of the trial could not be predicted because a novice lawyer was involved.

He said, "I'll be prepared to tell the judge how much time I'll take." He left the office feeling as he had when he left the sheriff's office—that neither of them thought much of his ability.

Conrad Gallahan put his head in his hands after T. C. Bruce walked out the door. The only thing worse than prosecuting a criminal who tried to defend himself was prosecuting a criminal who was represented by a lawyer who didn't know what he was doing. He got up from his chair and stalked down the hall to the clerk's office. "The judge will bend over backward to assure I don't take advantage of the inexperience of that young scamp. My work will be even harder." Hakes listened without comment while Gallahan paced around the office. "I just wish that my practice was good enough so that I didn't need the county attorney's salary. I'd quit this job in a minute."

Hakes knew that Conrad resented the fact that the young Bruce could run off to his father's ranch to enjoy life while the county attorney had to stay and prepare for a murder trial in addition to all of his other work. Hakes only said, "You ran for the job."

The frustrated lawyer growled something unintelligible and started back to his own office. At least, he would get some satisfaction from a conviction. The townspeople should then appreciate his abilities.

+++++++++

T. C. had left the clerk's office just before Gallahan walked in. He'd paused there just long enough to confirm that the judge would arrive in town the next week. From there, he went directly to Doctor Granby's

91

office. The doctor had cared for T. C. since birth and greeted him warmly. After the preliminary exchange, he answered T. C.'s questions.

"Yes, I examined the body when it arrived at my office. The cause of death was from knife wounds."

"Was there more than one wound?"

"Yes, and either the wound in the abdomen or the wound in the throat could have killed her."

"Did you see the knife that made the wounds?"

"No. The sheriff said that Lawrence Silverman was carrying a knife when he picked him up. The sheriff believes it was used to kill the woman, but I didn't see it."

"How long had she been dead when you first examined her?"

"I'm not sure how long she had been dead, but the condition of her body wasn't inconsistent with the sheriff's theory."

T. C. listened carefully to all that the doctor had to say and then thanked him for his time. He also reminded the kindly old man that the trial was coming up. The doctor knew that T. C. was worried about cross-examining him. He made light of the situation by saying, "Promise you won't abuse the man who helped you into this world."

T. C. promised to be fair. He left the doctor's office and tramped the six blocks to his parents' home for the noon meal.

At 1:30, he was back at the store to meet with Miss Spencer. He found her in the office and, just as she had promised, offered samples of her writing for him to review.

He nodded. One look confirmed that she would be able to produce the documents he would need. "Yes, your handwriting will do well."

"When shall I begin?" she asked.

T. C. had only thought in general terms of the jury instructions he would need to prepare, but he was embarrassed to tell her so.

"I think it would be well for us to go to the office of the clerk of the court and look at instructions from previous trials. That way you can see the required format."

Felicity was delighted at the suggestion and immediately asked permission from her uncle to leave the store. Permission received, she put on her bonnet and exited as T. C. held the door. When they passed out onto the boardwalk that led up the hill to the courthouse, she took his arm and strolled gracefully beside him.

Ride the Jawbone

Hakes seemed to know what was taking place. His greeting to T. C. was curt, but he almost bowed to Miss Spencer. Without being asked, he reached under the counter and brought out a court file from the trial of a man accused of burglary. He offered them the use of a table in the vault.

T. C. noted with some irritation that the offer was directed to Miss Spencer. Hakes placed the file on the table with it opened to the jury instructions. He stood in the doorway to the vault, leaning against the open door and watched them, working on his teeth with a toothpick, as they seated themselves and directed their attention to the file. T. C. wished Hakes would leave them alone, but didn't feel he could order the man around in his own office.

The jury instructions included the usual guidance about the duty of the jurors and stated the number of them required to reach a verdict. One set forth the requirement that a conviction could only be found if the defendant was guilty beyond a reasonable doubt. Another instruction defined reasonable doubt. T. C. explained to Miss Spencer that they would need jury instructions exactly like the ones in the file.

"I'll copy them in exactly this form," she assured him.

Miss Spencer was extremely interested in the way that the jury instructions were compiled and took time to read all of those in the file. When they had finished their inspection, T. C. thanked Hakes for his assistance. Miss Spencer also gave her thanks and said she would return with writing material to copy the instructions they needed. The clerk smiled a foolish smile and told her she would be welcome any time. He didn't even look at T. C. as the two of them left the office. His eyes were only on Felicity Spencer.

As T. C. walked Miss Spencer back to the store, he asked, "Will this work you are going to do for me interfere with your other duties?"

"My uncle won't complain. Don't worry about that."

At the doorway into the store, Felicity took his hand and thanked him for his explanations of the court system. Walking away, T. C. wondered how he had been so lucky as to find such an appealing creature to act as his clerk. He found himself whistling while he walked back along the boardwalk toward his parents' home.

May 29th

The Judge arrived earlier than expected and was at the courthouse on Tuesday afternoon in the last week of May. T. C. didn't need a formal notice of his arrival. The whole town knew of it. Early Wednesday morning, T. C. went to the store to visit with Miss Spencer, as had become his habit. He found her in the office with the jury instructions on the desk in front of her.

Before he could speak, she said, "There is something I've kept from you."

T. C.'s immediate thought was that she was about to tell him she was engaged to be married. He just stood there, staring at her.

"I know that Mr. Silverman tried to choke that man in the jail. The county attorney will ask the sheriff about it at the trial to show how violent Mr. Silverman really is. Hakes suggested that you make what he called a motion in limine to prevent that from happening. He gave me a file that had such a motion in it. I copied it for you to present to the judge this morning if you think it's worthwhile."

As T. C. reached for the document, his mind began to comprehend her suggestion. If the jury heard of Loco's attempt to kill a man right in the jail, they would have little hesitation to find him guilty of the killing of Penelope Burke. He read the motion and the supporting legal brief and saw that it was persuasive. They only required his signature for submission to the court. He glanced again at Miss Spencer to find her looking back at him, eyebrows raised, waiting for his reaction.

His anger rose at old Hakes for butting his nose into his business and at Miss Spencer for being so presumptuous as to prepare such documents without discussing the matter with him. Almost instantly, however, he understood that his anger came from embarrassment. He should only be angry at himself. Hakes and Miss Spencer should not have to do for him what he should have done without their suggestion. He smiled down at the helpful lady seated before him, complimented her on her initiative, and thanked her for her efforts.

"Would you like to accompany me when I meet with the judge and Conrad Gallahan?"

Her smile in response was worth the invitation.

Ride the Jawbone

As they walked along the boardwalk to the courthouse, he wondered how he would explain his desire to have Miss Spencer sit in on the pretrial conference that is normally limited to the judge, the clerk, and the lawyers. He finally decided to just be honest.

Hakes was triumphant when T. C. gave him the motion and brief for filing. He had been able to show T. C. that his age and experience trumped the young man's college book learning.

Conrad Gallahan couldn't hide his chagrin when T. C. handed him copies of the originals. "This should have been filed before the pretrial conference," he objected. "I should have been given proper time to respond."

Knowing what he said was true, T. C. answered, "I won't resist any reasonable request for time to respond." When Gallahan didn't answer, he asked, "Do you have any objection to Miss Spencer sitting in on the conference with the judge?"

Conrad started to voice an objection, but stopped, as if he suddenly realized how small-minded it would make him look. He finally shook his head and said, "It's perfectly fine with me, if the judge approves." Turning to Felicity, he added, "But you must understand, this is legal business and you're not a lawyer, so don't presume to speak."

The judge welcomed them into his office at 1:30 that afternoon. T. C. explained that Miss Spencer was acting as his clerk and asked if she could sit in on the conference. He added that she had prepared the motion and brief.

Smiling, the judge asked the county attorney if he had any objection. Conrad Gallahan scowled, but indicated he did not. Judge Henry picked up the documents, looked at T. C. and said, "Mr. Bruce, I see that you didn't take my suggestion and hire the clerk from Two Dot. After seeing Miss Spencer's work, I can understand why." Turning to the county attorney he asked, "You don't have any objection to the motion do you, Mr. Gallahan?"

"I certainly do. As you can see, your honor, it was filed just today. I've had no opportunity to review the brief and to respond. It's probable that the motion is not well taken and should be denied."

"Ah, c'mon, Conrad. We've been through this before. You know good and well that you can't use acts that occurred after the crime was committed as evidence against the accused. The only reason that you would want to introduce testimony that the defendant tried to choke someone while in jail would be to inflame the jury. You can have time to file a brief in response if you like, but I'll grant the motion either now or after you file a brief—and you know it. You also know I'll be right in doing so. So why don't you save yourself some time and effort?"

Conrad Gallahan hated to give up. "Well, Your Honor, if filing a brief is to be wasted effort, I guess I won't do it." Then, as an afterthought, he added, "I could go up to the Supreme Court on a writ. The Court may agree with me."

"You could, but you won't. Preparing such a petition and brief takes a lot of work, and you know it wouldn't be successful, so we all know you're not going to do it. The motion is granted. Now, let's get on with other matters. I find I have a conflict and won't be able to hear this case the last week of June. I can hear it if we start on Monday the twentieth of June. Would that date be all right with you, Mr. Bruce?"

T. C. was taken by surprise and could only nod his head in agreement. His mind was still focused on the judge's response to the motion. He had won a huge victory because of Miss Spencer's effort, and because Hakes had been helpful. He would have to make his appreciation known to each of them. That would be easy with Miss Spencer, but not so easy with Hakes.

While T. C.'s mind wandered, the judge asked, "And how about you, Mr. Gallahan? Can you be ready on the twentieth?"

"You know me judge. I'm always ready. I could try this case tomorrow if you want."

"Yes, you are always ready. I wish all of the lawyers in this judicial district were as good in that regard." The judge's head moved up and down as he spoke. "Well, tomorrow won't be necessary. We'll set the trial for nine o'clock on June twentieth."

He addressed the clerk. "Mr. Albers, send out the notices to the members of the jury panel right away, please." Turning to the lawyers again, he asked, "Is there anything more that we need to discuss before the trial, gentlemen?" After a very brief pause, he continued. "Good!" Reaching for Felicity's hand he said, "It was nice to make your acquaintance, Miss Spencer." Turning back to the lawyers he added, "I'll see you gentlemen bright and early on the twentieth."

Ride the Jawbone

With this dismissal, T. C. rose from his chair and stepped aside to allow Miss Spencer to exit first, and then waited for the two older men to follow her. As he left the room, he turned and said, "Thank you, Your Honor." Judge Henry nodded, dropped his eyes to his desk, and picked up another document. The murder was only one legal matter of importance in Meagher County that week.

T.C. felt jubilant when he exited the courthouse with his scrivener. "Miss Spencer, may I take you for an ice cream sundae to celebrate?"

Her look was a mixture of fondness and exasperation. "Oh, for heavens sake! You shall call me Felicity, and I shall call you Thad. Yes, you may take me for a sundae." And she again put her arm through his as they walked down the hill toward the apothecary. Glances of approval from those they passed along the way pleased T. C., who realized what a handsome couple they made.

+++++++++

As Conrad Gallahan trudged down the hall from the judge's office, he mumbled to himself, "That young fool should be doing everything in his power to delay the trial. The sooner the trial, the sooner the hanging. But that's his mistake, and I'm not obliged to tell him."

++++++++++

T. C. Bruce went to bed that night feeling smug. He had been successful in the first skirmish. It gave him confidence that he could handle the trial itself in a competent manner. But then, in the middle of the night, he awoke with a sudden, panicky recognition of the full import of the judge's ruling. Not only did that ruling keep the county attorney from introducing evidence of the actions of Lawrence Silverman during his stay in jail, but it also kept T. C. from doing the same. He could not ask the sheriff to tell about any of Loco's strange behavior in the jail—his yowling, his refusal to talk, the struggle to get him clean. He had intended to use the behavioral testimony as the basis upon which to ask the doctor if such behavior indicated insanity. Without that testimony, he had no basis to argue that Loco was insane and incapable of understanding the nature of his actions.

T. C.'s first reaction was anger at Hakes Albers. But he had not been forced to file the motion that Hakes had suggested. The more he thought, the more he realized they had not created a problem for him. Instead they had saved him from a terrible mistake. Had they not prepared the motion that he signed and filed, and had he tried to use the sheriff's testimony to show that Loco was crazy, the county attorney would have jumped at the opportunity to have the sheriff also tell of Loco's violence toward the other prisoner. T. C. sat up on the side of the bed and scratched his hair with both hands as he tried to think what to do next.

Chappy's suggestion came to mind. Deal with the facts. He must go to see Noseless Pete, get the pictures, and serve Pete with a subpoena to appear at the trial. The trial would occur earlier than he had told the sheepherder. He would leave on the morning stage for Dorsey and ride the Jawbone to Summit and then hire a horse to find his witness, the one who might be Loco's only hope to avoid the hangman's noose.

+++++++++

Felicity sat at the dressing table in her room that same evening combing her hair as she prepared for bed. Her mind replayed the day's activities, and she was glad she came to White Sulphur Springs, Montana.

She learned of their relatives in the west at an early age and started asking her father about Montana. When she reached her eighteenth birthday, her uncle wrote and invited her to spend the summer with him and his wife. They had no children and would welcome the opportunity to have a young person in the house. She traveled by train to Chicago and then on the Northern Pacific to Lombard, Montana. From Lombard she rode the Jawbone to Dorsey, where her uncle met her with his buggy. Because she had worked in her father's store at home, Felicity was able to help in the store in White Sulphur Springs. It was the perfect situation because it allowed her to quickly become acquainted with the people in town. And she had met Thad Bruce.

All she had intended to do was spend the summer with her aunt and uncle before going home to continue her education. But now the young lawyer was in her thoughts much of the day and before she slept at night. Tall and good-looking, he was always carefully dressed, and his manners were beyond reproach. He was serious, but pleasant to be with. Yet he seemed to lack self-assurance. She liked him—a lot. As the hair combing continued, she wondered what it would be like to be kissed by him, held in his arms, or even something more. At that thought she blushed. When she finished brushing the last of her locks, the modest young woman looked at her solemn face in the mirror and quietly whispered, "I think I will marry the handsome Mr. Bruce."

May 30th

T. C. arrived at Dorsey ahead of schedule, but a rock slide in Sixteen-Mile Canyon, made the Jawbone late again. When finally on its way, the engine belched black smoke and struggled mightily to climb the slope of the mountain. It arrived at Summit in the early afternoon. T. C. hired a saddle horse and rode to the Bakken Ranch. He learned that Pete was camped on the Bozeman Fork about two miles above its mouth. T. C. rode back down to Summit and stayed at the hotel. In the morning he rode eastward to where the Bozeman Fork entered the South Fork of the Musselshell. He followed the Bozeman Fork until he could see Pete's sheep wagon parked beneath a grove of quaking aspen trees. T. C. waited for the herder to return.

Near noon, Pete rode up to the wagon. His face was covered as before, and he remained on his horse until he recognized his visitor.

"You're going to make me testify at the trial," he said in a matter-of-fact manner and without apparent rancor.

T. C. smiled and asked if Pete had completed the pictures he had promised. The herder went into the wagon and, in short order, carried out a large sheet of paper affixed to wooden backing and covered with canvas. He leaned it against a wagon wheel and removed the covering. The picture was done in pen and ink. Colored chalk gave emphasis to the important features. Pete returned to the wagon for another.

The first of the pictures gave a broad view of the coulee and surrounding area where Pete had found the body. The second drawing showed the body in detail. T. C. asked the question that he would ask in court. "Do these pictures portray, with reasonable accuracy, the scene as it existed at the time you found the body?"

"Yes. They're not the same as a photograph, but they're reasonably accurate."

"I must have you testify to that fact at the trial."

Pete stared at him over the bandanna. "I've known all along that you'd want me to be there. But are you sure my appearance won't have the wrong effect on the jury? You know how you reacted the first time you saw what's left of my face. The jurors may find me so repulsive that anything I say may be disregarded or believed to be untrue."

T. C.'s first inclination was to downplay that possibility, but what Pete said was correct. "That may be. But the only way that I can get the pictures into evidence is to have you there to tell the jury that you made them, and that they are accurate. It may not be possible to convince the jury that Loco should go free, but it's a certainty that he'll be convicted if you don't appear."

"How can you work so hard to defend him when he probably is guilty? Why not just let him hang?"

T. C. used the same technique on Pete that the judge had used on him. "You said probably. You didn't say certainly. It's the difference between those two words that the trial is all about. Everyone may believe that Loco killed the woman, but the State has to prove it beyond a reasonable doubt. It's my task to be certain that the man is not convicted unless the State does its job. There's always the possibility that someone else killed her. If so, Loco shouldn't hang."

Pete reached under his bandanna to scratch his neck. "Well, no doubt you have a subpoena. I'll have to make arrangements with Olaf Bakken for someone to watch the sheep while I'm away. How long will the trial last, and how long will I be needed?"

T. C. thought for a moment, "Your actual testimony will only take an hour or so, but it's hard to know when it will be needed. I think you should plan on being away from here for at least three days." When he thought of his mother's admonition, he added, "You're invited to stay at my parents' home. Mother insists."

Pete looked off into the distance before answering. "I'll camp on Willow Creek. That's close enough to town so you can send word when you need me. That way I won't be a bother."

T. C. knew it was not being a bother that made the other man decline the invitation. He didn't press the matter, but instead mused aloud about the easiest way to get the pictures to town undamaged.

"Stop and tell Olaf Bakken that you need my testimony. He can haul the pictures to town for shipment to The Springs."

"Will he do it?"

"Of course. Olaf's a good man. He'll understand the reason."

Not another word was said about the trial while the men ate the food T. C. had prepared. The menu was the same as before—ham, fried spuds, and canned tomatoes. He wondered if a sheepherder ever got anything else.

T. C. rode back into Summit in mid-afternoon. The train would not arrive until late morning the next day. He purchased a tablet and a pencil and passed the afternoon composing an outline of the opening statement. He ate supper at the dining room, if one could call it that, in the Summit Hotel.

++++++++++

At supper time, Felicity knocked on the door of the Bruce home. When Mrs. Bruce answered the knock, Felicity presented her with a small cake that was fresh out of the oven. Mrs. Bruce invited her to come to the kitchen and cut two pieces from the cake for them to share. They sat at the table and visited. Neither of them mentioned T. C., but Mrs. Bruce understood the reason Felicity came calling. Felicity understood that she was welcome. As she was leaving, Mrs. Bruce gently touched her arm, saying, "You may call me Prudence."

June 1

After an early breakfast and with time on his hands until the west bound train arrived, T. C. walked along the railroad tracks to the place where the conductor said the body of Penelope Burke had been found. It had rained during the night, but the day was crisp and clear. Soon enough, he was standing where the tracks crossed the coulee. He could see the trees and willows that surrounded the hollow where a small watercourse was visible. The picture the sheepherder had drawn was an excellent portrayal of the location. As he took it all in, T. C. thought of a defense for his client that didn't rest upon insanity. With excitement he concluded there was a possibility that Lawrence Silverman wouldn't hang for the murder of Penelope Burke.

June 11th

The handwriting on the envelope addressed to Thaddeus C. Bruce, Attorney at Law, White Sulphur Springs, Montana was feminine and small. The letter inside read:

> Dear Mr. Bruce,
>
> I have been asked to sign a contract to teach at the Flagstaff school. I believe that I should have an attorney review the contract before I sign it to be certain that it is in proper form and that it is to my benefit. May I retain you for that purpose?
>
> I realize that you are busy now with the upcoming trial. I will call upon you after its completion unless I hear from you telling me that you do not wish to represent me in this matter.
>
> Yours truly,
> Sarah Kuntz

T. C. finally knew her last name.

June 19th

A stranger called at the Bruce house in White Sulphur Springs. When T. C. answered the knock, he said, "A man with a mask over his face stopped me on the road from the Musselshell, near where the road crosses Willow Creek. I thought I was about to be robbed, but he just asked me to tell T. C. Bruce that he was camped about a mile up the creek from the road." He looked T. C. up and down, and asked, "Is that you?" When T.C. nodded, the stranger turned on his heel and walked away, ignoring the thanks that T.C. called after him.

Pete's pictures arrived by stage, properly crated to avoid being damaged in transit. T. C. had long since finished preparation of the opening statement, had outlined proposed questions for witnesses and had prepared a rough version of a closing statement. Felicity had put the jury instructions and the verdict into proper form for presentation to the court after the testimony was completed. T. C. had given up going to see his client. The last time that he had gone to the jail, Lawrence Silverman would not even look at him. The sheriff promised, however, that the prisoner would be clean for his appearance in court. T. C. was as ready for the trial as he could get.

Supper the night before the trial was more elaborate than usual. Mrs. Bruce had prepared it with help from Felicity, who had become an evening fixture in the household. When T. C. returned from his trip to see Pete, Mrs. Bruce explained that Felicity was kind enough to help with the cooking. "I appreciate her help. Your mother is getting older, you know."

Enjoying Felicity's company, T. C. took advantage of it. As they ate the evening meal, they talked about the trial and little else. Felicity was excited, Mrs. Bruce worried, and Mr. Bruce confident.

T. C. didn't contribute much to the conversation. He was already suffering the nausea that bedevils a lawyer before a trial begins. He didn't have the experience to know that the feeling would disappear the first time he rose to his feet in the courtroom.

Felicity remained silent as T. C. walked her to the Spencer house after supper. That was fine with him. He couldn't speak to her about how nervous he felt. She lingered on the doorstep as he trudged away.

In bed that night, T. C. rehearsed the things he intended to say to the judge and the jury over and over again. Sleep did not come until two o'clock in the morning. He awoke at sunup, groggy and tired.

June 20th

The courtroom was crowded with people when T. C. arrived at eight thirty in the morning. All of the prospective jurors were there. It appeared that half of the folks in the county were in the courtroom or the hallway leading to it. People stood in clusters on the stairs and outside the building, visiting and waiting for the excitement to begin.

T. C. stood a moment at the double doors at the back of the courtroom. Benches aligned on each side of the wide aisle would seat about one hundred people, but only if they squeezed themselves together.

Two counsel tables stood near to one another in the area beyond the rail that separated the audience from the lawyers, the witnesses, and the jurors. The elevated bench that dominated the area allowed the judge to look down upon everyone else in the room. The jury box was to the judge's left.

T. C. put his materials on the counsel table closest to the jurors. He wanted the best view of the witnesses as they testified, while watching the jurors' reaction to their testimony. He decided to place Lawrence Silverman in the chair closest to the jury. That way, he could see his client while he was looking at the jurors. He, Felicity, and his parents had gone through the list of jurors the previous week and identified some that he should dismiss and some that they hoped to keep.

He turned away from his task to see his parents and Felicity pushing their way through the crowd. He'd asked Felicity to sit just behind him in the audience section and watch the jurors as the lawyers questioned them, in order to help him decide which of the jurors to dismiss with his peremptory challenges. Two of the town matriarchs had already firmly seated themselves in the place that T. C. would have preferred for Felicity. They scowled ferociously when it appeared they would be asked to move. Three older men, friends of Thad Bruce, solved the problem by surrendering their seats so that Felicity and T. C.'s parents were able to sit close enough. Before he could speak to them, the door that led from the courtroom to the judge's chamber slammed opened. Hakes stuck his head out and called, "Bruce! The judge wants you in here. Right now."

T. C. smiled a sickly smile at Felicity. He walked through the door that Hakes was holding and into the judge's chamber. Judge Henry sat behind his desk and Conrad Gallahan occupied one of the chairs facing him. When T. C entered the room, Conrad half rose from the chair, stuck out his hand, said, "Counselor," and sat down again. T. C. responded by saying, "Mr. Gallahan."

That customary exercise out of the way, the judge asked, "Gentlemen, are there any matters that we need to address before we begin the morning session?"

T. C. spoke first. "There are, Your Honor. I move the court for an order directing the sheriff to remove all of the shackles from my client before he is brought into the courtroom. The appearance of the man in shackles will give an impression to the jurors that he's guilty. He will be convicted before we start."

Conrad Gallahan rose out of his chair. "Just a minute," but the judge cut him off.

"Mr. Bruce, wasn't it just a few days ago that we heard about your man trying to kill someone with his bare hands? I'm not about to allow him to come into this courtroom, loose to the world, and have him try something like that again. The motion is denied."

He looked at each of the lawyers across from him and continued, "Anything further?" After the briefest of pauses he remarked, "No? Good! We will begin promptly at nine o'clock with the selection of the jury. Mr. Albers, please be sure that the sheriff has the defendant in the courtroom at that time, but not any earlier. Thank you, gentlemen and good luck. I'll see you out front in a few minutes."

T. C. hurried through the crowd, down the stairs, and out the back door where a path led to the outhouse. The trip gave him some comfort, but didn't do away with the queasiness in his stomach. As he worked his way back through the crowd toward the courtroom, he had to run the gauntlet of their comments.

Just as he reached his seat, the noise in the room hushed. He turned to see the sheriff directing Loco up the aisle toward him. The crowd separated before the accused man in a way that made T. C. think of the Biblical parting of the Red Sea. Loco was shackled hand and foot. The short chain connecting the leg clamps forced him to shuffle along, but he was cleanly dressed and his hair and beard were trimmed. He looked better than T. C. had ever seen him.

The way the people shrunk away on either side of the aisle and the looks of disgust on their faces made it clear that they were ready to hang the man, then and there. If the jurors were of the same mind, and there was no reason to believe otherwise, T. C. would be hard pressed to convince them to acquit, no matter what the evidence.

T. C. gestured toward the chair next to his own. Loco went to it and sat down without a word or any change in his facial expression. He glanced once at T. C., or at least T. C. thought he did, then turned to stare at the wall behind the Judge's bench. After Loco was seated, the noise level rose to an even higher pitch. The commotion didn't end until Hakes entered the room from the judge's chamber and cried in a loud voice, "All rise!"

The crowd came to its feet as Judge Henry strode through the door and climbed to his desk. He hit the bench once with his gavel, sank slowly into his chair and said, "Please be seated." T. C. turned to see that his client had not followed the lead of all others in the room, but remained in his chair. T. C. knew that one of the most difficult things he had to contend with was his client's intransigence.

The young lawyer didn't realize how long the preliminaries would take. First, the clerk was directed to take the roll of the members of the jury panel to assure that all of them were present. Some had to answer from the hallway. The judge ordered those into the courtroom, and others were asked to make room for them. There was grumbling among the ones dispossessed of their seats but, after some shuffling around, all the jurors were inside. One old fellow who was on the jury panel immediately rose to his feet and asked the judge if he could be excused because his wife had taken sick in the night, and she needed him at home. The judge granted his request, but admonished the others that all of them were needed if a trial was to be held. No more jurors asked to be excused.

Judge Henry directed the clerk to swear in the jurors who were on the panel. They all rose to their feet and, after Hakes read the oath, said in unison, "I do." Selection of potential jurors from the broader jury panel began. Each man whose name the clerk drew from a hat took a seat in the jury box until enough had been selected to assure that there would be twelve jurors left after the peremptory challenges were exercised. The jurors who couldn't find room in the jury box were directed to take seats in the first two rows behind T. C. Spectators who had come early to get good seats protested, but eventually moved to make room for the jurors. T. C.'s parents and Felicity had to surrender their seats. All of this took more time. When the final potential juror was seated, the judge nodded to the county attorney and said, "You may proceed, Mr. Gallahan."

The county attorney rose slowly to his feet behind the table where his papers and books lay scattered and began by introducing himself to the jurors. He next introduced the judge. He introduced the clerk and the court reporter. He turned to T. C. and introduced him as, "Mr. Bruce, who will represent the defendant." Last of all, he pointed at Loco. "The gentleman seated next to Mr. Bruce is the defendant, Lawrence Silverman." It seemed a waste of time because everyone in the room already knew the name of each participant.

Conrad Gallahan knew there were two ways to question potential jurors on voir dire. He could ask very specific questions of each one in an attempt to determine the bias, if any, that the juror held. Or he could ask general questions of the panel and then rely upon his familiarity with the jurors and the community to tell him which of them should be stricken. He was well acquainted with nearly all of the men on the panel. He picked up a list of the jurors and began to ask questions of the panel at large. "Do any of you know the defendant?" No one raised his hand. "Do any of you know anything about this case of your own knowledge? Not hearsay, but of your own knowledge?" No one raised his hand. Then he said, "I've done legal work for many of you. Would that fact influence you in reaching a verdict?"

Henry Wortman raised his hand and asked, "If I vote against you, will you still finish the contract that I hired you to do last week?"

There was laughter from the crowd. The judge looked at the county attorney, "That is a clear conflict of interest, Mr. Gallahan. I'll excuse the juror for cause. Do you object Mr. Bruce?"

T. C. did not.

"You're excused, Mr. Wortman. And you're free to leave if you wish. Or you may stay." The judge said. "Mr. Albers, call another juror." The man whose name was drawn took the empty seat.

The county attorney asked if any of the jurors knew T. C. About three-quarters of them raised their hands. He asked one of those, an older fellow, what kind of relationship he had with the young man. The man replied, "I know Thad Bruce and have known him for years. Mr. Bruce runs a good operation on the Mussellshell. I know that young man as his son. As far as I know, the boy is all right." Mr. Gallahan then asked if the others who had raised their hands had a similar acquaintance with Mr. Bruce, the lawyer. All of them nodded.

Finally, the county attorney told the jurors that the State had the burden of proving the defendant guilty beyond a reasonable doubt.

"But that doesn't mean we have to show you pictures of the defendant committing the murder. Proof can come from circumstantial evidence." He asked if they would accept that as the law if the judge so instructed them. When there was again a general nodding of heads, he asked the entire group if each of them felt that he could decide the case on the evidence presented in court. The heads nodded some more. Gallahan turned to the judge. "Pass the jury for cause, Your Honor."

T. C watched with interest. In his only experience at a jury trial, the lead attorney had asked very pointed and personal questions of each potential juror. He had expected something similar here and planned to simply ask additional questions of a juror who worried him. Thus, he hoped to weed out any juror who was unquestionably prejudiced.

When the judge looked at him and said, "Mr. Bruce, you may begin," he hardly knew what to do. He rose from his chair, smiled at the men in the jury box, and at the juror in the first chair.

"Mr. Collins, you understand that Mr. Silverman is innocent of any crime as he sits in the courtroom today, don't you?"

Mr. Collins looked at him for a moment and then said, "I guess so." T. C. continued. "Mr. Collins, the defendant, Mr. Silverman, has been charged with a crime, but no one has proven that he committed it. The burden is upon the State to prove his guilt beyond a reasonable doubt. If the State does not do that, you must find that he is not guilty. Do you agree with that?"

Collins nodded. "Yup. I understand that Conrad has to prove it."

T. C. addressed the man in the next chair. "Mr. Johnson, if it is shown that Mr. Silverman did kill Miss Burke, and if it is also shown that he didn't know what he was doing at the time, you couldn't vote to convict him, could you?"

Mr. Johnson reared back in his chair and shouted, "I sure as hell could! If that old devil is going to run around killing people, we should hang him. The sooner the better!"

Before he had completely finished, the judge's gavel came down with a bang that startled T. C. and everyone else in the room. All of their eyes turned to Judge Henry who was leaning over the bench and pointing at Mr. Johnson with his gavel. "I will not tolerate profanity in this courtroom. And you know that, Knute. Now, you're excused from this jury. Step down from the jury box."

Ride the Jawbone

Judge Henry turned to look first at the jurors remaining in the box and then at those seated in the audience section. "Each of you is to disregard the remark of Mr. Johnson. And I don't want to hear any more profanity in this room. Is that clear?" No one said a word. The room was absolutely silent until the judge turned to the clerk and said, "Mr. Albers, draw another juror." When the next juror was sitting in the seat vacated by Knute Johnson, the judge spoke again, this time in his ordinary soft voice. "You may continue, Mr. Bruce."

T. C. glanced toward the other counsel table. Conrad Gallahan was leaning back in his chair with a smirk on his face.

T. C. was so non-plussed by the judge's outburst that he limited his questions to those having to do with the burden of proof and the presumption of innocence. He asked questions of several more of the jurors, all of whom assured him that they understood that Loco was not yet guilty in the eyes of the law. There was an inference in the answers of some of them that they felt that he would be guilty soon enough.

Finally, he said to the group as a whole, "Would any of you answer any differently than those who have been asked questions?" No one said a word.

T. C. decided to rely upon his parent's knowledge of the people in the community to make his jury selections. He turned to the judge and said, "Pass the jury for cause, Your Honor." The only reason that he said those words was because Conrad Gallahan had said the same thing. T. C. assumed it was the proper way to end his voir dire of the jurors.

The judge nodded. "Very well." He turned to the men in the jury box. "Gentlemen, I'm going to ask the lawyers to meet with me in my chambers for a little while, so court will be in recess. During the recess, you are not to talk among yourselves nor with anyone else about the case. And don't leave the courthouse. We'll only be in recess for fifteen minutes or so. The bailiff will call you back in when we are ready to begin again." With that said, he banged his gavel with much less vigor than before and rose from his chair to leave the room.

As T. C. reached to pick up his papers, his eyes fell upon his client. The man was still sitting as before, just staring at the wall in back of the judge's bench with apparent indifference to the things going on around him. T. C. smiled at his parents and Felicity, and headed for the judge's chamber. He had no idea what the judge wanted to see the lawyers about.

"Well, gentlemen, let's select a jury." Judge Henry was leaning back in his chair with his hands folded over his paunch. "Mr. Albers, please give each of these gentlemen the jury selection sheet."

At the trial in St. Paul, the jury had been selected in the courtroom and T. C. had expected that to be the process today. But this was better. No one but those in the room would be able to see him perspire as he made his selections of jurors for dismissal. The Judge looked at him and said, "You understand, Mr. Bruce, that you get two peremptory challenges for each one the State gets?"

"Yes sir. I get ten." The truth was that he and his parents could not identify ten in the jury pool that they felt would not be fair. He would strike the ones that they were worried about and go from there.

"All right, Mr. Gallahan, your first selection."

The county attorney did not hesitate in saying, "Juror number eleven." And old John Tew was gone from the jury.

"Mr. Bruce, your selection?" There was a faint smile on the judge's face as he said it.

"Juror number fourteen." T. C. got rid of the husband of the woman who had insulted Mrs. Bruce when T. C. had first taken on the defense of Loco.

"And you're second selection, Mr. Bruce."

T. C. chose juror number two as his second choice for removal. After that, Conrad Gallahan made a selection. T. C. hesitated when it was his turn again. He glanced at the judge and found him looking at the clock, fingers drumming on the arms of his chair. Clearly, he wanted the process to move along rapidly. T. C. hurriedly made a selection and then was not sure if he had chosen correctly. By his next turn, he was confused and could not remember the names of those he and his parents had decided should be stricken. He couldn't even remember the ones they concluded would be good jurors. He wished Felicity were here. She had written down the names of the jurors as their names had been drawn and matched them to the numbers. He was sure she would remember the choices he was supposed to make. But she wasn't, so he floundered along, picking numbers that represented names and hoping that he would manage to get rid of the three or four men he and his parents had decided should be removed.

The process continued until each attorney had used all of his peremptory challenges. Those who had not been eliminated from the list constituted the jury that would hear the case.

Back in the courtroom the judge asked the clerk to read the names of the selected jurors and direct them to sit in the jury box as their names were read. He told the remaining members of the jury pool that they would receive their juror's fee from the clerk in the mail. Finally, he asked Hakes to read the oath to the jury. Each man held up his hand and, at the end, they all said once again, "I do."

++++++++++

Felicity studied the men in the jury box and thought they looked like a group of huge magpies. Each was dressed in a black suit with a white shirt and a black tie. Each had carried a black hat into the room and placed it on the floor beside his chair. Each face was gravely solemn. Old Milton Anderson, a one-legged friend of Thaddeus Bruce Sr., sat at the end of the front row next to the witness chair, his crutch propped against the back wall. They all looked ancient to her. Only Selmer Green was less than sixty years of age and he was at least fifty.

T. C. looked at the jury too, but only saw a wall of people. Their faces and their names did not register. His mind couldn't focus. While he wondered if he had chosen correctly, he heard the judge call a recess for dinner.

"Return promptly at one thirty," Judge Henry ordered. The gavel banged again and everyone in the room rose to leave. The sheriff and two deputies ordered Loco to rise. When they led him back down the aisle, the crowd parted to let him through as it had before.

T. C. found his father waiting for him. "The women went to fix dinner," the elder Bruce explained.

+++++++++

T. C. couldn't eat. His stomach wouldn't let him even think of food. While the others ate, he sat at the table agonizing over his actions of the morning and the things he would be faced with when he returned to the courtroom. His parents and Felicity chatted about the conversations that went on during the morning, and about a thousand other things of no interest to T. C. When dinner was finally done, T. C. headed for the door to return to court. His father followed, leaving the two ladies behind to clean up the dishes.

T. C. walked slowly so his father could keep up as his game leg looped to the outside of his stride. Halfway to the courthouse, he asked his son, "Why didn't you get rid of Norris Thorpe? He's a great friend of Conrad Gallahan, as I mentioned to you." T. C. groaned, understanding why he had been suffering since the morning session. He had forgotten to strike the one juror that they had all agreed should not stay on the jury.

++++++++++

The clerk called out, "All rise," when the judge entered the courtroom. Judge Henry looked around and then said, "Let the record show that the defendant is in court and the jurors are all present. Mr. Gallahan, you may begin your opening statement."

The county attorney moved his square body to stand in front of the jury box. His opening statement was simple. "The State will show that the defendant, Lawrence Silverman, killed Penelope Burke by stabbing and slashing her with a knife. He then threw her body from the Montana Railroad train. The body rolled down the slope, to a place where it was eventually found by a sheepherder.

The first witness will be the conductor who saw them both on the train. He'll tell you of the actions of Lawrence Silverman toward the dead woman. Mrs. Watson, the proprietress of the hotel where the victim had been staying will also testify. She'll identify jewelry found upon the person of the defendant as a brooch belonging to the victim. Doctor Granby will testify as to the nature of the wounds, and, finally, the sheriff will tell of the capture of the defendant." He finished by saying he was confident that the evidence would convince the jury that the defendant should be convicted of murder in the first degree.

The judge spoke in a soft voice, "Mr. Bruce."

T. C. took a deep breath and pushed away from the table. "Gentlemen of the jury, the burden is upon the State to prove each and every element of the crime of murder. It must also prove each and every fact that the State has alleged in its complaint. Mr. Gallahan has just told you what the State must prove. And the proof must be beyond a reasonable doubt. You are not allowed to speculate or decide by conjecture. If the State fails to prove anything that the law requires, including every fact that Mr. Gallahan has just described to you, you must find the defendant not guilty. And if the facts show that it would have been impossible for Mr. Silverman to have committed this horrible crime in the manner the county attorney has just set forth, you must acquit him. The facts will, I am sure, lead you to that conclusion." T. C. sat down, relieved to have the task out of the way. He didn't think that it made any impression on the jury at all.

The judge nodded in his direction, and then turned to T. C.'s adversary and said, "Call your first witness, Mr. County Attorney."

Conrad Gallahan stood. "The State calls Anthony Prato."

T. C. turned to see the witness rise from one of the benches. It was the conductor who had been on the train when he first saw Sarah—the one who had been so eager to talk of the murder. The portly, red-faced man made his way to the clerk's desk and raised his hand to be sworn. He then climbed into the witness chair. The county attorney stepped around the table to face the witness, hands clasped at his waist. "Please state your name and place of employment for the court record, sir."

"My name is Anthony Leo Prato. I work for the Montana Railroad as a conductor."

"Mr. Prato, were you the conductor on the westbound train on April eighteenth of this year?"

"I was."

"Is there any particular incident that occurred on the train on that date that sticks in your mind?"

"There is."

"Please tell the jury about that incident."

"A woman I now know to be a Miss Burke was in the rear car and started to go to the forward car. That man," he said, pointing at Loco where he was seated beside T. C., "was coming down the aisle the other way at the same time."

Gallahan looked upward at the judge. "May the record show that the witness pointed at the defendant, Your Honor?"

"So ordered."

The county attorney shifted his eyes back to Prato. "What happened then?"

"The lady tried to step by him, and he said something that must have offended her. She spat at him and called him a stinking old man."

"What happened next?"

Prato scowled at Loco. "He leaned closer to her and said something else. That's when she stepped back and swung her purse. She hit him along side the head with it." The frown changed to a crooked smile.

"What did the defendant do?"

"He doubled up his fist and raised it like he was going to hit her back."

Gallahan let the jurors think about that for a long moment. At last he asked, "What did you do at that point?"

"I got between them and told him to leave her alone and to sit down and be quiet." The conductor glared at Loco as he said it.

T. C. glanced at his client. Silverman was still staring at the wall, apparently unmoved by the things that the conductor said—if he was listening at all.

The county attorney, too, glanced at Loco. Then he asked Prato, "Did he do as you told him to do?"

"Well first he growled, 'I just might kill that damn woman!' But then he walked to the rear of the car and took a seat."

Gallahan walked back to his table, picked up a tablet, glanced at it and then turned again to the witness. "Where along the rail line did this occur?"

"Shortly after we left the station at Lennep."

"Mr. Prato, I assume the train traveled its usual route from Lennep to Dorsey. Am I correct?'

The conductor shifted in the witness chair. "The train has to follow the track. So, yes, we finally got to Dorsey."

"Was the defendant on the train when it got to Dorsey?"

"He was,"

"Was Miss Burke on the train when it reached Dorsey?"

"No, sir. I didn't see her again after we left Summit."

Gallahan stepped back and crossed his arms. "Did you see the lady get off the train at Summit?"

"I did not. And I was standing on the station platform where I would have seen her if she'd left the train."

The county attorney stood silently for a long minute to let the jurors reflect on the full import of that statement. Then he whirled and strutted to his chair. As he passed by T. C., he muttered, "Your witness."

T. C. asked two questions of the conductor. "Mr. Prato, are you sure that Mr. Silverman was on the train when it left Summit and when it arrived at Dorsey?"

The conductor looked at T. C. as though he had been insulted. "I said so, didn't I? Yes. He was on the train." The last was said with some heat in his voice.

"Mr. Prato, did you see Miss Burke on the train after it left Summit?"

The conductor stared at him for a moment and then responded, "No. I didn't see her after the train left Summit, but I was busy collecting fares. He killed her and threw her from the train right after we pulled out of town. I didn't have a chance to see her."

T. C. felt that he had blundered by giving the conductor the chance to tell the jury that he was sure that Loco had killed the woman. Collecting his wits, he asked the court to instruct the jury to disregard that portion of the statement as unresponsive to the question and containing speculation. Conrad Gallahan grinned at T. C.'s discomfort but made no objection. Judge Henry directed the jury as T. C. asked. The judge then turned to the conductor and said, "Just answer the question and don't volunteer information."

But T. C. had no more questions of Mr. Prato.

The sheriff was the next witness. He told of receiving word of the killing, going out to meet the wagon coming from Summit to pick up the body, and taking it to the office of the doctor. He also told of the arrest of Lawrence Silverman and finding a knife in his possession. He and his deputies conducted an extensive search of the defendant and his belongings and, he said, found a woman's brooch in his warbag. Both the brooch and the knife were presented to the sheriff to identify. After the identification, they were offered into evidence by the county attorney without objection from T. C.

The Judge called a recess. T. C. was surprised to find that half the afternoon had passed. He welcomed the respite from the intense concentration the proceedings required, listening to each question asked by Gallahan to decide if he should object. If an objection was needed, he had to be ready to state the legal reason. He had to listen carefully to each answer given by the witness so he could be ready to ask further questions along the same line on cross-examination. All the while, he watched the judge and the jurors to gauge their reaction to the proceedings as they went along. He tried to glance at Loco from time to time. His client deserved some attention.

After he'd relaxed in his chair for a minute or two, he looked at his client more carefully. Loco was behaving as before—sitting still and looking at the wall. A deputy came and asked Loco if he needed to go to the privy, but the man didn't answer. T. C., reminded of his own need, made a hurried trip out back.

When court resumed, it was T. C.'s turn. He began by asking the sheriff, "Did you actually see the location where the body was found?"

"No. Mr. Bruce, I did not."

"Who picked up the body from where it was found?"

The sheriff replied. "I don't know." Then he paused before he went on. "It's my understanding that several people went to the site when they heard of the murder, but I don't know who actually got there first or who picked up the body."

T. C. stepped back and clasped his hands behind his back. "Sheriff, when you went to arrest Mr. Silverman, where did you find him?"

Shea's voice remained calm. "I found him down by the lake north of town. He was sitting on a bench in his shack, scraping the hide of a coyote. The shack isn't much. It looks like it could fall down any minute." Shea rubbed his left hand across his mouth. "The place stunk to high heaven."

T. C. glanced at his client. No reaction from Loco to the sheriff's remark. He turned back to Shea. "What did you do when you found Mr. Silverman?"

The officer shifted in the chair. "I stood in the doorway and informed him he was under arrest. Then I told him I was going to take him to jail."

"What was Mr. Silverman's response?"

"There wasn't any."

"You mean he didn't speak?"

"That's right. He didn't say a word."

T. C. glanced over his shoulder at his client, then turned back to the witness. "Did he resist?"

Shea leaned slightly forward. "No, he didn't."

"What did he do?"

The sheriff shook his head once. "Well, when I told him to 'come on', he just got up off the bench. Then he walked along beside me to the jail. I locked him up once we got there."

"Did you have to put him in manacles to get him to go with you?"

"No, I didn't. He didn't argue or anything."

"Did he speak to you at all during the walk?"

Shea leaned slowly back in the witness chair. "Never said a word."

"Sheriff, do you have any way to connect the knife to the murder?"

"The knife appeared to be covered with blood, and it appeared to be the kind that was used in the killing."

"But doesn't Mr. Silverman make his living as a trapper? And wouldn't it be natural for the knife to have blood on it?"

Conrad Gallahan was on his feet. "Objection. Mr. Bruce has asked multiple questions. How is the witness to know what to answer?"

"The objection is sustained." The judge's tone was kindly. "Please ask one question at a time, Mr. Bruce."

T. C. swallowed and asked again, "Sheriff, didn't Mr. Silverman make his living as a trapper?"

"Yes, sir."

"And wouldn't it be natural for the knife that he owned to have blood on it?"

117

The sheriff thought for moment and then said, "That would be logical."

Finally T. C. asked, "Isn't it true that there must be hundreds of knives in the area, any one of which could have caused the wounds that killed the victim."

After the sheriff agreed, T. C. said, "Thank you, sir," and sat down. There was no redirect examination of the sheriff by the county attorney. T. C. wondered if he'd accomplished anything at all with his questions.

Next came the doctor who explained that he examined the body when it was brought to his office. He described the wounds in great detail. The knife had entered the abdomen in an upward thrust and pierced the lower left chamber of the heart. In addition, there was a slash wound across the throat that severed the main arteries and the windpipe. Either one of the wounds would have been fatal without the other.

T. C.'s questions on cross-examination focused on the knife. "Doctor, did you actually see the knife?"

"Yes, I did. The sheriff showed it to me a few days ago."

"Can you say with certainty that the knife that is the State's exhibit was the one that killed Penelope Burke?"

"No, I cannot."

"How long had she been dead when you examined her body?"

"It's hard to tell, but she would have died about the time she was alleged to have been thrown from the train." T. C. realized, too late, that he should not have asked that question. All he could do was return to his seat and say, "No more questions, Your Honor."

Again, there was no redirect examination by the county attorney. T. C. thought he'd done more harm than good for his client.

Finally, Charity Watson was summoned. She identified herself as the one who ran the Wilson Hotel in Two Dot and said that Penelope Bruce had been a guest for about two weeks before her death.

When questioned by the county attorney, she said, "Miss Burke told me that she was going west for a few days, but she said she would return. She asked me to hold her room."

When she was shown the brooch taken from Loco, Mrs. Watson identified it as one she had often seen Miss Burke wearing.

When it was his turn, T. C. smiled at the witness. "Mrs. Watson, did you talk with Miss Burke when she left the hotel to take the train from Two Dot? On the day of her death, that is?"

"Why, yes, Mr. Bruce. We visited for a few minutes when she dropped off the key."

"Are you certain she was wearing the brooch at that time?"

Mrs. Watson frowned, put a finger to her lips and looked off into the distance. At last she turned back at T. C. to say, "I think so."

T. C. moved one step closer to the witness chair. "I didn't ask if you thought she was wearing the brooch. I asked if you are certain she was wearing it."

Charity Watson scowled. "No, Mr. Bruce, I'm not certain she had it on. But I think so."

T. C. nodded, then asked, "Did Miss Burke leave any belongings at the hotel when she left?'

"She left a small trunk and another bag. After I heard of her death, I moved them from the room so I could rent the room to others."

"Since you learned of the sheriff's investigation into the death of Miss Burke, have you looked through her belongings that are still at your hotel to see if the brooch is still among them?"

Her scowl was fierce. "No I did not! The belongings were personal to her. I wasn't about to dig through them. It wouldn't be right."

T. C. smiled to show he understood. But then he asked, "So, Mrs. Watson, you really don't know if the brooch that is an exhibit at this trial—the one the sheriff found on Mr. Silverman—is the one you saw Miss Burke wearing in Two Dot?"

"No, Mr. Bruce. I don't." Before T. C. could stop her, she turned to the jurors to say in a firm voice, "But that brooch was unique. I've never seen another like it."

T. C. immediately asked the judge to direct the jury to ignore the witness's last statement.

Judge Henry turned to the jury and said, "So ordered."

When T. C. indicated he was finished with his cross-examination of Mrs. Watson, Conrad Gallahan rose to his feet and stated with great solemnity, "The State rests, Your Honor."

The Judge nodded to him and turned to T. C., saying, "You may call your first witness, Mr. Bruce."

T. C.'s stomach turned to ice. His first and only witness was camped on Willow Creek, two miles east of town. He had not anticipated that he would need to have Pete in the courtroom so soon. Just as he was about to rise to his feet to try to explain this to the judge, the county attorney saved him.

"Your Honor, it's four o'clock, and I've been told by my clerk that another criminal matter requires my attention. Mr. Bruce has subpoenaed only one witness. It seems probable that we will finish with testimony early enough tomorrow to get the matter to the jury in the afternoon. That being the case, would it be possible to recess for the night and begin again in the morning?"

"Is that correct, Mr. Bruce? Do you have only one witness?"

"Yes, Your Honor. I have no objection to recess at this time. And I agree with Mr. Gallahan that we should be able to finish with the testimony by noon tomorrow."

The judge looked at the clock and thought for a moment, then turned to the jury and announced that court would be in recess until nine o'clock in the morning. He again admonished the twelve black-coated men not to discuss the case with anyone, not even their wives. He banged his gavel while rising from his chair and descended from the bench.

The sheriff and his deputies took Loco away. It was of fleeting interest to T. C. that the jurors waited to leave the jury box until the defendant and the officers were out of the room.

T. C. was exhausted. He turned from the counsel table and smiled at Felicity, realizing how much comfort her presence in the courtroom gave to him.

As he walked through the gate in the barrier that separated the working section of the courtroom from the audience section, his father reached up and put his hand on his shoulder. It remained there as they made their way out into the corridor where the crowd was standing. T. C. ignored those who tried to talk to him. He just wanted to get away to a place where it was quiet and he could rest. He and his father pushed through the crowd and into the street. Once in the street, however, he told his father that he couldn't rest. Pierre Bouteron must be found and told to be in court by nine o'clock the next morning. T. C. would have to ride to Pete's camp.

Ride the Jawbone

As he, his parents, and Felicity walked the boardwalk toward home, his mother heard what he was saying. She stopped them in their tracks, turned to her husband, and spoke with the determination that seemed to have possessed her since her son got involved in the defense of Lawrence Silverman.

"Thaddeus, when we get to the house, you hitch up your buggy and go find that man and tell him to be here in the morning. Thad's tired and needs to think about the things that happened today, and he needs to plan for tomorrow. We'll wait supper until you get back." That said, she turned, locked arms with Felicity, and marched purposely along the walk.

Mr. Bruce nudged his son as he hurried along, game leg swinging to the side. "Neither one of us had better argue with her."

June 21st

The night was not restful for T. C. His mind wouldn't let go of the things that had happened during the day. The whole sequence of events played over and over again in his thoughts, no matter how hard he tried to put his mind at rest. He attempted to think of the questions he should ask Pete on the morrow, but those, too, eluded his efforts. He was locked into a continual memory scroll of the questions asked of the witnesses and of answers given. From time to time he would doze, but peaceful sleep never arrived. At six o'clock, he climbed out of bed feeling as if he hadn't slept at all, but the day was here. He had to begin again his effort to save Loco—whether he was ready or not.

The crowd arrived at the courthouse before T. C. When he walked into the courtroom, he saw Pierre Bouteron sitting at the counsel table where he and Loco sat the day before. Pete's back was to the room, but T. C. could tell he was carefully dressed in a black suit. As the lawyer walked up the aisle, he could also see the knot of a black bandanna at the back of Pete's head.

The herder rose from the chair and took T. C.'s hand in greeting, but was careful to keep his back to the room full of spectators. As Pete sat down again, T. C. thanked him for coming, but got no further with the conversation before the sheriff and his deputies brought Loco into the room and directly to the table where Pete and T. C. were seated.

Understanding that Pete didn't want to sit among the spectators, T. C. stood to allow Loco to have his chair. Loco ignored the herder and gazed at the wall.

The jurors began filing into the jury box just as Conrad Gallahan walked to his place on the other side of the room. He placed his materials on the table and glanced at the sheepherder with a quizzical look on his face. At that moment, the clerk said, "All rise!" as the judge entered the courtroom and mounted to the bench.

"Good morning, everyone." The judge scanned the room and said, "Let the record show that the defendant is present with his counsel. The county attorney is present and the jury is in the jury box." The judge cast a questioning look at the man wearing the bandanna. He turned to T. C. and said, "Mr. Bruce, are you ready to proceed?"

"Yes, Your Honor. The defense calls Pierre Bouteron."

Pete rose. There was a murmur from the audience as he turned his head partially to the crowd.

Conrad Gallahan had been staring at the witness since he first arrived. With a look of determination, he stood and walked briskly toward Pete. "Your Honor, I don't know what Mr. Bruce is up to, but we don't need any masked witnesses in this trial." With that, he reached up, grasped the bandanna by its bottom and yanked it down to Pete's neck. The face that he exposed so startled him that he took a step back and then just stood there, mouth hanging open. Pete reacted involuntarily and looked to his left at the county attorney. By doing so he allowed those on the left side of the room to see his face. An audible gasp reverberated through the room. Pete then turned to his right. That movement exposed his face, not only to the jury, but also to the remaining members of the audience. The gasp was heard again.

T. C. looked quickly at the jury. Each of them sat stony faced. None of them showed any reaction. It amazed T. C. that not one of the jurors had reacted as had the spectators.

Just as he was about to object to the action of Conrad Gallahan, the judge spoke in the same scathing tone that he had used the day before when he chastised the potential juror for using profanity. Leaning forward over the bench, he said, "Mr. Gallahan, you are admonished never to do such a thing again. It's clear why this witness is dressed as he is." His face wore an angry scowl and he pointed at the county attorney with the handle of his gavel. "You will not make decisions for this court. If you believed that the face of the witness should be exposed, you're obligated to ask the court for an order to that effect."

He glared at Gallahan and added, "And you know that, sir."

Turning to T. C. he continued. "Now, Mr. Bruce. You should not put the court nor the county attorney in the position that you just did. Your obligation was to tell us of the condition of the witness and to explain what he wished to do." Finally, turning to Pete, he spoke in a much more gentle tone. "Mr. Bouteron, let me apologize for the actions of Mr. Gallahan. If you wish to replace the kerchief, you may do so." After a pause, he continued, "Now, please raise your right hand so that you can be sworn."

Pete pulled the bandanna back up to cover his face, swore to tell the truth, and mounted to the witness stand. At first he looked straight ahead, but then he turned toward the jury. He turned to T. C. only when the questioning began.

"Will you state your name for the court record, please?"

"My name is Pierre Bouteron." The voice was clear and not muffled at all by the cloth covering his mouth.

"What do you do for a living, Mr. Bouteron?"

"I herd sheep for Olaf Bakken."

T. C. hesitated for a moment and then asked, "Would you care to tell the jury how your face came to be in the condition that it is?"

Pete stared at T. C. over the top of the mask for a long time before he answered. "No sir. I would not." His voice was flat as he said it. T. C. had offended the man and wished he could take the question back. Instead he forged ahead.

"Where were you on April eighteenth of this year?"

"I was herding sheep near Summit."

"Did anything out of the ordinary happen to you that day?'

"I came across the body of a dead woman lying below the railroad tracks near town."

"Can you describe the body as it looked when you found it?"

"She was lying on her back with one arm across her abdomen. The other arm—her right arm—was stretched out almost straight on the ground. Her clothes were all in place, except for her hat. The hat was not on her head, as one would expect it to be. It was lying partly on her face and partly on the ground beside her head."

"What kind of a hat was it?"

"It had a broad, flat brim and was blue in color."

Pete looked at T. C. as each question was asked, and then looked at the jurors while he answered. The jurors, all of whom had seemed bored at times the day before, showed their interest in the testimony by leaning forward to listen. Conrad Gallahan did not appear to be concerned about the testimony. His hands, always in motion, were now moving less than at times when he was agitated. Loco just sat as he had throughout the trial, looking at the wall. He didn't give the impression that he was listening to Pete at all.

T. C. pressed on. "Describe the face of the victim, please."

"Only half of her face was showing when I looked at her. The hat covered the other half. What I could see appeared normal, except that the birds had pecked out her eye." Hearing that, some of the jurors who had been leaning forward to listen, leaned back in their chairs. Others just shifted in their seats.

"Mr. Bouteron, how do you pass the time when you're not occupied by the care of the sheep?"

Pete thought for a moment before he answered. "I suppose you are asking what my hobby is. I like to draw and paint pictures."

"What kind of training have you had in the arts?"

At that question the county attorney rose from his chair to say in a loud voice, "Objection. Whatever this man does in his spare time is of no consequence to this court. It's irrelevant."

T. C. turned to address the Judge. "Your Honor, the witness has utilized his talent for the arts in a way that will be of help to the court and to the jury. That will be evident in a minute."

"Very well." The Judge nodded as he said it. "The objection is overruled. You may answer the question, Mr. Bouteron."

"I received training in the arts at St. Louis University."

"Mr. Bouteron, did you prepare a picture that portrays the body as you found it that day?"

"I did."

T. C. walked to the rail and asked his father to hand him the picture that was leaning against the wall. Mr. Bruce removed the butcher paper that covered it and passed it over the rail to his son.

The picture was large—about two feet by four feet—so it was not easily handled. T. C. was careful to hold it so that the jurors did not see the painting as he carried it to the counsel table. The county attorney, however, was sitting where he could see the picture clearly. His hands began to flutter about. He wiggled in his chair, craning for a clearer view.

T. C. first carried the picture to the table where the clerk was sitting and asked Hakes to mark it as an exhibit. Hakes put a letter "D," then a dash and then a letter "A" on the lower corner of the picture in black ink. When that was done, T. C. returned to the counsel table and placed the picture so that Pete, the judge, and Conrad Gallahan—but not the jurors—could see it. T. C. felt that by tantalizing them, he could increase their interest.

"Mr. Bouteron, is this the picture you produced?"

"It is."

"Does the picture portray with reasonable accuracy the body of the victim as you found it on April eighteenth?"

"Yes, sir. I believe that it does."

"Your Honor, I offer Defendant's Exhibit A into evidence."

Conrad Gallahan was on his feet in an instant. "May I inquire of the witness, Your Honor?"

"You may."

"Mr. Bouteron, you are not asking the jury to believe that this is the same as a photograph—that every detail is exactly as it was on the day that you found the body, are you?"

"No, sir, but the picture is accurate enough for anyone to understand and appreciate what I saw."

T. C. smiled to himself at the answer. It was perfect.

The county attorney thought for a moment and then looked impassively at the judge and said, "Your Honor, I have no objection to the admission of the exhibit into evidence, but for demonstrative purposes only."

T. C. was quick in his response. "The picture is offered only for demonstrative purposes, Your Honor."

The judge pursed his lips, nodded his head and said, "Very well,

Defendant's Exhibit A is admitted without objection. You may proceed, Mr. Bruce."

T. C. stepped forward and turned the picture so that the jurors could see for themselves the figure of the woman lying on her back. The hat covered one side of her face, just as described by Pete. The empty eye socket would surely catch the attention of each juror. The effect was just as T. C. had hoped. There should be no question in the mind of any juror that the picture depicted the body of the victim as the sheepherder had found it. He allowed them to look at the picture for a full minute without interruption, and then carefully placed it upon an easel where it remained clearly visible to the jurors and to the audience as well.

Only then did T. C. return to his questioning of the witness. "Please describe the place where the body was located."

"It was close to the bottom of a coulee near a small spring. I would guess that it was about two hundred feet downhill from the railroad."

"Was the body lying exactly in the bottom of the coulee?"

"No, sir. It was about four feet above the bottom and on the south side of the coulee."

"Describe the plants that were growing in the area, please."

"Well, there are thick willows and some cottonwood trees growing around the area above the spring. There are willows on each side of the spring and around the little stream that runs from it. The willows grow further down the hill on the south side than they do on the north side. The trees and brush form a kind of question mark around the water in the bottom of the coulee."

"Mr. Bouteron, did you also prepare a picture of the general area where you found the body?"

"Yes, sir, I did."

T. C. turned to look at the judge. "One moment, Your Honor?"

Judge Henry, by now obviously interested in what would come next, shifted in his chair and mumbled, "Of course."

Once again his father handed T. C. a picture. This one was much larger than the last—about three feet by five feet—so he had some trouble in manhandling it over the rail. When he had it fully in hand, he made no attempt to shield it from the view of the jury. With some awkwardness, T. C. managed to get it over to Hakes to be marked as

Ride the Jawbone

Defendant's Exhibit B. Leaving the picture resting against the clerk's desk, he returned to the counsel table to question the witness further.

Conrad Gallahan was on his feet even before T. C. could ask Pete if he was the artist who painted the picture.

When the question was asked and answered, Gallahan spoke again. This time the pitch of his voice had risen and his hands were waving about. "Your Honor, I will stipulate that Mr. Bouteron painted the picture and to any further foundation as to authenticity. But I object strenuously to the introduction of the picture into evidence. The picture may or may not be accurate and, if it isn't, it may seriously mislead the jury."

The judge exhibited some impatience. "Mr. Gallahan, I appreciate your willingness to stipulate as to foundation, but the exhibit has not as yet been offered into evidence so your objection is premature and is overruled. You may continue, Mr. Bruce."

When T. C. asked the next question, he looked at the jurors rather than at the witness. "Mr. Bouteron, is there anything either left out of this picture or put into this picture that is materially different than that which existed on April eighteenth?" T. C. cast a quick glance at Gallahan who was still standing in front of his chair at the other counsel table. His face was growing red and his whole body now shook with slight, but agitated movement. T. C. looked back at Pete, and then at the jury, as Pete answered.

"As I told the other lawyer when he asked about the first picture, the jurors can look at this picture and understand what I saw."

Conrad Gallahan yelped, "Objection. The answer isn't responsive to the question. I move that the answer be stricken and that the jury be instructed to ignore the answer."

The judge's impatience was even more evident as he leaned forward to say, "Mr. Gallahan, the answer is responsive enough. Your objection is overruled. Continue, Mr. Bruce."

"Your Honor, I offer Defendant's Exhibit B into evidence."

"Objection!" the county attorney shouted again.

This time the judge had a scowl on his face. "Your objection, Mr. Gallahan, is overruled and the exhibit is admitted." Then, turning he spoke in a more gentle voice, "Please continue, Mr. Bruce."

T. C. knew he had better get to the purpose of the picture without further delay. He said, "Mr. Bouteron, will you please step down from the witness chair and by reference to the picture, tell the jury where the body was lying when you found it?"

Pete rose from the chair and walked to the picture. His posture was erect and, but for the mask over his face, he was a man of imposing appearance. He pointed to the drawing.

"Mr. Bouteron, please show the jurors where the trees and brush that you described are located in relation to the body."

Again, Conrad Gallahan shouted, "Your Honor, may I have a continuing objection to this line of questions?"

"Yes, Mr. Gallahan, you may have a continuing objection. Mr. Bruce, go ahead."

After Pete pointed to the trees and brush, T. C. continued. "Mr. Bouteron, from your observations that day and from your common knowledge, would it have been possible for the body to have rolled down from the train track, to have penetrated the brush, and to have ended up at the location that you found it?"

This time the voice of the county attorney was a high pitched screech. "Objection, Your Honor! Mr. Bruce is asking this witness, who is not qualified as an expert, to give an opinion as to a possibility. The rules of evidence clearly prohibit such testimony."

T. C.'s response was given in a calm voice that contrasted sharply with that of his adversary. "Your Honor, Mr. Bouteron was there. He's a man of ordinary intelligence and can reach conclusions from his observations that any other man of ordinary intelligence can reach. It doesn't take special training or education to know whether or not a body could roll down a hill and through some brush. Or, if it didn't roll through the brush, it would then have had to roll around the brush, down to the bottom of the coulee and then up hill again. That is what the witness will tell us the body of Penelope Burke would have had to do to get where he found it."

Turning quickly to Pete he asked, "Is that correct, sir?"

"Your Honor," Gallahan screeched even louder, "The only way for the jury to know for themselves is for them to have been there. They can't rely upon the opinion of this sheepherder to tell them what could or could not have happened. I ask you to direct the jury to disregard the statements—the testimony, Your Honor—of Mr. Bruce. Mr. Bruce is not a witness in this trial. He can't testify as he just tried to do."

Before the Judge could respond, T. C. acted. "Your Honor, Mr. Gallahan is right. The jurors should make their decision based upon their own observations. I move that the jury be taken to the site to view it for themselves."

"Just a minute, Mr. Bruce, I haven't ruled on the last motion and that motion is granted." Turning to the jury, he said, "You are instructed to disregard the statement of Mr. Bruce about what the body could do. He is not a witness. You will be given a written instruction to that effect before you begin your deliberations." Turning back to the county attorney, "Now, Mr. Gallahan, what is your response to the motion for a site visit?"

"I resist the motion, Your Honor. It isn't necessary. It will only confuse the members of the jury. It will cost the county money and the county commissioners won't like that. The jury can reach a verdict based upon the evidence presented here in the courtroom." He seemed almost to be pleading.

The way that the judge reared back in his chair before he spoke told T. C. that he'd made up his mind. "Well, Mr. Gallahan, you objected on the basis that the jurors would be misled by the picture. The location of the body and whether it could have gotten there from the train are squarely before the jury now. It's my view that the only way to allow the members of the jury to make an informed decision is to take them to the location. And we will do so tomorrow, assuming, Mr. Bruce, that you will be finished with your case?"

"Yes, sir. I have no more witnesses."

"Do you have further questions for this witness?"

"No, Your Honor. I do not."

"Mr. Gallahan, do you have any cross-examination?"

Conrad marched back to his chair behind the counsel table, turned to the judge, and growled, "No sir."

"All right. Gentlemen, we will take the jurors to the site tomorrow. Mr. Gallahan, you may present any rebuttal testimony when we return." He rubbed his head as he thought. "Now let's figure out how we're going to do this. Where's the sheriff?"

Sheriff Shea stepped forward from the place at the rear of the room where he had been standing throughout the trial.

"Ah, there you are, Sheriff. We'll need buggies to take the jurors, the defendant, and the rest of us to the site tomorrow. Will you go to the livery stables and find out how many they have available to rent?" He paused for a moment and then raised his hand as if to stop the man, even though the sheriff had not yet moved from his place along the wall. "On second thought, some of the jurors can ride horseback and may prefer to do so." He turned to the jury and asked, "How many of you have horses that you could ride to the site tomorrow?"

All of the jurors raised their hands. "Well, well! That will simplify matters considerably." Then, looking at Milton Anderson, the one-legged juror, he observed, "Milt, you don't need to ride a horse even if you want to prove to me that you can. We'll make room for you in a buggy." Then, turning back to T. C. he said, "Mr. Bruce, the defendant will ride in a buggy with two of the sheriff's deputies. Do you have any objection to that?"

T. C. looked sideways at Lawrence Silverman to find that he had not changed his expression. T. C. shook his head to indicate that he had no objection. Remembering that the court reporter needed a verbal response for the record, said, "No, Your Honor. No objection."

Turning to the county attorney, the Judge asked, "Any objection, Mr. Gallahan?"

"I object to the whole proceeding, Your Honor. But I have no objection to your suggestion that the defendant go in a buggy with the deputies, so long as they are careful in guarding him." There was resignation in his voice, and when he finished speaking, he slumped into his chair with his arms hanging at his side. For the first time since the trial began, his hands were not fidgeting.

"Very well, then. Sheriff Shea, please rent a buggy for the deputies and the defendant." Turning then to Pete, he said in a gentle voice, "Mr. Bouteron, we will need you at the scene, of course, to show the jury where the body was lying when you found it. Do you have a horse to ride?"

Pete turned in the witness chair to face the judge and spoke from beneath his mask. "Yes, sir. I rode my horse in here this morning, and I can ride with you tomorrow."

Ride the Jawbone

"Thank you, sir." The judge turned back to the others. "Let me warn the lawyers and the jurors that I will have no volunteer testimony while we are at the site. I'll ask any questions of Mr. Bouteron that I believe to be appropriate. You jurors are to remember my admonition not to discuss the case among yourselves or with anyone else until all of the evidence has been presented. Will you all do that?"

All of the jurors' heads bobbed up and down. The judge then looked beyond T. C. to Thaddeus Bruce. "Thad, if I remember correctly, you have a good buggy that has seats for six. And you have a fine team to pull it. Am I right?"

Mr. Bruce rose slowly from the seat and said, "Why, yes, Your Honor. I do have a good team and buggy. Do you need them?"

"I need a buggy for the lawyers and for me. We'll also take Mr. Albers with us and we'll give Milt Anderson a ride. The reason for this arrangement is to assure that there is no accusation that either lawyer talked to any juror during the trip. They will both be with me. Is that fair, gentlemen?"

"Yes, Your Honor," T. C. responded promptly. The county attorney nodded, then mumbled, "Yes."

Judge Henry turned back to Mr. Bruce and said, "If you can have the buggy ready in the morning, we will all appreciate it."

The judge looked out at the audience. "It's important for everyone to remember that we will still be in court tomorrow. Those of you who wish to do so may travel along with us, but you must not interfere in any way with our activities. You are to stay away from the jurors and from everyone else connected with the court."

Turning again to Sheriff Shea. "Sheriff, it's another of your responsibilities to assure that everyone follows my instructions." After another look around the courtroom, the Judge added, "All right. Court is adjourned until tomorrow morning at eight o'clock when we will reconvene in front of Smith's livery stable. I want you all there on time, and we will travel together from there to the place where that poor woman's body was found. Sheriff, be sure that the group all stays in a bunch. Round up as many additional deputies as you need for that purpose. I'm sure that you have some men who provide help to you when you need it. Hire them. The county commissioners won't like it at all, but do it anyway. That's an order. Are we all agreed?"

When no one disagreed, he ended the session by saying, "Good. I'll see you all in the morning." He rose to leave the bench, then stopped and turned to the jury once more. "It will not be necessary to dress for court tomorrow. Wear something that's comfortable for travel. I plan to do so. That goes for the lawyers, too." Then he banged his gavel, ending the court session for the day.

June 22nd

Everyone appeared at the livery stable at the appointed time, and the assemblage moved out smartly toward Dorsey. T. C. drove his father's buggy with the Judge, Hakes Albers, Milton Anderson, and Conrad Gallahan as his passengers. Pete, kerchief over his face, was riding his horse next in line. One of the special deputies rode between him and the jurors who, except for Milton Anderson, traveled on horseback in a group. Behind them came the buggy with Lawrence Silverman and the two regular deputies whose duty it was to guard him. Sheriff Shea, riding a large and colorful pinto horse, had stationed himself behind the buggy carrying the defendant. By doing so, he could separate the official court party from the crowd of spectators tagging along.

East of Dorsey the grade in the wagon road leading to the town of Summit became increasingly steep. T. C. slowed the horses from the trot that had been the pace from White Sulphur Springs. The day was warming fast, and sweat was running down the back legs of the team. The animals continued to walk briskly upward toward the place where the road approached the railroad track, a short distance from Summit.

Pete moved ahead of T. C.'s buggy, leading the group toward the coulee where he'd found the body—the same coulee the conductor had pointed out to T. C. from the train a couple of months before. An area had been cleared of sagebrush immediately adjacent to the railroad track and they followed it southward a short distance. Pete turned his horse downhill and the others followed. Those driving buggies had to seek a passage through the stumpy sagebrush that grew here and there along the path of travel. Pete didn't go far before he stopped, looked back at the judge, and pointed down into the bottom of the coulee that lay ahead. When T. C. pulled the sweating horses to a halt, the judge climbed down, stretched his back, and stepped off to the side where he could address the crowd as they assembled nearby.

"All right. You jurors get down and follow me. Deputy, get some help and hold the jurors' horses. Sheriff, bring the defendant up here so he can see what's going on." Then he turned to Pete, "Now, Mr. Bouteron, please show us where the body was located when you found her. And, when you get down there, you might stretch out on the ground and show us how she was lying."

Pete stepped down from his horse, handed the reins to T. C., and trudged away. The jurors and the crowd stood on the north side of the coulee, looking south. They watched with interest as Pete made his way toward the spring. He had to go around some low brush that extended down the north side of the coulee for a short distance. T. C. smiled to himself. The scene was just as Pete's picture showed it. The jurors kept looking back toward the railroad and down toward the brush that blocked the way to the place where Pete was heading.

The sheepherder crossed the little stream that flowed from the spring and took three steps upward and stopped. He looked back at the crowd of people watching him from above and pointed downward to a place near his feet. Then he got down on the ground and stretched out on his back with his head pointed uphill and away from the stream. He crossed one arm over his chest and extended the other out on the ground just as his picture had portrayed the woman's body.

There was silence for a moment as each onlooker contemplated the situation that must have existed when the victim was found. A loud growl caused them all to look back just in time to see Loco leap into the air and fall prone to the ground. His body rolled down the hill about five feet and lodged against a sage bush. Before anyone could move, he was back on his feet. Letting out another roar, he threw himself down and was rolling again. His body made about one and one half revolutions and lodged against another sage bush. He rose immediately and opened his mouth for another shout. But before he could either yowl or move, a shot banged out of a deputy's rifle. When Loco went to the ground that time, his body lay crumpled in a contorted position and he stayed where he fell. The only sounds that came from his mouth were a gasp and a grunt.

There was absolute silence until the sheriff shouted, "George, you damn fool! All he's trying to do is show us that a body couldn't roll down this hill!"

The judge moved the fastest. He was at Loco's side before anyone else. He peeled off his coat as he knelt down on the ground. Loco looked upward at him with one eye, the other looking off into space, and pointed at his right leg. Blood soaked through the cloth halfway between his knee and his hip. The Judge looked for the sheriff.

Before anyone else could say a word, Conrad Gallahan recovered from the shock of the shooting and yelled, "Mistrial! I demand a mistrial!"

The judge didn't even look at him as he said, "Shut up, Conrad." He saw the sheriff moving his way and barked an order; "Get the shackles off this man." He pulled a knife from his pocket and began to cut away the leg of Loco's pants to get at the wound. Once that was done, he could see that the bleeding was not excessive and that no bone seemed to be broken. Off came the judge's shirt, which he tore into wide strips. The sheriff helped the judge wrap Loco's thigh with the pieces of the material. When it was done, the judge got to his feet. "Sheriff, get your men and load the defendant into the buggy right now. Be careful when you do it." He looked down at Loco and asked him if he could make it to town.

Loco did not respond right away, but finally nodded his head. Judge Henry stared at the man for a second, then nodded back and turned again to the sheriff. "Start for White Sulphur Springs, and don't stop till you get there. Then get him to the doctor."

Two deputies hoisted Loco to his feet, got one of his arms around the shoulders of each of them and half dragged him to the buggy. After a struggle they succeeded in stretching him out on the back seat. The sheriff and a deputy climbed in. The sheriff took the reins and hazed the team around to follow the track the way that they had come.

T. C. and all of the others stood almost motionless from the time Loco started his ruckus to the time that the sheriff got the buggy going. Then the noise of many voices rose over the landscape.

The judge silenced the crowd. "You jurors ride back to town and don't talk about what happened here or talk about anything else having to do with this trial until I tell you that you can. The deputies will ride with you. Court will reconvene in the courtroom at nine o'clock in the morning. Be there." He looked over at the one legged juror, "Milt, come along now. Let's get in the buggy."

Looking at T. C. and Conrad Gallahan he said, "Let's get out of here." He waved his arm at the clerk of court. "Hurry up, Hakes." The judge started up the hill at a brisk walk toward their buggy. As he walked, he stuck his necktie in the pocket of his coat and put the coat on over his undershirt.

Pete had risen from the ground when Loco was shot and started back up the hill. He ran and caught the judge and lawyers as they reached their buggy. The bandanna still covered his face. "T. C., am I done? Can I go back to my sheep or not?"

The judge paused in his climb and looked back at the witness. "No, Mr. Bouteron, you are not done till I say so. Please be in court in the morning. You're still under oath and still on the witness stand." There was some impatience in his voice.

T. C. looked at Pete and shrugged. He picked up the reins as the others climbed into the buggy.

June 23rd

Conrad Gallahan made his motion for a mistrial in the judge's chamber the first thing in the morning. The judge listened to him without interruption. When the county attorney was done, the judge didn't even ask T. C. to respond. Instead he said, "I've thought about the matter over night and have concluded that the demonstration given by the defendant didn't mislead the jury. Unless the demonstration misled the jury, there's no basis upon which to grant the motion for a mistrial." He paused and looked at Gallahan. "For that reason, the motion is denied."

Gallahan inhaled as though to argue the point further but then seemed to think better of it. Instead he said, "I won't cross-examine Mr. Bouteron, and I have no rebuttal witnesses."

When T. C. heard that, he heaved a silent sigh of relief.

The judge told Hakes to tell the jurors it would be an hour before court reconvened. He gave each lawyer some time to read through the jury instructions prepared by the other. The judge, the county attorney, and T. C. Bruce then reviewed the offered jury instructions. One item at a time, the instructions were argued and settled.

The defendant walked with a severe limp when the deputies brought him to the courtroom. T. C. was glad to see that he could walk at all. Loco had on a new pair of pants and, for the first time in court, he didn't have shackles on his ankles. The crowd gave him an even wider berth than usual when he limped along the aisle from the rear of the courtroom to the front. The judge climbed to his bench and the day's court proceedings began.

Pete sat at the table next to Loco. The same cloth covered his face, and he was prepared to take the witness stand again when the county attorney formally announced that he had no questions of Mr. Bouteron. The judge turned to Pete, told him that he was dismissed, and thanked him for appearing. As the sheepherder made his way out of the courtroom, some of those in the audience swiveled their heads to get a good look at him. He kept his eyes straight ahead to the courtroom door and stepped through without a backward glance.

The jury instructions were read aloud in solemn tones by the judge. When he finished, Conrad Gallahan rose slowly to his feet to make his closing argument. The main thrust of the argument was that Lawrence Silverman had the means, the motive, and the opportunity to kill Penelope Burke. He was found in possession of a knife that was of the kind that killed her, and he had her brooch in his possession. The only way that he could have gotten the brooch was to have taken it from her. The county attorney admitted that it may have been difficult for the body to roll down the hill to the place where Mr. Bouteron said he found it, but maybe Mr. Bouteron's memory was faulty. Maybe the body was farther up the hill. In any event, no one else had any reason or opportunity to kill the victim, so it had to be the defendant.

The time that T. C. both anticipated and dreaded finally arrived. As he pushed himself to his feet to begin, his stomach was in a boil. He had never been so nervous in his life. It was all he could do to keep his legs from shaking. His client's life could very well depend on the things he was about to say.

He felt the eyes of his parents and Felicity upon him. He realized it was not the outcome that mattered to his father so much as that he did well and was comfortable with his effort. T. C.'s mother, on the other hand, wanted her son to win. She had come to view the county attorney as an enemy. She wanted him destroyed. It showed in her posture. Her hands were gripped tightly together and her face bore a stern resolve.

Felicity was nervous because she knew T. C. was nervous. But she was proud that he was properly groomed and dressed. His suit, like those of others in the room, was black, but his was finely tailored and carefully pressed. His tie was knotted perfectly. And his sandy hair was clean, parted on the right, and neatly combed. She couldn't help but compare T. C.'s appearance with that of Conrad Gallahan.

Conrad wore a black suit, too, but it was the same one he had worn throughout the trial. His pants and his coattails were wrinkled from sitting in the chair. His hair was combed straight back and had a greasy look about it. She thought, "If looks matter, Thad will win." She appreciated that he stood perfectly erect and gave the appearance of complete confidence. When he began to speak, she held her breath and said a silent prayer.

"Gentlemen. You remember what the county attorney told you at the beginning of this trial. He said that the State would prove that Lawrence Silverman killed Miss Burke and threw her body from the train. In that statement, he told you what he was obligated to prove. And the judge,"—T. C. nodded toward the bench as he said it—"has reminded us again, in the jury instructions, that the proof must be beyond a reasonable doubt. You've seen where Mr. Bouteron found the body. Think what the body must have done if it fell from the train and ended up where it was found. It would have had to roll downhill through the sagebrush, turn ninety degrees to the left, roll further down the hill, cross a stream, and then roll uphill. Then, it had to turn itself perpendicular to the slope of the hill at the place where it came to rest. Then the body had to place its hat carefully in such a way as to cover half of its face."

T. C. moved away from the chair in front of which he was standing and faced the jurors from the center of the space before the bar. "Think about it. Miss Burke was either murdered where her body was found, or her body was carried to the place where it was found. There is no other way that it could have gotten there. But this man," T. C. said as he pointed to the defendant, "didn't do it. Lawrence Silverman was still on the train. That's what the conductor told you. Remember what else the conductor admitted. He said he wasn't sure that Miss Burke was on the train when it left Summit." The young man paused for effect. "You have no reason to disbelieve the conductor. After all he was a witness called by the State."

T. C. was warming to his task. "The county attorney spoke of the knife found in Mr. Silverman's possession. I don't know how many of you own a skinning knife, but I suspect that most of you do. Such knives are as common as dirt in this county." He waited a heartbeat and then went on. "Let's consider the brooch. Miss Burke evidently owned a brooch like the one found on Mr. Silverman. No one has told you that there is only one such brooch. Maybe there are several of them. It's possible that Miss Burke"s brooch is still among her belongings. No one has testified to the contrary."

T. C. walked over and stood across the table from the defendant. He stretched his arm out toward Loco and put his hand palm down on the table's flat surface. He continued to face the jurors. "Mr. Silverman was on the train between Lennep and Summit. He apparently had a disagreement with Miss Burke. That and the brooch are all there is to tie him to her. That's not enough to convict any man of murder. We all have faith in your good judgment. There is more than reasonable doubt. Mr. Silverman should be acquitted." He stopped speaking, stood looking from one juror to another for some time before he turned, stepped around the counsel table and settled in his chair. His part of the trial was finished. There was nothing more he could do to save his client. Relief washed over him like a giant wave. He didn't even look at Loco to learn if the man reacted to his efforts in any way.

Conrad Gallahan heaved his square body upright and advanced toward the jury as though he was headed for a fight. "Gentlemen. No one saw Miss Burke leave the train at Summit. Therefore, she must have been on the train when it got to the spot above where the body was found. Since that's the case, someone on that train murdered her. There was no one other than the defendant with the motive to kill her. You remember that I told you at the beginning that I couldn't bring photographs of the murder being committed. But that doesn't mean that the defendant didn't do it." He closed his argument with a strident voice. "Lawrence Silverman is often called Loco. He's capable of committing this monstrous crime. He needs to be convicted and punished. You on the jury are the guardians of our society. It's your duty to return a verdict of murder in the first degree."

T. C. rose halfway out of his seat to object to the county attorney's inflammatory statement, but before he could say a word, the judge gestured to him, indicating that he should save his breath.

Judge Henry turned a steady gaze upon the jurors, "Gentlemen, Mr. Gallahan has intimated that the defendant is crazy. There is no evidence in this case about his mental condition. You are instructed to ignore those statements during your deliberations and consider only the evidence." He swiveled in his chair to look at Hakes, "Mr. Albers, do you have the exhibits ready for the jurors to take to the jury room?"

Hakes stood and said, "Yes, sir."

The judge turned his attention to the sheriff at his place at the rear of the courtroom. "Sheriff, you are to take the jurors to the jury room so they can begin their deliberations." Then, turning back to the jurors, he instructed them one last time. "Follow the Sheriff, gentlemen. He'll show you where to go. When you reach a verdict—and remember that it must be unanimous—knock on the door to the jury room and tell the sheriff."

He looked at the clock on the wall at the back of the courtroom. Before the jurors could stand, he added, "If you don't complete your deliberations before noon, the sheriff will take you to the Sherman Hotel to get something to eat. The county will pay for it." Looking at the lawyers he said, "Is there anything more, gentlemen? If not, court is in recess until we hear from the jury."

As T. C. watched the deputies lead Loco away, he wondered what could be going through the mind of his client. Until yesterday, he had not given any indication that he was the least bit interested in the outcome of the trial. Yesterday his actions showed that he did know what was at stake, and that he wanted to influence the outcome. T. C. decided that Lawrence Silverman may be strange, but he wasn't crazy. He knew what he was doing all of the time.

He wondered if the jury would find Loco's demonstration persuasive—if his argument had made any impression at all upon the jurors. If not, Loco was heading for the gallows. He thought of Norris Thorpe, the one juror that his parents believed would surely favor the prosecution. For the first time the full impact of that failure hit him, and for a moment he couldn't get up from his chair.

++++++++++

The jurors reached their verdict in less than an hour after they had eaten the noon meal, paid for by the county. T. C. sat at the table in his mother's kitchen when a deputy knocked on the door and told him that the Judge wanted him back at court. T. C. hurried back to the courthouse as fast as he could walk, his parents and Felicity almost running along behind him. When all of the trial participants were once again in their places and the gallery was full to overflowing, the judge climbed to the bench. After noting that the defendant was in court accompanied by his attorney, he directed the sheriff to bring in the jury. When they were seated, Judge Henry turned to the jurors and asked, "Gentlemen, have you reached a verdict?"

The man who rose to answer for the jury was Norris Thorpe. A chill shook T. C. He was certain that Thorpe had convinced the others to accept Conrad Gallahan's argument and convict Loco. Mr. Thorpe addressed the Judge with a simple, "We have, Your Honor."

"Are you the foreman, Mr. Thorpe?"

"I am, Your Honor.

"Please give the verdict to the clerk." Turning to Hakes, he said, "Bring the verdict to me, Mr. Albers." Hakes took the verdict form from the foreman and walked it to the judge. Judge Henry read it carefully and then handed it back to Hakes. "Please read the verdict, Mr. Albers."

Hakes gathered himself up in all of his dignity, turned to the audience, and read in a loud voice, "We, the jury, find the defendant not guilty."

Before anyone else could move, Loco rose from his chair and limped over to the sheriff. He stuck his arms under the sheriff's nose. His voice, when he spoke, was a course command. "Take these off!" T. C., and everyone else in the room, was startled by his action and by his voice. The sheriff turned to the judge for instruction. The judge, eyebrows raised in the astonishment felt by all in the room, nodded. The shackles came off and Loco turned to leave. The crowd parted hurriedly to allow him to get to the rear of the courtroom. He limped down the stairs and out of the building without another word.

Ever since T. C. had first seen the man in the jail cell, he'd wondered if Loco could talk. Now he knew.

When Loco was out of sight, all of those in the crowd began talking at once, and the noise filled the room. The judge beat on his bench with the gavel to quiet them down. When order was restored, he thanked the jury for doing their duty, told them they would be paid by the county for their efforts, and declared court adjourned.

T. C. didn't feel elation. He felt empty. Felicity was the first one to reach him, and his parents were right behind. His father grabbed him by the shoulder with one hand and reached to shake his son's hand with the other. Thaddeus Bruce wore a wide smile as he offered his congratulations. T. C.'s mother patted his arm and beamed. He rose from his chair without quite knowing what to do next. It was at that moment that Felicity moved so close to him that their bodies were touching. Face turned upward and smiling a radiant smile, she said, "I'm so proud of you!"

She reached to pluck an invisible speck of lint from the lapel of his coat. It was a gesture of possession that every woman in the room instinctively understood. It told each one of them that T. C. Bruce belonged to her.

T. C. had no idea that he had just been claimed as surely as though he'd been branded.

+++++++++

Sarah watched from the rear of the room. She came to town hoping to speak once again with the young man with whom she had ridden the stage to Martinsdale. She saw Felicity's gesture and understood exactly what it meant. She was too late and her opportunity was gone. Sarah left the building and walked directly to the hotel to make arrangements to take the stage back to the Morton ranch the next morning.

She had hoped to find a man who shared her interests and who would be kind and gentle like the Reverend Dorman. She thought she might have found him in T. C. Bruce. The scene that she'd witnessed in the courtroom told her with finality that she would never be Mrs. Bruce.

141

Should she go back to Iowa and marry Oliver? He was not very bright. He would have no idea why she needed to have books in the house. There would be no stimulating table conversation. But Oliver was not cruel like her father. As an only son, he stood in line to become one of the biggest landowners in the county. He could and would provide for her. And she would inherit her parents' farm when they were gone. She would keep the ownership of that land to herself. It would bring in money that she could invest as the Dormans did. With the income from the investments, she could buy the things that she wanted without asking Oliver. She vowed that if she had a girl, that child would receive an education. She promised herself that her daughter would enjoy things beyond the farm. As all of these thoughts coursed through her mind, a tear trickled down her cheek.

Later that evening, having dried the tear and scrubbed her face, she went to the dining room for something to eat. While she was finishing her meal, a man she had never seen before approached the table where she was sitting alone. He was tall, well dressed and about the same age as the Reverend Dorman. He was nice looking, with regular features and a sandy mustache. When he spoke to her it was in a soft, polite way.

"Please forgive me if I introduce myself. I'm Gordon Jordahl from Tennessee, and I'm told that you are looking for a teaching position. I came to Montana to buy land, and I found a place near Bozeman that's just what I need. I have a small son back home who is without a mother. When he's in Montana, he'll need someone to care for him and to teach him."

Sarah looked up at him as he spoke. When he finished, she returned her gaze to her plate.

When Sarah didn't respond, the man asked, "May I sit with you so we can discuss a teaching arrangement?" Sarah hesitated for a moment and then nodded once. When seated, Gordon Jordahl asked, "Would you consider such a proposal? I am willing to pay more than the ordinary teacher's salary, and I can give you references."

Sarah glanced sideways at him and said, "I'm willing to discuss it. When would you bring your son to Montana?"

Gordon Jordahl smiled.

Ride the Jawbone

The stage for Martinsdale, carrying Sarah, passed T. C. as the young lawyer rode eastward along the road out of town. Sarah, caught up in thought about the man from Tennessee, didn't see him. T. C. paid little attention to the stage as it passed. He was headed for Pete's camp.

The herder's teepee was set up on the bank of Willow Creek. Pete was pouring water on the fire in preparation for his trip back to the Bakken ranch when T. C. rode in. The young lawyer got down from his horse and stood with his hand resting on the saddle horn, while he told the sheepherder of the verdict. Pete listened without comment. He looked squarely at T. C. over the cloth covering his face and asked, "If Loco didn't kill her, who did?"

June 25th

T. C. was in a state near to euphoria. On reflection, he never really thought he would be successful in defending Loco. It seemed certain that the man would be convicted. Through luck, and the help of others, T. C. had convinced the jury to let Loco go. His euphoric feeling was tempered by a concern about the public reaction to his efforts. He didn't venture out of the house till the second day after the trial.

When T. C. started to the post office to pick up his parents' mail, he wondered what kind of reception he would get from those he would meet on the street. The town had been ready to hang Loco before the trial began. Now they had been deprived of that pleasure. It would only be logical that they would blame him for the loss.

On Main Street he met the wife of the operator of the livery stable. She stopped him with a smile. "You did a grand job, young man. I'm sure that your mother is proud of you." She patted his arm, and, as she walked away, she added, "She should be."

Next he encountered one of the jurors. T. C. nodded a greeting as they approached one another, not knowing what else to do. The juror stopped and stuck out his hand. "T. C., you did fine. You made old Conrad look foolish." Before T. C. could respond, he added, "I hope you'll be opening shop here in the Springs rather than in Two Dot. We need a smart young fellow like you in this town." After listening to those remarks, T. C. felt a little smug.

When he neared the cobbler shop, the proprietor hurried out and grabbed his coat sleeve. "You're the talk of the town, T. C."

Before he could say more, the owner of the building where the cobbler shop was located ran up to them. "This man hasn't paid the rent. I'm hiring you, T. C., right now, to sue him for the rent and to get him evicted from this building."

The cobbler continued to hang onto T. C's sleeve as he shouted, "You get the hell out of here, Herman. I got to T. C. first. I've already hired him to represent me. You're too late."

"Like hell I am! I'll show you!" The owner pulled back his arm and swung his fist at the cobbler, nearly striking T. C. in the jaw.

The cobbler ducked the blow and grabbed the other man in a hug. They fell to the ground and rolled around in an attempt at wrestling. T. C. watched for a minute in astonishment and then reached down and tugged at the coat of the one who was on top to try to separate them.

Almost instantly he realized how foolish they all looked and stepped back, chuckling as he brushed dust from his hands—just as the sheriff arrived on the scene.

"OK, boys, that's enough." They both recognized the sheriff's voice and gave up the struggle. As the two men scrambled up from the ground, each was shouting that he had gotten to T. C. first. The sheriff had dealt with that kind of scuffle many times. He got between them and told them both to go on about their business. They did so, but not before they exchanged some final angry words. The only damage that either man suffered in the fray was dirt on his clothes.

Sheriff Shea watched the cobbler duck back into his shop and the owner stomp up the street. He pushed his hat back on his head and looked at T. C. out of the corner of his eye. "Well, young man, you got old Loco off and that seems to have brought you some notoriety." He laughed quietly and then continued. "Those two are only the first ones who will be wanting you to save them from their follies." His look turned serious. "Anyway, Loco's gone—disappeared. I guess he didn't kill her. But I sure can't figure out who did, if he didn't." The sheriff lifted his hat to scratch his head. "Maybe you have some idea who did it and how it happened."

"No sir, Sheriff. I have no idea who killed her. Have you investigated any other possibilities?"

"I don't know of any other possibilities to investigate. Until someone gives me something new to go on, I've got other things to do." The sheriff looked at T. C. for a moment before he turned to leave. "You did a good job. I was sure we'd convict him."

T. C. carried the mail back to the house and handed it to his father. As the older man sorted through the flyers and other impersonal items that were mixed with the letters, T. C. told him of the ruckus between the two men on the street and of the reaction of the others that he had met during his walk. "It seems strange that they accepted the verdict without anger when they all were so anxious to hang Loco before the trial began."

"Son, people like a winner. They may still think that Loco killed that woman, but they also know that the proof wasn't good enough. You get the credit for that." He tore open an envelope as he spoke. "There'll be some who complain, but they'll direct most of their complaints at the county attorney. Conrad will be busy explaining why it wasn't his fault."

June 26th

A day later, T. C. walked Felicity to the hotel for dinner. They met Conrad Gallahan tramping along the boardwalk. He tipped his hat to the young lady and offered his hand to T. C. "Congratulations, Mr. Bruce. I didn't get to say that in the courtroom after the trial. You performed well." Then, just as T. C.'s father had predicted, he began his explanation. "The sheriff should've done a better job of investigating. He should've gone to the place where that woman's body was found, and he should've asked Mrs. Watson to search that woman's belongings to make certain that there wasn't another brooch." He looked from T. C. to Felicity and back. "Well, I suppose he does the best he can. And I'm stuck with it." With another touch of his hand to the brim of his hat, he stomped on down the street.

When he was safely away, Felicity couldn't suppress a giggle. "He should have personally made certain that all those things were done, shouldn't he?"

The giggle made T. C. grin. "Yes, I suppose he should have seen to that. But he didn't." He stuck out his elbow for her hand. "Let's forget all that and just enjoy the day."

He escorted Felicity back to the store after the meal, and then found himself without anything to do. For weeks the trial had filled his mind. Now it was over. He began to think about the ranch and realized how much he wanted to get back there so he could be a part of them. The trial had been exciting, but the ranch was home.

While he ambled toward his parents' house, one of the town merchants stopped him. "I'm having trouble collecting some bills. I understand that you'll be setting up shop here in town. I hope you get going soon, because I need your services." The man then walked up the street without another word. He'd all but ordered T. C. to get busy and start practicing law. The trial had made everyone in the community aware that he was a lawyer. Now, it seemed, they assumed that he would be hanging out his shingle and taking on the representation of clients. But the ranch was his interest, at least for the moment.

T. C. had not forgotten Sarah. She said she would contact him about reviewing a contract after the trial, and he expected to hear from her any day. It would be pleasant to visit with her in a setting that was private, one that would allow him to learn more about her. He would explain the need for a thorough review of the contract as a means of prolonging their visit. Maybe she would even smile. Back at the house he went to his room to compose a letter.

> *Dear Miss Kuntz,*
> *I plan to return to our ranch for a while. If you still wish to have me review the contract for you, I could meet you in the lobby of the hotel in Martinsdale at a time that you select. If it would be more convenient for you, I could travel to the Morton ranch just as easily. Please let me know your preference.*
> *Your servant,*
> *T. C. Bruce*

He addressed the letter to Miss Sarah Kuntz, care of Willard Morton, at Martinsdale, Montana.

Ride the Jawbone

Late that afternoon, he told his parents that he would return to the ranch. He intended to ride back the next morning. His mother cast a sharp glance at him and said, "Have you told Felicity of this?"

"Why, no. I hadn't thought to do so."

"She'll be here soon to help with supper."

T. C. took that to mean that he should tell Felicity of his plans that evening. He supposed that was proper. After all, she had been his clerk and was of much help in his effort to save Loco. He did have some obligation to her.

It was while they were eating dessert that he mentioned what he intended to do. She was silent for a moment as she looked at him. "How long will you be gone?"

"I don't know. Probably until the haying is done in the fall." He rubbed his cheek and then added, "I may come back to town sooner than that if there's a need. Sometimes Seth sends me in for business reasons. He doesn't like to travel."

Felicity looked down at her plate and then back at T. C. again. "It would be nice to see your ranch."

It wasn't T. C.'s ranch, and he was about to say so when his father latched onto Felicity's suggestion.

"Of course, you should see the ranch. We'll make that trip just as soon as it can be arranged. I've been promising Seth that I'd go down there anyway. And your aunt and uncle will go with us, I'm sure. I'll talk to your uncle about it tomorrow."

The situation was out of T. C.'s hands. The whole bunch would be traveling to the ranch sometime soon, but he would leave it to Seth and Mrs. B. to deal with the visit of such a throng. He found it disconcerting when Felicity said as he left her at her door, "I will miss you very much."

June 27th

T. C. got a late start. He ate his noon meal at Copperopolis and reached the Hall Ranch in late afternoon. The day was hot, and both the horse

147

he was riding and his packhorse were sweating. Mrs. Hall said that they did indeed have a room for him, so he unsaddled the horses and turned them into a corral for a roll. He fed them the grain and hay that Mr. Hall provided and headed for the house. At supper, he spoke of Sarah Kuntz. "There was a young lady here when I came through on the stage a while back, and I understand that she has agreed to be the teacher at your school this fall. What can you tell me of her?"

Mr. Hall answered. "She passed through on the stage to the Springs a few days ago and then was on the stage going east again a couple of days later. She's not much of a talker, but she told us she was still considering the offer when she came through going to town. She was real quiet on the way back and didn't say a word about the job. We'd like to know if she really wants to teach at the Flagstaff School."

T. C. didn't know if he should say anything about Sarah's request that he review the contract. "She told me on the stage ride that she was staying at the Morton Ranch. Have you tried to contact her there?"

"No. We figure that she'll get back to us eventually and let us know her decision. We need to know pretty soon, though. If she doesn't want the job, we need to look for someone else."

T. C. changed the subject by asking about the hay crops in the area. That led to the usual discussion of ranch conditions that took up the rest of the meal.

June 28th

As they were drinking a last cup of coffee after breakfast, Mr. Hall began his litany. "That Missourian up above is stealing all the irrigation water even though I have the first water right on the creek. He got away with it this spring, but I won't put up with it another year. I've got to get our water rights adjudicated so I can have a water commissioner appointed. When you get your office set up, please let me know."

Here it was again, another person wanting something from him now that he was a lawyer. "I'm not sure what I'll do. Right now I'm headed for the ranch to help with the summer work. I'll let you know if I start to take on legal work."

"Please do. I've known your father for years. I'm sure that you're the best one to handle this for me."

T. C. paid the bill for the food and lodging and started on his way. He was anxious to get to the ranch and away from anyone who wanted legal service. Right now, all he wanted to do were the things that he had always done before he graduated from law school.

Riding down the countryside, he wondered why those who knew and admired his father automatically assumed that he would be a good lawyer. At mid-afternoon he topped the ridge and looked down on the Bruce Ranch headquarters. It was good to be home.

++++++++++

While T. C. settled in at the Bruce Ranch, Sarah rested quietly in her room at the Morton Ranch, thinking about Gordon Jordahl. He had gone to great lengths to tell her of his plans. The land he had purchased was out of Bozeman about three miles. It was his intention to build a house in town in which he, his child, and a teacher could live. He described the house that he had in mind. The feature of most interest to Sarah was the library. He had a large collection of books that he would bring to Montana. His manner was gentle and courtly.

When she seemed hesitant about taking the position, he suggested that she travel to Bozeman to learn about that town, and to look at the land that he had purchased. She could help him pick out a lot for the house. When Sarah would not immediately commit herself, he suggested that she take time to think about it. He had to make a trip and would be gone for a few days. If she decided to travel to Bozeman, she should write to him in care of general delivery. He would meet her at the train. She could make her decision at that time.

Gordon Jordahl was obviously well educated and seemed to care very much about his child. Caring for one child and one man would not be nearly as hard as teaching at the Flagstaff school. He had offered her more money. But she didn't know anything about him.

She decided to go to Bozeman. Before she went to bed, she wrote two letters, one to Gordon Jordahl, the other to T. C. Bruce.

July 2nd

The haying would start after the Fourth of July holiday. Seth and all of the other ranchers knew that there was little sense in starting before that. The hay crew needed some time to party and then to sober up. The men who were not with Chappy on the roundup had spent the days before the holiday servicing and repairing haying machinery. Three mowing machines, two dump rakes, three bullrakes and an overshot stacker were used to put up the hay. All of them, as well as some spares, were checked for broken parts, greased and oiled. The harness for the horses was also oiled and mended. T. C. worked along with the others. He was glad that neither Seth nor any of the crew had made much of the outcome of the trial. They were just glad to have another person to help with the work.

The merchants of Two Dot planned a great celebration for the Fourth of July. The activities were scheduled to begin at noon with a potluck in the open area behind the livery stable. A town band had been organized to perform while the crowd was eating. Horace P. Smith, the lawyer from Harlowton, was invited to give the address after the meal. The saloon keeper would provide the prizes for horse and foot races. After all, he stood to do a good business with the crowd that would be in town. Finally, there would be fireworks at dark. Everyone in the upper Musselshell Valley would be there.

The roundup of cattle in the lower river valley always shut down for the holiday. The men would head for some town to whoop it up. Most would come to Two Dot.

T. C. could hardly wait. It was fun to gather with friends and neighbors for such celebrations and this was the first really big affair to be held in the new town. He was sure that Chappy would ride in from Flat Willow Creek. From him, T. C. could get a report on the calf crop that was born to the Bruce cows still running on the open range. And maybe Chappy would tell him of the problems and disasters that always seemed to plague the operation. He was never sure how much information he would get from the ranch foreman. But he looked forward to the conversations just the same.

Ride the Jawbone

After breakfast Seth announced that he had received a letter from T. C.'s father. The Bruces and the Spencers were coming for a visit and would arrive on the train in Two Dot on July tenth. That required some preparation. Since there were not enough bedrooms in the house to take care of all of them, the men would sleep on cots in tents. The women would get all of the space in the house. Mrs. B. muttered about getting the house clean and preparing special food for the guests. T. C. assured her that his parents knew what it was like to be busy taking care of a haying crew and that no extra effort need be made. She paid no attention to him.

Seth was not as anxious as T. C. for the holiday to come. He'd told the men that they could have the holiday off. That meant that he must milk the dairy cows and do the other chores without help. He knew that all of them would imbibe plenty of liquor. At least one day after they came back to work would be a waste while they nursed their hangovers. One or more of them might not make it back at all.

He understood what it was like to be young. Seth asked T. C. to take a buggy to Two Dot to fill Mrs. B's list, and bring groceries back to the ranch after the celebration. Seth was giving T. C. an extra day away from the ranch. He would take the opportunity and enjoy it.

July 3rd

T. C. stopped the team at the top of the hill, overlooking the town of Two Dot. The road before him led downward until it became the main street. The panoramic view disclosed the stage stop near the bottom of the hill. The doctor's house stood beyond, surrounded by a fenced yard. A large general store was farther along on the west side of the main street, and, beyond it, a butcher shop and a ladies dress shop. Next in line was the saloon, then the post office, with the barbershop adjacent to it. At the far end of the street stood the hotel. On the east side of the street were the livery stable, the café, and some small houses and cabins. The railroad ran east and west across the main street north of all of the buildings.

T. C. reflected for a moment upon the rapidity with which the newly created town had grown. Before the railroad came, there was nothing where the buildings now stood. Only three years later it was bustling with activity and showed signs that it might become the largest town in the county. That was the hope of the merchants who were sponsoring the Fourth of July festivities. Even though it was just approaching mid-day, T. C. could see several horses tied to the hitching rack in front of the saloon. Buggies and wagons, with teams hitched to them, were gathered near the depot. Evidently the train was expected soon. If so, it was late, as usual. A new platform for the band was under construction in the open space behind the livery stable. T. C. saw three men pounding nails into the structure and could hear the banging of their hammers.

He urged the team into their normal trot down the hill toward the livery stable. T. C. pulled the buggy next to the building, unhitched the horses, and made arrangements for their care. He hoisted his war bag containing shaving gear and dress clothes onto his shoulder and headed for the hotel. He wanted to rent a room before they were all taken.

Mrs. Watson stood behind the registration counter when he walked in. T. C. wasn't certain of the reception he'd get from her. She'd been a witness for the prosecution, and the prosecution had lost. Her smile was pleasant, however, and she pushed the registry book toward him. He smiled and reached for the pen.

Mrs. Watson spoke first. "Well, maybe that man didn't kill her. I don't see how he could have done it, since he was still on the train. She must have gotten off at Summit and then something happened. We probably will never know."

T. C. finished signing the registry. "Mrs. Watson, do you still have the belongings she left here?"

"Like I said in court, I moved her small bag and trunk to my quarters so I could rent the room. They're still there."

"Have you looked through them since the trial? There may be something that would help in finding the killer."

"T. C. Bruce, I did not go through her things. It still doesn't seem right. Besides, it might be against the law."

"Well, somebody needs to look. Maybe there's something in the bag or trunk to tell where she lived and who her relatives are. They surely should be told about her."

Ride the Jawbone

The frown became more fierce. "I'm not going to do that. I'm just not going to paw through that poor woman's clothes and other things." The last was said with great emphasis.

"How about if I help you? We can look together. And I'll make a list of everything we find. We can send the list to the sheriff. That way, if anyone ever asks, the information will be available."

Mrs. Watson frowned some more. "Well, someone should do something. But I can't do it now. With the celebration and all, I'll have my hands full. We can do it after everyone leaves."

T. C. smiled again. "All right. We'll go through her things before I head back to the ranch." He thanked the proprietress, picked up his bag, and headed for the stairs.

T. C. crossed the street to the cafe for something to eat. After finishing his meal he stood on the boardwalk watching the crowd as it gathered. People were streaming in on horseback, in wagons, and in buggies. Some even walked into town from down the river. Tired of watching the passing scene, T. C. began the rounds to see if Chappy had arrived. He drank a beer with acquaintances in the saloon and visited with others on the street. He spent time at the cafe drinking coffee with young men who, like him, were in town for the celebration. The afternoon passed without the appearance of the foreman.

After supper T. C. found himself in the small lobby of the hotel with two of his father's friends. They wanted T. C. to tell them all about the trial, and then, as soon as he was finished, their conversation turned to the old times, the times before the Musselshell country was full of people. T. C. heard stories about Indian raids, about the beginning of the Musselshell roundup, and about Harlow's tribulations in building his railroad. They spoke of their journey to Montana before the turn of the century. One of them had come by wagon along the Overland Trail from Missouri. The other had arrived on a steamboat at Fort Benton. Each tried to outdo the other with yarns of scary incidents that happened along the way. All of this was fascinating to T. C., and he remained there listening until the older men finally wearied and gave it up for the night. Only then did he climb the stairs to his room to go to bed. Tomorrow he would find Chappy. Tomorrow the real fun would begin.

July 4th

T. C. woke at the accustomed hour. He shaved and dressed in his good clothes, then hurried down the stairs and across the street to get his breakfast. At the café, he found Chappy sitting alone at a table in the corner, hands wrapped around a coffee mug. The foreman jerked his head to indicate that T. C. should join him. A waitress stood ready to pour coffee as he pulled out a chair. She took their orders and went on her way. Apparently Chappy had been waiting for T. C.'s arrival.

After the first brief exchange of greetings, the conversation died. T. C., knowing that Chappy disliked idle chatter, sipped his coffee and chewed on his ham and eggs. When they finished and the plates were pushed aside, Chappy reached for his Bull Durham to roll a cigarette. Only when he had the cigarette glowing did he look across at T. C.

"So you got old Loco off." And, after a long drag on the cigarette, he spoke through the smoke. "Well, then, who killed her?"

There again was the question that seemed to be on the minds of every person who spoke to T. C. about the trial.

"I don't know who killed her. The sheriff doesn't seem too interested in trying to find out anything more, unless someone gives him something to go on. And I suppose he's right. There doesn't seem to be anyone else who could have done it."

Chappy always got right to the point. "Have you tried to find out anything about the woman? Someone might've had a reason to kill her."

T. C. wondered why it should be his responsibility to find the murderer, but he didn't argue with Chappy. "No. I haven't done anything to find the one who killed her, but Mrs. Watson has a bag and a trunk that Miss Burke left at the hotel. She never looked into them. I said I'd do it with her before I go back to the ranch."

"What did the doctor say about her? He examined the body, didn't he?"

"All he talked about were the knife wounds that killed her." It had never occurred to T. C. to ask about anything else that the doctor might have found. What else could there have been?

"Who did she talk with while she was here in town?"

"I don't know. It really isn't my job to find out." T. C.'s patience was wearing thin.

"Maybe not, but someone should dig into it." T. C. thought about that. Chappy was right. Someone should try to find the killer. It just wasn't right to let a murderer get away. But he didn't need any more lectures from the foreman, so he changed the conversation. "How has the roundup gone? What kind of percentage will the calf crop be?"

Chappy was also willing to forget the murder. "Things have gone good, so far. There are more small operators who've turned cattle out on the range, so that slowed things down some. Many of them didn't even send a rep, much less provide riders."

"How did our cows do? Was the calf crop normal?"

"About normal. It's still cheap to run cows down there where a lot of the range isn't fenced yet. The calf crop doesn't have be too good to get along." This remark sounded strange to T. C. After all, it was his father, not Chappy, who stood to gain or lose from the calf crop. But what the man said was correct.

"Is Beaver Nelson the roundup foreman again this year?"

"Yup. But he says that he's going to give it up. It doesn't make any difference. The roundup can't run much longer anyway. Soon there'll be too many fences everywhere."

The conversation drifted to other things as they finished their coffee. T. C. paid the bill for both of them, and they headed up the street toward the speaker's platform was located. Even at that early hour, people were gathering. As they walked along in silence, T. C. decided that he really would try to learn more about Penelope Burke.

The band began playing long before noon. Planks had been placed across sawhorses to make tables, and women were covering the tables with vast quantities of food. The area between the livery stable and the platform was crowded with people. T. C. didn't know most of them. They came from the ranches in the valley and from the new towns that had sprung into being with the arrival of the railroad. There were women with children hanging onto their skirts, a few young single women, many young men, and a few old men. They were dressed in every kind of attire from the finest clothing to the roughest and most ragged. Every one of them seemed to be caught up in the excitement of the celebration.

Finally, the owner of the general store mounted the platform, waved his arms for the band to stop its blaring, and yelled out, "Silence, please, everyone! Our minister will ask the blessing." Every man in the crowd removed his hat, and each person stood quietly with bowed head while the minister asked God to bless America, its leaders, its lands, its waters, its people, its government, its health, its wealth. Finally, he got around to asking God to bless the food that they were about to eat. Only when his voice became hoarse from shouting did he stop praying.

The band started playing again as the great rush to the food began. Women dished out victuals to those who walked the length of the tables holding out metal plates. The plates were carried to open spaces where people sat in clusters on the ground to enjoy the meal, the company, and conviviality that such a gathering provided in ranch country.

T. C. spent the morning moving from group to group hoping to find Mr. and Mrs. Morton. He was certain that they would come to town for the day. He was just as certain that Sarah would be with them. This would be the perfect opportunity to spend time with her in a social setting. The eating began, however, and there was no sign of the Mortons or of Sarah, so he sought out Seth and Mrs. B. who'd traveled to town in a buggy that morning.

Near the edge of the crowd Mrs. B. had spread an old blanket on which were scattered huge baskets containing an enormous amount of food. They were joined in the meal by Mr. and Mrs. George O'Toole. The conversation was of ranch matters and of the happenings in the community. T. C. enjoyed it, but felt it would have been better if the Mortons and Sarah were among those gathered for the day.

When most of the crowd had been fed, the storekeeper again stopped the band and, in his loudest voice, introduced Horace P. Smith. The speaker was described at great length as one of Montana's finest lawyers, a defender of the weak and the helpless, a student of government, the next state senator from Meagher County, and perhaps the future governor of Montana. The assembled crowd clapped politely, but the attention of most remained on the food. Mrs. B. turned to T.

C. and asked, "Why are we listening to him? You're the lawyer that everyone is interested in today."

T. C., filled with food, smiled at the complement. He focused his attention on Horace P. Smith. Some day, he might be asked to make a speech, and he needed to know what was expected. The political aspirant began by thanking everyone for attending, then launched into an oration that went on for nearly an hour. He could have saved his breath. Most of those in the crowd stopped listening shortly after he began. T. C. tried to concentrate on the things that Horace P. was saying, but soon he, too, gave up and let his attention drift.

When the speaker finally ran out of breath and walked from the platform, there was polite clapping, which probably indicated more that the crowd was glad he was finished than appreciation for his remarks. The storekeeper thanked him profusely, and then announced that the children's foot races would be held along the road to the schoolhouse. The whole crowd moved to watch and cheer as children competed in both short and long races for prizes provided by the storekeeper.

Next on the agenda was the horse race. Things were getting serious. The race was to run straightaway along the main street of town from the river on the north to the bottom of the hill on the south, a distance of about a half mile. The crowd moved in a group toward the finish line marked by a rope laid across the street in front of the stage stop.

There were seven horses in the race. Each had its supporters who wagered among themselves and solicited wagers from anyone else who might be interested. The saloon keeper's helpers had been busy pouring beer out of kegs arranged conveniently near the finish line. The judgment of some of those who were placing bets was at least slightly clouded. Spirits were high as indicated by shouting and laughter as the horses and their riders lined up for the start.

Those standing near the finish line saw the smoke from the starter's pistol and watched the horses begin the run toward town before the noise of the gunshot reached them. Most of the riders rode bareback, stretched out low over the necks of their steeds. The seven came charging across the railroad tracks in a group, but then two of them, one a jug-headed black and the other a rangy roan, began to pull away from the rest. When they passed the doctor's house the two were well ahead of the pack, with the roan slightly in the lead. As they approached the finish line, the black laid back his ears and surged up alongside the leader. The rider of the roan horse, seeing that he was about to lose the race, slashed with his quirt at the face of the other rider. That poor fellow instinctively leaned away to avoid the blow and, in doing so, pulled his mount off-line—and the race was over. But it was only the beginning of the excitement.

Every person in the crowd saw what had happened, most of them certain that the black horse would've won but for the foul play of the rider of the roan. When the backers of the roan demanded that the losers pay off the bets, the losers refused. Hot words were exchanged, and soon the words turned into blows. In minutes the noisy quarrel degenerated into a general riot. Half drunken men were swinging fists at each other, some were grappling and wrestling on the ground, and still others were stomping and kicking those who were grappling and wrestling.

The storekeeper apparently thought it was his responsibility to stop the carnage, so he pulled out a pistol and fired a shot into the air. That frightened those among the women and children who were not already frightened, but didn't faze those who were mixing it up.

Sheriff Archibald Shea was an old hand and knew about celebrations. He'd taken the precaution of attending this festival in the company of two of his deputies. These three stalwarts had prepared for just such an occurrence by securing pick handles, and they had experience using them. They came charging up the street, sheriff in the lead, and waded into the mob. Each had a two-handed grip on his pick handle and none of them was reluctant to clobber any one of the crowd who was within reach. Most of the time, they aimed for the head.

T. C. hurried to the edge of the throng when the ruckus began and moved farther away as the fighting grew more fierce. He stood at a distance and watched the deputies methodically swing their peacemakers, hearing the thud of wood on human skulls. He was appalled to see men fall to the ground unconscious and wondered if some of them might be killed by the force of the blows.

The tactics of the sheriff and his deputies were effective. The rioters, or at least those who were still standing, scattered to get away from the abuse that the lawmen were offering. At last the peace officers stood nearly alone in the middle of the street. Stretched out around them were four still bodies. T. C. glanced about for Chappy and found him leaning against the corner post of the fence at the doctor's house, picking his teeth with a piece of grass.

The sheriff looked around slowly and carefully to be certain that the fight had gone out of all the combatants and then tromped off down the street, deputies in tow, without another glance at the forms on the ground. Chappy waited till the officers were on their way and then walked over to one of the bodies and rolled the fellow over on his back. When he did so, the man began to moan and reached for his head with both hands. Chappy straightened up and waited for the wounded one to recover full consciousness. Then he grabbed the fellow by the arm and helped him to his feet. Only after the drunken soul was standing did T. C. recognize him as one of the Bruce ranch hands, the burly fellow who had been working on the ditch as T. C. passed by earlier in the year. With T. C. following behind, Chappy led the inebriate along the street to the livery stable, up the stairs of the stable to the hayloft and directed him to stretch out on the hay.

Chappy fetched some water from the well and vigorously scrubbed away the blood and grime from the cut and bruised face of the man. A long deep gash ran along the side of the fellow's head at the hairline. The foreman went about the task cleaning the wounds without apparent concern about additional pain he might be inflicting. T. C. noticed that the ranch hand's fists were bloody and bruised. Obviously, he had been an active participant in the brawl. When Chappy had done as much for the man as the circumstances allowed, he ordered the battered individual to rest. The combination of too much to drink and of the beating he had received made it easy for the man to accept the order. He was already beginning to snore when T. C. followed Chappy down the stairs. Out on the street, Chappy spat once and said, "It happens every time he gets drunk."

After the Main Street battle ended, older men returned to their families and began to load belongings in buggies for the ride home. Cowpunchers, ranch hands, and sheepherders, on the other hand, headed for the bar. Chappy wasn't among them. T. C. leaned against the livery stable door and watched the foreman saddle his horse for the return to the roundup camp at Flat Willow Creek. The last thing the foreman said to T. C. before he turned and rode away was, "You can tell me what you find out about the Burke woman when I get back to the ranch."

The crowd of revelers reassembled on the street in front of the saloon after the end of the fracas over the horse race. The drinking continued unabated. They all seemed to be enjoying the camaraderie until it was broken by Sven Olson who spotted Anders Anderson and hollered out the old Scandinavian taunt:

Ten thousand Swedes
Ran through the weeds
Chased by one Norwegian!

Anders couldn't let himself and his homeland be slandered. His reaction was immediate. He threw his beer mug with perfect aim. The mug caught poor Sven squarely on the forehead and dropped him to the ground in a heap. A standerby thought that Anders' reaction was uncalled for and jumped on the back of the Swede. In an instant, the melee was resurrected and men were yowling and brawling as though the last ruckus had never stopped. Sheriff Shea and his deputies charged from the back of the hotel, pick handles in hand, and waded into the fray as before. Heads cracked and men yowled until, after a time, some modicum of quiet descended on the street once again. But the drinking didn't stop.

That night in his bed in the hotel room, T. C. listened to the noise that continued in the street below. The drinking had its effect. Drunken cowhands shouted and cursed, windows were broken, and the sheriff continued his relentless pursuit of peace by breaking the heads of the brawlers. Real quiet did not come to Two Dot until the light of dawn began to make its appearance.

The Fourth of July festivities had been a huge success.

July 5th

T. C. and Mrs. Watson stared at the trunk sitting on the floor, each of them expecting the other to make the first move to open it. Finally, T. C. tripped the latch and pulled up the lid. There were two compartments, one much larger than the other. The large one held clothing, the other women's toiletries. T. C. moved back from the trunk to let Mrs. Watson handle the dead woman's belongings. He was embarrassed to touch anything so feminine.

Mrs. Watson pulled up a chair and reached for the first garment, a wine colored silk dress. She unfolded it slowly and held it at arm's length. After careful inspection, the gray haired woman refolded the dress and placed it on a nearby table. She examined each garment in turn while T. C. watched. The dresses were all fashionable and of quality material. Beneath the dresses were blouses and skirts and beneath the blouses were undergarments. When Mrs. Watson began to inspect the undergarments, T. C. turned and walked to the window. The hotel proprietress chuckled softly as she continued her inspection.

With the clothing removed, Mrs. Watson found several books lying on the bottom of the trunk. She ignored the books, and instead turned her attention to the smaller compartment. T. C. glanced back from time to time to watch the process. Mrs. Watson removed more intimate articles and placed them on the table. Opening a small case, she found that Penelope Burke owned a variety of jewelry pieces. T. C. moved closer to watch intently as Mrs. Watson removed the pieces, one by one. When the packet was empty, Mrs. Watson sat back in her chair and looked at T. C. in silence. The brooch wasn't there.

With a frown on her face, Mrs. Watson then picked up the smaller bag and sorted through the things that it contained. The brooch wasn't in the bag either. She looked T. C. in the eye. "That filthy man had her brooch!"

The implication of the remark was clear. Maybe Loco did commit the murder after all. T. C. sat down to contemplate that possibility. His thought turned to the dead woman. Leaning forward with his elbows on his knees and his chin in his hands, he asked Mrs. Watson, "What was she like?"

"Miss Burke? She was quiet. And she was neat and tidy. What do you mean?"

"Was she quarrelsome? Or was she easy to be around?"

"She was quiet. I don't know any other way to describe her."

"How long was she here?"

"She came in on the stage from Big Timber two weeks before she left town on the train. She paid in cash. She asked me to hold the room for her when she left." Mrs. Watson shuffled her hands around on her skirt. "She sure didn't plan to get killed."

"How did she pass the time while she was here?"

"She read a lot. She would go for walks. Once I saw her walk down toward the river. Another time she walked beyond the schoolhouse toward Big Elk Creek. She went across the street to the cafe for meals." Mrs. Watson frowned. "That's about all I know."

"Who did she talk to? Did anyone call on her?"

"She was pleasant enough and spoke to those who spoke to her on the street." A frown furrowed Mrs. Watson's brow. "Except for that man they call Loco!" After an instant the frown disappeared and she continued, "Only one person called on her that I know of. A man—a stranger to me—came to town one day. He drove to the hotel in a buggy and went to her room without asking which room was hers. I'm sure that she must have written to him about it." A quizzical look crossed her face before she continued. "You know, she went to the post office each day like she was expecting mail. I don't know if she got any, but the postmaster should remember."

"Tell me about the man who called on her."

"Well, he didn't stay in her room for more than five minutes. Then they went out to his buggy and drove away somewhere north." Mrs. Watson's brow furrowed as she thought. "It may have been a rented buggy." She paused, and then said, "They were gone for a couple of hours. When they got back, he dropped her off here and drove up the street. I didn't watch to see whether he left the buggy at the livery stable or not. He may have rented it in Big Timber. I don't know where he came from or where he went." She paused again in thought. "Miss Burke looked angry when she got out of the buggy."

T. C. leaned forward in his chair. "What did he look like? How old was he? How was he dressed?"

"Well, he was older than she was, but not much—maybe forty years old. He was good looking, and he was dressed very nicely. I can't tell you much more than that."

"You say he was older than she was. How old was she do you think?"

"It's my guess that she was not yet thirty."

T. C. got up from his chair. "I think I'll talk to the postmaster. Maybe he'll remember if she got any mail. If so, he may remember where it came from. She has a mother and a father somewhere, and they'll want to know what happened to her."

The postmaster seemed insulted when T. C. asked about the dead woman's mail. The old fellow had been accused of reading the postcards that came through his office. He growled, "I never pay any attention to the mail that people send or receive. That's their private business."

"Well, I'm trying to locate her family so I can let them know what happened. I thought that you might be able to help."

The bald-headed man relaxed. "I suppose you're right. We should try to find her folks." He scratched the top of his head for a moment. "She sent one letter that I can remember. I think it went to Tennessee, but I'm not sure. I can't remember who it was sent to. I think she received two letters. They both came to her care of general delivery. I don't think that either one of them had a return address." He shook his head as he finished. "That isn't much help, is it?"

T.C. agreed that it wasn't much help and turned to leave. Before he reached the door, the postmaster reminded him that he should pick up the mail for the ranch. From the mailbox he extracted the usual business and personal letters for Seth and Mrs. B. There was a letter, addressed to him at White Sulphur Springs, which had been forwarded. The return address showed that it was from Sarah. There was a letter, also addressed to him, in his mother's handwriting. His first inclination was to open Sarah's letter right there. But he decided to wait to read it in the privacy of his room. He put the mail in a paper sack that the postmaster handed to him, said his thanks, and went on to his next stop.

The proprietress of the cafe, a tall woman with a wrinkled face, was pleasant and talkative. "Yes, Miss Burke ate here while she was in town. She always asked for the best things on the menu and always paid cash. She never failed to leave a tip, either." Before T. C. could ask the question, she answered it. "She never ate with anyone else. She was pleasant when people spoke to her, but didn't encourage conversation." She inclined her head to one side. "Her dress was always fashionable and immaculate. She was a handsome woman." None of that information was of much help to T. C.

As he left the cafe to go to the livery stable, Mrs. Watson called to him from the hotel steps. T. C. trudged across the street, and she met him on the boardwalk. "I found this in one of her books." She handed T. C. a piece of paper. The letter was in a steady, masculine hand.

Dear Penny,
> *I suggest that you contact a lawyer there to deal with him.*

Dad

Below that in a firm feminine hand, written diagonally across the bottom of the page, were the names of all of the lawyers in Meagher County.

Justin Potts
Conrad Gallahan
Horace P. Smith.
Thaddeus C. Bruce, Jr.

They stood on the boardwalk staring at one another. T. C. spoke first. "Was there an envelope with the letter?"

"No. The sheet of paper was by itself, in a book, like she had used it for a bookmark."

"And there isn't any date on the letter."

Mrs. Watson smiled. "No, but he told her she should find a lawyer there. It must have come to her while she was here in Two Dot."

"What kind of books were those? I didn't even look."

"They were good books, no dime novels. Ivanhoe is the name of one of them. Some of the stories by Longfellow. She must have been well educated. At least, the way she spoke would make me think so."

T. C. contemplated that information for the briefest of moments, then thanked Mrs. Watson for her efforts. He turned to begin the walk to the livery stable but after taking two steps the young man turned back. "We didn't find any money."

"No. We didn't."

"You said she paid cash?"

"Yes. She always paid in cash. Sometimes it was in hard money, and sometimes in paper money."

"If she had cash, she must have taken it with her. I wonder if the sheriff found any on her body or in her purse." When T. C. finally tramped away, he left Mrs. Watson standing on the boardwalk with a puzzled look on her face.

The operator of the livery stable was skeptical. "No, I don't remember renting a buggy to anyone like that. But we can look back through my records." He shuffled through his daybook and found an entry showing that a team and buggy was rented to one Gordon T. Jordahl on about the date that a man called upon Miss Burke. "Now I remember. I did rent a buggy that day."

"Where did he come from?"

The operator rubbed his unshaven jaw. "I don't know where he came from or where he went. He just walked in the door and asked to rent a buggy. I made him pay in advance, of course, and he paid in greenbacks. When he brought the team and buggy back, I got busy putting the team away and didn't watch where he went."

"Can you describe him?"

"No. I don't remember much about him. He was pretty well dressed. Just kind of an average sort of man, I guess."

"How old was he?"

"I suppose he was forty five years old or so, maybe forty. I'm not good at guessing ages."

T. C. removed his hat and scratched his head along the hat line, replaced the hat and said, "Thanks for the help." After the livery stable operator replaced his daybook, the young lawyer said, "I guess I'll take my team, get the groceries, and head on back to the ranch."

Before he left town, he returned to the post office, bought paper and a stamp from the postmaster, and wrote a note.

Dear Felicity,
    Would you be kind enough to ask the Sheriff if they found any money on the body of Miss Burke or in her purse? I am anxious to see you and will enjoy showing you the ranch.
      Your friend
      Thad

T. C. dropped the letter in the mail slot, climbed into his buggy and started for the ranch. As he reached the stage station, it occurred to him that the attendant might remember Gordon Jordahl. He pulled up the team and made his entry to the small building. The attendant was reading a paperback entitled "Ranch Romances" while resting on his back on one of the benches. T. C. didn't waste time. "Do you remember if a fellow came in on the stage from Big Timber about April fifteenth? He was about forty years old and his name was Gordon Jordahl."

The attendant didn't even rise from the bench. "I can't keep track of everyone who comes and goes in this town. I have no idea who might have come in on the stage that long ago." He scowled at T. C. and returned to his reading. T. C. considered a retort, gave it up, and stomped off toward his buggy. The fellow was insolent, but he was also right. How could he be expected to remember whether or not some stranger had come to town almost three months ago?

In his room that evening, T. C. opened the letter from Sarah.

> *Dear Mr. Bruce,*
>   *I may not take the job teaching at the Flagstaff school. For that reason I will not require your services to review the contract. I may need help with another matter later. If I do, I will contact you.*
>
>   *Yours truly*
>   *Sarah Kuntz*

T. C. was terribly disappointed. He thought of Sarah's closeness on the stage ride and along with it came remembrance of the warmth they shared under the robe and of the tingle he felt with her thigh rubbing against his. T. C. hadn't realized how much he had hoped to see Sarah Kuntz once again.

Then he opened the letter from his mother. It contained a single sheet of paper on which she had written:

> *Thaddeus,*
>   *Who is Sarah Kuntz?*
>   *Mother*

Ride the Jawbone

The train arrived in Two Dot near six o'clock in the evening. The first one down the step was Felicity. She hurried to T. C. and put one hand on each of his arms above the elbows. The top of her head—it just reached to his shoulder—was tipped back so she could smile up at him when she said, "Hello, Thad. We came to see the ranch." Her smile was as delightful as T. C. remembered. Embarrassed as he was by her attention, when he looked down at the smile a sudden temptation arose to put his arms around her waist and pull her to him. With some effort he backed away and solemnly replied, "It's nice to have you here. It will be fun to show you around."

Next off the train was Mrs. Spencer. Seth offered his hand to steady her as she stepped to the ground. After Mrs. Spencer came Mrs. Bruce, and then the men. Mrs. Bruce greeted Seth and Mrs. B. warmly and introduced them to the Spencers. Her short greeting to her son told him that something was amiss. He wondered if he was to get a scolding of the kind he suffered during his childhood—and he wondered what he might have done to deserve it.

Mrs. B was, as always, worried about getting everyone fed and suggested that they eat at the cafe before starting for the ranch. The eight-mile trip in the buggies would take at least two hours.

When they entered the cafe, Mrs. Bruce led the older people to a table for six. That left T. C. to find another table where he and Felicity could sit together. They settled next to the wall and away from the others.

Felicity was almost breathless. "I got your letter yesterday and talked to the sheriff before we left. He said that Miss Burke had over five hundred dollars in her purse and he's still got it. He said that he won't let go of it till Judge Henry tells him what to do with her things." T. C. was listening with his hands folded together on the tabletop. Felicity reached out and put her hand on his. "I decided to talk to the doctor, too, in order to find out what else he could tell us from his examination. The doctor said that she was a mother, or at least that she had borne a child."

"How could he know that?" T. C. liked the feel of her hand.

167

"Because she had stretch marks on her stomach." T. C. reacted to that bit of information by pulling his hands quickly away. He wished that he hadn't asked. That was a matter that women should discuss among themselves, a matter no woman should discuss with a man. "Thad, why would anyone kill her and not take her money?" T. C. wondered the same thing, but now he found there were a lot of things to wonder about. "Mrs. Watson and I looked through her belongings at the hotel. We didn't find the brooch. I guess that Loco really did have it. We found a letter that was sent to her from her father, but it didn't have a return address nor did it have his name. He told her she should get help from a lawyer in dealing with a man." T. C. looked away from her for a moment. "I'd like to be able to find her family and tell them what happened."

"Thad, we have to find out who killed her. It isn't right to just let her murderer get away." There was real determination in her voice and a look in her eyes that was different from the usual sunny glow.

He leaned forward with hands on the table once again. "A man came to see her at the hotel. No one seems to know who he was or where he came from. It appears he was somewhat older than Miss Burke. According to Mrs. Watson, they went for a buggy ride together and then he left town—right after the buggy ride. No one else in Two Dot seems to know anything about him. And no one seems to know much about her. The postmaster said that she sent one letter and received two. We only found the one in her trunk." He smiled and gave her hand a tentative pat. "There isn't much to go on to find the murderer." The feel of her hand made it difficult for him to concentrate on Miss Burke and her murderer. Other thoughts came creeping into his mind.

They arrived at the ranch about nine o'clock that evening. Arrangements had been made for sleeping, with a tent for the men set up near the front of the house. Because Felicity would be sleeping in T. C.'s bed, he'd spent lots of time cleaning the room in preparation. Mrs. B. had cleaned it some more.

++++++++++

168

Ride the Jawbone

When Felicity snuggled under the covers that night, her thoughts were of T. C. Bruce and they were thoughts that she would never share with others—especially her aunt and uncle.

July 11th

The visitors upset the ranch routine. Ordinarily T. C. drove a bull rake, but he was needed to help entertain the guests. Seth had to put one of the mowing machine operators on the bull rake so that the hay stacking could continue. That meant that the men driving the dump rakes would soon catch the mowers and then the stacking crew would soon catch the dump rakes. But the guests were of first importance.

Mrs. B had to feed the visitors as well as the crew. Mrs. Bruce and Mrs. Spencer understood that their presence created an additional burden and joined in the work. The table was not large enough to feed the men and the guests at the same time, so Mrs. B. suggested that the guests eat first. Mrs. Bruce would have none of it. She reminded everyone that the men who did the work had to be properly fed and the others could wait. So, after the haying crew ate their fill, the table was cleared and reset for the guests. T. C. ate with the guests, his mother seated on one side and Felicity on the other.

Seth offered to drive Mr. Spencer and Mr. Bruce around in a buggy to look at the hay crops. Mr. Bruce said he would enjoy such a tour, but that T. C. could hitch the team and do the driving. That way they wouldn't interrupt Seth's activities. T. C. was glad to have the opportunity and hurried off to the barn to harness the horses. When he pulled the buggy up in front of the house, his father and Mr. Spencer were ready to go—and so was Felicity. With the young lady on the front seat beside him and the two older men in the rear, T. C. began a tour of the meadowlands below the buildings. His father made comments occasionally as they traveled, and Mr. Spencer asked a question from time to time. Felicity was full of questions and kept T. C. busy answering them as they drove along. They watched the haying crew move the hay from the fields and create a stack. The machinery and the organized manner in which the men went about their work fascinated the young woman who had been raised in town and had never seen such activity.

The mowing machines, each pulled by a team of horses, cut the tall hay and left it lying flat on the ground. After the hay had cured in the sun for a day, dump rakes, also pulled by a team of horses, dragged the hay into long windrows and then dragged the windrows into bunches. The bull rakes, powered by two horses, pushed bunches of hay onto the teeth of the overshot hay stacker. A long cable and a series of pulleys allowed a team of horses to hoist the hay up and over so that it dropped onto the growing haystack. On top of the hay pile, two men used pitchforks to move the hay about in order to make a square and uniform stack. When finished, the stack would stand about twenty feet tall. The work was hard on the men and brutally hard on the horses. Both men and horses had sweat pouring off them in the day's heat. But it was the irreplaceable hay that kept the livestock from starving through the winter. So the work went on no matter how hot the days might be.

Felicity was glowing with enthusiasm when they returned to the house. She looked from one man to another and asked if she could see more of the ranch. The men assured her that it would be arranged.

T. C. spent the next two mornings driving the older men around the ranch. They seemed to be comfortable with one another and to enjoy discussing changes they had observed over a short period of time. The haying operation was modern and efficient. They compared it to the way hay was harvested only a few years earlier when men pitched the mown hay into wagons by hand, then hauled it to a boom pole stacker where it was again pitched by hand into a sling. The sling then carried the hay to the stack where the sling was tripped to drop the hay. It was then pitched by hand to make a square stack. The modern method was easier on the men, but the horses had to do more work.

They also discussed Mr. Bruce's decision to fence the whole ranch and to use purebred bulls exclusively to breed his cows. Mr. Spencer asked about the cost of the fencing and the cost to purchase the bulls. He wondered how much the selling weights of the cattle could be increased and if the price received for the cattle would increase because of the breeding program.

Ride the Jawbone

At first T. C. viewed these questions as somewhat impertinent. But he soon realized that Mr. Spencer was a businessman who understood the need to make a profit. His father did not seem to resent the questions and even encouraged them. All of this discussion was part of a larger exchange about the modernization of the world. The railroad through the valley was just one more indication of how rapidly things were changing. It brought new people to the valley, and with them came new ideas. The future appeared bright to the old friends and, on occasion, they would jokingly tell T. C. that he would be around to enjoy the interesting world to come while they would pass on and miss the fun and excitement that was just over the horizon.

During one of the excursions, T. C. took them to the boundary line between the Bruce ranch and the O'Toole ranch and pointed out the vast acreage that could be irri d between the fence line and the river. His father had already figured out the same scheme and acknowledged that they should try to acquire the O'Toole property if it came up for sale. The three men sat in the buggy for some time and discussed the possible price that the O'Toole ranch would command and how the purchase could be financed. T. C. listened intently to the observations of Mr. Spencer, who seemed to view matters from a different perspective than the ordinary rancher. He emphasized the need to be certain that any new acquisition would pay for itself and cautioned T. C. and his father not to buy land just because it was near at hand and because it seemed like a good idea. While Mr. Bruce didn't need that reminder, it was a good business lesson for T. C.

+++++++++

Felicity stayed at the house in the mornings and helped the women with their never ending labors. Each afternoon, T. C. handed the young lady into the buggy to show her more of the ranch. Once they drove to the top of the Butte, and ate a picnic snack that Felicity had packed in a basket. From there they could see the Porcupine Butte and, far in the distance, the Beartooth Mountains. Another time they watched the small waterfall in Sawmill Canyon. He showed her his favorite fishing hole, the best place to watch for deer, and the spring that bubbled up water that tasted better than any other.

Their conversation often turned to the stranger who had called upon Penelope Burke at the hotel in Two Dot. They wondered who Gordon Jordahl really might be. But more than anything else, they discussed possible ways to find him. The conversations, however, didn't lead to any real solution.

In the evenings, they ambled along the creek and listened to the sounds of the birds. Felicity walked gracefully beside him with her arm through his. On those occasions, T. C.'s thoughts were not of Penelope Burke, Loco, or Gordon Jordahl, and certainly not of Sarah Kuntz.

They took their usual walk the evening before the guests were to return to White Sulphur Springs. When they were safely out of sight of the house, Felicity reached up and put her arms around T. C.'s neck. Then she stood up on her tiptoes, pulled his head down and kissed him. T. C. reacted instinctively, pulling her body tightly to his. The kiss lasted only a second. Then she pushed herself away, smiled her glowing smile, and turned to walk back toward the house without saying a word. T. C. started to follow, then stopped to watch her movements. For the first time, he stared unabashedly at the graceful way that her hips moved as she strolled along.

Even though it was not the first time he had kissed a pretty girl, his emotions were in turmoil. He wanted the moment to continue. He wanted them to remain where they were so that he could hold her some more. But she strode toward the house. There was nothing to do but run to catch up. When they reached the door she turned, looked up at him, and softly said, "Good night," as though the kiss had never happened. T. C. was left with his arms reaching out to the place where she had just been standing.

T. C. Bruce was no longer thinking of Felicity as a friend.

July 14th

As his parents and their guests were preparing to leave, T. C.'s mother took him aside and demanded to know the identity of the woman named Sarah from whom he was receiving letters. T. C. didn't lie, but he didn't elaborate either. He explained that she was someone who had asked him to review a contract and he had written to her to arrange a time and place to meet. He didn't mention the stage ride or the feelings that he'd experienced while riding with Sarah. Those feelings seemed of less importance after the kiss of the night before.

"Why was she staying at the Morton ranch?"

"She was looking for a teaching position, Mother, but she may have changed her mind about an offer to teach at the Flagstaff school."

"How did you meet her?"

There was some exasperation in his voice when he answered, "Mother, we rode the stage together. That's all. I guess she was like the others who think I'm a good lawyer just because of the recent trial."

Apparently satisfied, his mother bustled away to finish packing.

Not long after the conversation with his mother, his father led T. C. to the horse barn on the pretext of looking at a horse. "Son, Seth just told me that he and Mrs. Black want to leave this fall. He'll stay till the hay is up and until the beef roundup is finished, and then they plan to move to some land they purchased south of the river east of Harlowton. He assumes that you'll be here to look after things. I don't know what your plans are." He leaned with one hand up against a post, his face grave. "Do you know what you intend to do?"

T. C. was speechless. It had never occurred to him that Seth would leave any time soon. Expecting the manager to remain for some years yet, he had given no thought at all to the notion of managing the ranch. To avoid an answer to his father's question, he posed a question of his own. "You know that mother wants me to practice law, Papa. If I stay here, what will I tell her?"

"The decision is yours, not mine and not your mother's. You should do what you want to do. We will both accept your decision. If you want to practice law, we'll help you get setup wherever you want to be. I'll find someone else to manage the ranch. If you decide to stay here, it would please me greatly, of course. But you shouldn't make your decision based on my wishes."

"Papa, I haven't thought about it enough. But I'll make a decision soon and tell both you and Mother."

"That's fine, but I need to know before too long. If I have to find another man, I must start before a lot of time goes by."

Thaddeus Bruce put his hand on his son's shoulder as they left the barn and kept it there as they walked toward the house.

Much as he tried, T. C. couldn't concentrate on his choice of a vocation. His thoughts were focused on Felicity. The ruminations that flew though his mind were not about the opening of a law office or of the management of a ranch. They were of schemes to get her alone and hold her close again—hold her for a long time—and of other exciting things they might do.

On the return trip to Two Dot, Felicity sat on the front seat of the buggy, but kept her distance from T. C. Her uncle and aunt were in the rear where the behavior of the young people could be easily observed. T. C. sat squarely on his side of the buggy seat, barred by propriety from even touching Felicity's hand. His parents, together with Seth and Mrs. B. followed in another buggy.

At the station, T. C.'s parents and the Spencers climbed the steps to the passenger car, but Felicity lingered behind. She put her hand on T. C.'s arm and said, "I'll tell the sheriff what you learned about Miss Burke." She started up the step and then turned to him once more. "The ranch is wonderful. Perhaps I can visit again?"

Before T. C. could answer, she was up the stair and in the car. He stood immobile as the train started up the track. T. C. Bruce surely wanted Felicity Spencer to visit the ranch again—soon.

July 15th

Chappy and the others who had been on the calf roundup on the lower Musselshell rode into the ranch late in the evening. After caring for his horses and before doing anything else, Chappy took T. C. aside. "Mrs. Watson from the hotel sent you this letter. She gave it to me instead of putting it in the mail."

T. C. tore the envelope and pulled two pieces of paper from it. The first was a note signed by Mrs. Watson.

> *Dear Mr. Bruce*
> *I found this envelope in the pocket of one of her dresses when I was folding them to put them away. It shows an address that may be from her father.*
> *Charity Watson*

Ride the Jawbone

The envelope's return address showed a street in the town of Oxford, Tennessee. At last T. C. had a way to find the family of Penelope Burke. That evening he wrote a letter to "Mr. Burke" at the address shown on the envelope. It occurred to him later in the night that Burke may have been the murdered woman's married name. But the letter should get to the address and should be opened by someone who knew her, someone who would learn that she was dead.

The next morning he told Chappy what he and Mrs. Watson had learned. Chappy listened and then asked, "What if the address is for the man who called on her, rather than for her family?" T. C. gave thought to that possibility, but decided to send the letter anyway. At least someone would get it and that might lead to more information.

He also wrote to Felicity to tell her what he was doing, and to tell her that he missed her. And while doing it, he wished he knew a way to convey his real feelings.

July 16th

Sarah arrived at the train station in Bozeman at 3:00 in the afternoon. Because she'd written to Gordon Jordahl to tell him the date and time of her arrival, she stepped from the car expecting to see him waiting for her. Despite the fact that he had assured her he would meet the train whenever she arrived in Bozeman, he was nowhere in sight.

As she looked about, wondering what to do, a cabby approached her, hat in hand. "Excuse me, Miss. Can I give you a lift uptown. It's quite a walk from here."

She hesitated only a moment and then nodded her head. The cabby picked up her valise, threw it in his hack, and helped her onto the seat. As they approached the main street, the cabby turned and asked, "Where to, Miss?"

"Please take me to the hotel." She didn't know what else to tell him.

"There are two hotels, Miss. The Bozeman is the best. You should stay there."

"That will be fine."

175

When he handed her down from the cab, the driver said, "That will be four bits, ma'am."

Sarah looked at him with a blank face for a heartbeat, and then dropped a coin in his outstretched hand. Fifty cents was a lot of money.

The Bozeman Hotel was an imposing brick structure, five stories high, more luxurious than anything Sarah had ever seen. The clerk was polite and said, yes, they had a vacancy and a single room would cost one dollar a night. She signed the registry card and handed the man one of the precious silver dollars from her purse. He selected a key, picked up her bag and headed for the elevator. Sarah had never seen such a device, and caught her breath as it started its climb to the third floor. The clerk stood with his hand out after placing her bag on the floor near the bed. She didn't know what he expected, and looked fixedly at him with her arms clasped defensively across her chest. He turned to leave and mumbled with much sarcasm, "Well, thank you, too."

The room was tastefully furnished, with a large bed, two chairs, and a dressing table with a large mirror. Pictures decorated the wall. She opened a door to find a private bathroom. At least she could enjoy the luxury of a bath in the large tub. That brought some consolation for the money she had spent. But where was Gordon Jordahl?

He appeared at her table when she was eating the evening meal. "Please forgive me. I was out at the farm making arrangements for the sale of the hay and was unable to get away in time to meet the train." His smile and manner were as she remembered, and he did seem sincere in his apology. She gestured with her head to indicate that he should join her. "I'm glad that you're registered here. The other hotel isn't any place for a lady. In the morning, I'll come by to pick you up and we'll ride around town. You'll like Bozeman. It's the nicest city in Montana." When Sarah said nothing, he continued. "We can drive out to the farm, too. It isn't very far, and I'll show you a lot that I'm considering as the place to build the house."

"Are you staying here at the hotel?"

"No. I'm staying at the farm. There's an old house there that's good enough for me, but it wouldn't be adequate for you. I want my son to live in a nice home, which is why I plan to build. We can talk more

Ride the Jawbone

about that tomorrow." He stood, smiled some more, and said. "I'll come to the hotel at nine o'clock. Please be ready."

As he walked away, Sarah whispered to herself, "At least, he should have paid for my meal."

July 17th

Sarah first sat quietly in a chair. Then she rose to stride impatiently about the lobby. Jordahl was late again. He arrived at ten and was all apologies as he walked her to the waiting buggy. As they drove west on Main Street to its corner with Central an electrical trolley rattled along a track in the middle of the street. The horses pulling the buggy paid it no attention.

Sarah had never spent time in such a large town and marveled at the many stores and shops. She hoped to walk the street later in the day just to look in the windows. Three blocks up Central, her escort pointed to an open lot that was surrounded by magnificent homes. "That's where I hope to build. What do you think?"

Sarah looked at the nearby houses. All of them were large and elaborate. "Would the house that you build be like the others?"

"I hope to build one that will be the nicest of all. I've talked to a local architect about the design and have inquired about builders. It will take more than a year to finish. But I'm sure that you will like it. And it will provide a proper setting for you to teach my son."

"Where will you live until it's finished?"

"I've looked at houses to rent and haven't found the right one yet. But I'll keep looking. It'll be big enough so that you can have a proper room for yourself and a room to use for teaching."

"What else will I be expected to do?'

"Provide company for my boy, and maybe some company for me, if you are willing to do so. I'll hire a cook and a housekeeper. I don't expect you to do those things." The skin at the corners of his eyes crinkled nicely when he smiled. "My principal interest is in the well-being of my son."

They traveled south to the farm country beyond the city limits.

Sarah's companion pointed to a large building with a steeply pointed tower that stood near the edge of town. "That's the state college. They're planning more buildings to go with the three they've built so far. It only began a few years ago." Sarah had never seen a college.

"Who goes to the college? Can anyone attend?"

"Yes, it's open to anyone who has finished high school. And they teach a preparatory course for those who haven't attended high school." He turned to smile at her again. "Where did you go to college?"

Sarah didn't want to disclose her lack of formal education, but she wasn't going to lie. Her reply was brief. "I didn't go to college."

Gordon Jordahl flapped the reins to hurry the horses along and didn't pursue the matter any further. Sarah wondered why not. It seemed he would want to know about her education, since he was asking her to teach his son. But she was relieved that she didn't have to tell him how scanty that education had been.

About three miles in the country, Jordahl stopped the buggy and pointed. "This is the farm. It's one hundred sixty acres of good ground, and it has plenty of irrigation water. The buildings are in bad shape but they can be fixed up. I've always wanted a farm and now I have one."

The soil was black and rich, just like the farm ground Sarah remembered from Iowa. The first crop of alfalfa hay had been cut and stacked, and the second crop showed green and rich. The buildings were located along a small stream and were protected from the wind by a growth of large cottonwood trees. It was indeed a lovely setting.

"Will you be a farmer, then?"

"No. I intend to have someone else do the farming for me."

"If you're not a farmer, what do you do?"

He smiled at her again. "I had an investment business that I sold. It's the money from the sale that paid for the farm and will pay for the house. There'll be enough left over to provide income to live on."

The notion of investments had interested Sarah ever since she lived with the Reverend and his family. "How will you invest your money?"

"Probably in government and corporate bonds. I want it to be safe, but I also want to get a reasonable return."

Sarah had never allowed the money she earned to get out of her hands. She had converted her earnings to greenbacks and still kept it in a belt around her waist. She realized the money should be invested in such a way as to produce some income, but the thought that it might be lost kept her from parting with it, even for investment purposes.

Mr. Jordahl turned the buggy and began the return trip to town. As they rode along he continued to tell her of his plans for a new life in Montana for himself and his son. She finally asked, "What is your son's name?"

"He's named for me. His name is Gordon, Junior. Everyone calls him Gordy."

"Who is caring for him now?"

"I left him with a cousin. I hope it isn't too long until I can have him with me again. But I can't bring him here until there is someone to help care for him and to teach him." He looked sideways at her. "It's up to you, you see. If you agree to accept my offer, I can then move forward with my plans. I'm excited about a new life here in the west."

Back at the hotel, he helped her to the ground. As she turned to thank him, his hand touched her on the waist and slid down to her hip where the money belt rested, for only the shortest of moments. Sarah was not a stranger to men who attempted to paw her. But his touch was gentle, and the indiscretion seemed accidental, so she ignored it.

As he walked her into the lobby, she said, "Thank you, sir, for the ride. Will I see you for dinner?"

"Please forgive me. I'm meeting with the man who's putting up the hay on the farm. I have to decide when to sell it." He stood with his hat in his hands. "Please think about my offer. I hope, of course, that you'll accept. I'll come to the hotel in the morning and you can tell me your decision."

Sarah, left with the remainder of the day to fill, began strolling along the main street of Bozeman. She hurried past a butcher shop and a cigar store with clouds of smoke wafting out of its open door. She stopped at the window of the jewelry store to look at the rings and necklaces on display. She wandered the aisles of the dry goods store where she lifted, poked, and prodded at the merchandise on display. She passed the saloons without a glance at their dark interiors. The foul smell that came from each of them made her want to hold her nose. Three grocery stores were favored with her attention. She passed a doctor's office, the offices of two lawyers, and a real estate office.

At the millinery, Sarah wandered in to look at hats on display.

The proprietress, large and overweight, came forward before Sarah was completely through the door.

"M'lady is interested in the latest fashion?" Sarah nodded and tried to pass by to the shelves where the merchandise was displayed. The heavy woman persisted.

"M'lady is lovely and should have the finest of hats. Let us try some on." She gently pushed Sarah along to a chair in front of a tall mirror and began bringing hats for her to admire.

Sarah felt an obligation to be honest. "I only walked in to look. I have no need to buy a hat."

The storekeeper wouldn't be deterred. She insisted that Sarah try on hats, one after another. All the while she commented on Sarah's appearance.

When Sarah said once again that she wasn't interested in buying a hat, the woman's demeanor suddenly changed. Her voice became businesslike and serious. "My goodness but you are a handsome woman. Have you thought of modeling clothes? I would pay you to model hats for me while a photographer takes pictures that I can use for advertising." She stopped, finger held against one cheek, and then continued. "I'm sure that Mabel at the woman's clothing store would do the same." She stepped closer and said, "I'm Nettie Overton." She waited for Sarah to respond with her own name.

Sarah's gaze shifted from her reflection in the mirror to the reflection of Mrs. Overton. "How much would you pay?"

"I can pay fifty cents an hour for the time you actually spend with the photographer." She frowned and then continued. "That's an awful lot of money, but your face has unique beauty. It makes almost any hat look appealing."

Sarah looked back at herself in the mirror and contemplated the words "unique beauty." A smile touched her lips, a smile that lasted only a moment. Then Sarah turned to speak directly to the proprietress of the store. "I'm only visiting in town, but I may settle here in the future. I'll keep your offer in mind."

She removed the hat carefully, handed it to Mrs. Overton, replaced it with her own, and walked quietly from the store.

The carefully tailored clothing she wore, coupled with her lovely countenance and graceful bearing, gave the impression of a person of importance. She had learned well from Reverend and Mrs. Dorman the role of a gracious lady.

++++++++++

Sarah ate a small meal in a cozy café near the hotel. As she picked at the food her mind traveled to the large structure that Jordhal said was a college. The trolley appeared to run near to it. Maybe she could ride that electrical contraption to the main hall and ask questions—learn more about what it had to offer. The hotel clerk said, "Yes, indeed, the trolley would take you directly to the corner close to the main hall." At her inquiring look, he added, "The trolley? It's free to anyone who wants to ride. All you have to do is get on at any street corner. It stops at all of them."

At the front of the hotel she watched as an elderly man clambered slowly up the trolley step and followed him a moment later. The operator gestured with a thumb toward the seats in the back, so she slipped into one next to a window. A bell clanged and the ride began. The ride was more smooth and less noisy than she had expected. Sarah watched with interest as people got on and off at each stop—businessmen, women with small children, some who had the appearance of vagrants. At the corner of Main and Central a slender young man of medium height, wearing tailored clothes and a bowler hat, stepped lightly up the trolley step. He had a ruddy complexion and sported a sandy mustache. As the man angled by in the aisle, he smiled downward at Sarah and touched his finger to the brim of his hat. From the reflection in the forward window of the trolley she watched him take a seat four rows behind her. His suit coat was of light brown tweed. A large bow tie, the color of dark chocolate, contrasted sharply with the white shirt. Not the drab black suit she was accustomed to seeing on the men of the area. He must be from somewhere other than Montana. As Sarah continued to watch, the man dragged a pipe from a pocket, looked down at it for a second, and then seemed to decide that the trolley was not a proper place to light up. He stuffed the pipe back in the pocket, leaned back in the seat, and brushed once at his mustache with a finger. A dandy. That was the word that came to Sarah's mind, one she'd heard the Reverend use in describing such a fellow. That man fancies himself a dandy.

Their conveyance moved slowly southward along Grand Avenue. Sarah gazed at magnificent homes similar to those she'd seen along Central Avenue while on her buggy ride with Jordahl. She concluded there must be real wealth in Bozeman.

Soon enough the bell clanged again and the trolley came to a stop on a corner a short distance from the towering college main hall. Sarah stepped gently down the step to the ground to look around at her surroundings. In the near distance to the right was another large brick building with another a bit farther away to the left. A great open area of carefully groomed grass, accented by thriving decorative bushes and flower beds surrounded the buildings. But what to do now?

The man in the bowler alighted from the trolley after her, nodded to her once again, and turned to walk off in the direction of some houses that were clustered nearby. The look of confusion on Sarah's face must have been apparent because, after three steps, he stopped. Turning back, doffing his hat, he smiled and said, "You look lost, ma'am. May I help you in some way?"

Sarah stopped breathing and clutched her purse close to her chest. She'd never seen this person before. Could she trust him? Then, an inward smile, he can't be dangerous. He's just too gaudy. She nodded her head. "Perhaps you can." A breath. "I'd like to look at the college, and I don't know where to begin."

His wide smile revealed white teeth with one incisor that seemed to protrude slightly from the rest. "My name is Joshua Farley. I'm a professor at the college." He waited for her name in response. Sarah wasn't ready to tell a stranger anything about herself and stood silent, still firmly clutching her purse. Farley broadened the smile. "Well! If you wish to see the Montana Agricultural College, allow me to escort you." He moved closer to Sarah and poked an elbow in her direction. She hesitated and then quietly rested her hand on his arm. When he gently placed his hand over hers, she almost pulled away. He smiled downward at her again. "It's a beautiful day for a stroll. Let's enjoy it."

Joshua Farley proved to be a talker. "That building with the spire is called Main Hall. It's where the president of the college has his office and where the other administrative offices are located. The library is on the second floor."

"Is it a large library?"

Ride the Jawbone

The question brought a chuckle from Farley. "I'm a graduate of Harvard, which has one of the most extensive libraries in the world. So, to me, the library here is almost insignificant." He stopped walking to look down at her face again. "But this is a brand new college and the library and everything else about it will grow and get better. It's why I'm here. It's exciting to be part of something at the beginning. Everything at Harvard is old. The buildings are old. The professors are old. Even the ideas are old." Farley began the stroll again. "My father is a physician in Peabody. His family has lived there forever. And my mother came from Newton. Her parents are old New England too. All of their thoughts and ideas seem to be old. They look backward more than forward. I need new and exciting things."

He looked off into the distance as the stroll continued up toward the Main hall. "I read about the founding of this school in a university journal and immediately applied for a professorship. You see, I'd always wanted to come to the west, and here was an opportunity." He moved his hand from hers and waved it wide at the mountains that surrounded the valley. "I was raised in New England. We have mountains there but nothing like the ones we see. Here they seem to rise straight up from the valley floor." Another wave of the hand, this time toward the broad farm lands beneath the mountains. "There is nothing in the east to compare with those fields and pastures."

Sarah wasn't as much interested in the surroundings as she was in the college and this man's relationship to it. "You are a professor?"

"Yes. It will be my first year to teach at this institution. My degree from Harvard is in the humanities, and I'm to teach the social sciences to the undergraduates." A pause and another smile for Sarah. "Since the college is so new, there aren't any graduate students as yet. But before too long there will be."

Sarah, of course, knew nothing about different classes of students. She remained silent. When they approached the steps leading up to the big doors of Main Hall, she stopped to ask, "May I see the library?"

"Why, of course." He led her up the stairway, stepped aside, and held one of the doors to allow her to pass. The entryway was cloaked in gloom. This time he took her elbow in one hand and pointed upward along a staircase with the other. "It's up there."

From another hallway they entered a large high-ceilinged room that was lighted by tall windows along the south and west sides. Stacks of bookshelves that reached almost to the ceiling ran in parallel lines the length of the room. Each shelf held books and books and books. Sarah ran her eyes along the rows in awe. At a high desk just beyond the entrance an older woman wearing severe clothes frowned at them. Joshua smiled his smile at the lady. "Good afternoon, Miss Sunderland. I'm showing Miss …." He turned with a quizzical look to Sarah. "I'm sorry. I don't know your name."

She looked from Farley to the librarian and back. "My name is Sarah Kuntz." Sarah's voice was very quiet.

Farley smiled again at Miss Sunderland. "As I began to say, I'm showing Miss Kuntz about the college. She's particularly interested in the library."

The scowl deepened. "Well, show her, but remember the rule about silence so as not to disturb others."

Hand again on her elbow, Sarah's escort moved in the direction of a corridor between the shelves. At the far end, he stopped. This time his chuckle was almost a giggle. Then he whispered, "Miss Sunderland is accustomed to students who sometimes disrupt her quiet. This is her domain, and she's not about to let that happen with you and me."

Sarah's focus was only on the books. She echoed his whisper. "Can anyone come in here and read?"

"Well, all of the students can surely do so. And I suppose there is some arrangement to allow the townsfolk access. I haven't been here long enough to know all the rules."

"So if I was a student I could read as many of these books as I wanted?"

Now his look at Sarah was more sober. "Are you thinking of enrolling here?"

"Perhaps."

"Well! I didn't realize that was the reason you are interested in Montana Agricultural College." A hand again grasping her elbow. "Let's go outside where we can talk in a normal voice."

On the sidewalk Farley turned to face her squarely. After running his eyes over her features, he blinked once and mumbled. "My goodness! You are lovely." Then his face reddened in embarrassment. "Forgive me, please, for being so forward. I know better."

Ride the Jawbone

Sarah's mind was on the idea of spending time at this school and reading in that library. His unthinking complement didn't even register on her mind. "Can a woman attend here?"

Farley quickly recovered from his embarrassment. "The college offers courses in the domestic sciences for women."

"What do you mean by domestic sciences?"

He thought for a moment. "They teach young women to be good housewives."

She gave him such a look that he hurriedly stammered, "And such other things as proper nutrition and how to maintain proper sanitary conditions."

"In other words, they teach women how to do what women must always do. What is the benefit of college to any woman in that?"

He struggled for an answer, then offered in a meek voice, "I'm sure that women are allowed to enroll in other courses as well."

"Mr. Farley, I hope so."

Joshua Farley was now thoroughly nonplussed. To cover his discomfort he reached again for her elbow but she pulled away. "You've been most kind, sir, to a stranger." She extended her hand. "I've taken too much of your time, and I must be on my way back to the hotel."

The young fellow with the ruddy good looks grasped the hand in one of his and placed his other over the top. "The pleasure has been mine." He pursed his lips before asking, "May I see you again? Perhaps for dinner this evening?"

"I think not, sir. But I do thank you again for your kindness."

He released her hand and reached to extract a small tablet from the inside pocket of his suit coat. "Let me at least give you my name in writing so that you don't forget me." With that he scribbled across a sheet from the tablet, ripped it off and handed it to her. His name —*Joshua G. Farley*—was produced in a scrawl. After the name he'd written in the same scrawl, *Professor of the Humanities*. It was not the neat script that Sarah expected from an educated man. Nonetheless, she tucked the paper in the top of her purse, thanked him one more time, and strode away to catch the trolley that was now approaching from downtown.

+++++++++

185

That evening in her room, she thought through the day's events. Gordon Jordahl was a handsome and charming man. His speech told her he was well educated. He must have the money he spoke about. After all, he bought one hundred sixty acres of land. Still she felt something was amiss. Why didn't he show her the buildings at the farm? Why hadn't he offered to take her to dinner? His offer of employment was attractive, but there was something peculiar about the man and his story.

Her thoughts turned to Joshua Farley. He was attractive in a shallow kind of way. And he made it clear that he was interested in seeing more of her.

The day had been educational. There was indeed a college in Bozeman, Montana. She might take classes at the college. Those classes would allow her access to the hundreds of books in that library. Her thoughts flowed along. There might be work that she could do there to earn money while she took the classes. There must be a dining area for the students. Maybe she could cook. Or wait on table. Or maybe she could teach, possibly secure a position at a country school nearby. From the milliner she'd learned there were other ways to earn money.

Then there was Jordahl. Surely caring for his son wouldn't require all of her time. Perhaps he would not only allow her time for classes at the college but help with the cost. After all, he said he had that kind of money.

All the while the sight of the long, tall shelves lined with books never left her mind. The library at the college was wondrous indeed.

++++++++++

That evening, seated alone in a saloon and sipping whiskey, Gordon Jordahl smiled to himself. "I was right about that woman. She has money."

July 18th

As she watched him walk toward her across the hotel lobby, Sarah realized that his suit, shirt, and tie were the only ones that she had ever seen him wear. The usual smile brightened his face. "Have you had breakfast?" When she nodded that she had, he continued, "Good. Then let's walk down by the creek. It's a beautiful day."

The morning was cool and pleasant. Behind the hotel, the creek flowed past some houses and then into an open park. A bench provided a place to watch two ducks as they paddled in the water. When they were comfortable, Gordon Jordahl asked if she had made a decision.

"It is not a decision to make hurriedly. I'll go back to the Morton ranch and then decide."

His smile faded for a moment and then returned. "I can understand your need for time." He rose from the bench. "I'll travel to the ranch in a couple of weeks so that we can discuss it further." As they walked slowly back toward the hotel, he mentioned the house again. "The architect needs an advance before he'll begin his work. The final payment from the sale of my business will arrive at the bank later this week, but right now I'm embarrassed to be without the funds to pay him." He turned and took both of her hands in his. "Would you be willing to lend me five hundred dollars for a few days? I'll pay interest—ten percent interest." The look on his face was earnest. "I'll repay you, with the interest, when I call upon you again at the Morton ranch."

Sarah pulled her hands away. She had learned enough from the Reverend to know that ten percent interest was exorbitant. Four percent was the rate that banks paid. "Why would you pay that much interest?"

"I want to be fair to you. And it will only be for a short time." He leaned toward her as he continued, and his voice became insistent. "I'll give you a mortgage on the lot, but it will take a lawyer a day or two to draw it up. I'll sign it and send it to you as soon as it's finished."

Sarah's money was hard earned. She would not give it to a bank, and she would not give it to a man she hardly knew. "I'm sorry. I must keep the little money I have in order to care for myself."

Anger flashed in his eyes for a fleeting moment. Then the smile returned. "Well, the construction of the house will be delayed, but I guess that isn't the end of the world." He put his arm around her waist again as they walked along. "I really hope you will come to Bozeman to teach Gordy. He needs someone like you, since he's without a mother."

Sarah stepped out of his grasp. "What happened to his mother?"

His face turned grave. "I hate to talk about her tragic death."

"I'm sorry." She didn't know what else to say.

When they reached the entrance to the hotel, he removed his hat and held it in his hands. He spoke in a most sincere voice. "I suppose you could take a teaching job at a school near the Morton ranch. But do you really want the work involved? You'll not only teach several children in many different grades, but do all of the other work as well. You'll have to clean the school and even haul the coal for the stove." He looked at her intently. "And it will be lonely in a teacherage that's a long way from town." He returned his hat to his head and grasped her hands. "Teaching Gordy will be much better."

Sarah drew her hands away. "Mr. Jordahl, I told you I would think about it. I'm not going to make the decision now. If you want to visit me at the Morton ranch in two weeks, you may do so. I'll have decided by then."

He tipped his hat, smiled at her again, and abruptly walked away.

Sarah watched him go. Gordon Jordahl had not paid for any part of the trip that she had taken at his request. And she would have to pay for a train ticket tomorrow.

+++++++++

Jordahl, though frustrated, was certain he could talk Sarah out of some of her money when they met again. Until then he wasn't quite broke. There was a little money left from that girl in Big Timber who had let him live with her. Then he made the trip to Two Dot to see Penelope. She kicked him out, but not before he'd almost persuaded her to loan him a few dollars from her savings. And the widow with whom he was staying in Bozeman seemed willing to continue to provide room and board, at least for a time. As he tramped up the street from the hotel toward the saloon, he wondered, "What do you suppose Penelope named that brat? It could've been Gordy." Then his thoughts turned to her death. "When I left Two Dot, she said she'd give me fifty dollars as soon as she could get it from her bank. Then she changed her mind." He walked through the saloon door. "Well, I can't get it from her now. I wonder what they did with her money after they buried her." He scowled as he added, "Too bad they didn't convict that cockeyed old devil. Then I wouldn't have to think about it any more."

July 26th

T. C. spent several days trying to come up with a reason to go to the Springs. The excuse, when it came, was one he didn't want.

The most experienced and skilled of the ranch hands drove the mowing machines and the bull rakes. The dump rakes were generally driven by the younger and less experienced of the workers. The younger workers also got the most dependable of the horses. But no horse is absolutely reliable.

The son of the barber who had a shop in Harlowton drove a dump rake. He was seventeen years old, full of enthusiasm, and an excellent worker. One of the horses he drove was black and the other a bay. Seth called them Nip and Tuck. They were lively, but gentle.

His hay rake was a two-wheeled implement. A metal framework, to which spring steel teeth shaped in a half circle were attached, connected the large wheels. The ends of the teeth, dragging along the ground, gathered up the hay. When enough hay had been gathered in the teeth, a trip device, actuated by the operator, raised the teeth and allowed the hay to drop in windrows behind the rake. The driver rode on a metal seat fastened to the main framework by means of a piece of heavy flat spring steel. It was not a comfortable ride.

Early one morning before the team had worked long enough to become tired, the barber's son was raking near the brush along the creek. A young fawn, hiding in the hay, didn't move until Nip was directly over it. The tiny terrified animal leapt to its feet with a bleat, and its ears touched the bottom of Nip's belly.

The horse snorted, jumped, and kicked and took off running as hard as he could run. Tuck, frightened by the actions of his partner, joined in the race. The hay rake dragging behind them shook, rattled and banged. The noise frightened the two horses even more, encouraging them to run faster. The barber's son hauled on the lines in an effort to stop the team, all the while doing his best to stay on the seat. The rake

189

bounced over the rough ground and the curved teeth flopped up and down each time a wheel hit a bump. The boy was in danger of falling off in front of the teeth and either find himself rolling along as though he was a bundle of hay, or perhaps have the teeth drop on him and leave him with severe body punctures. He managed to stay aboard as long as the wheels bounced into the air one at a time. When the rake crossed an irrigation ditch and both wheels dropped down and back out of the ditch at the same time, the jar threw him high into the air. He landed on the ground on the back of his head and neck.

Nip and Tuck continued to run, but Nip, who was the fastest, was outrunning Tuck. They continued in a circle that became smaller and smaller until they finally stopped.

The boy lay still where he had fallen.

The other workers heard the racket and saw the team pounding across the field but there was nothing they could do to stop the runaway. The horses pulling the other implements snorted and danced around and all of them required the careful attention of their drivers to prevent them from joining in the race. As soon as possible, T. C. and one other man handed the care of their teams to those who had jumped down from the haystack. The two men ran to where the fallen driver lay, his body in a grotesque twist. The boy's eyes focused on T. C., and he started to speak. But at that moment, the other ranch hand grabbed the injured fellow's feet and attempted to straighten his crumpled body. The young man uttered a small groan and simply stopped breathing. He lay silently on the ground with his eyes open, never breathing or blinking again.

Chappy rode to town to telegraph the news to the barber. Seth, with help from other hands, loaded the boy into a buggy and drove to Two Dot in the afternoon. The barber wasted no time when he got the news. He met them at the store and claimed the remains of his son.

The entire Bruce Ranch crew attended the funeral and burial in Harlowton the next day. After the burial, Seth gave a check for the boy's wages to his father. The check was in the amount of thirteen dollars.

Ride the Jawbone

July 29th

T. C. packed the few things he needed on the back of his saddle. Before he left to report the death of the hay rake driver to his father, he sought out Seth. "Papa says you plan to leave the ranch. I haven't the slightest idea how to keep the ranch books. I don't know how to go about hiring a crew, and I don't have any experience in bossing men. If you leave, the rest of the crew may leave with you."

"T. C., you'll probably find the crew will change. That's just the way it goes. You can find men in Two Dot or Harlowton or Martinsdale or White Sulphur Springs. All you have to do is look. I'll show you how I keep the books. It isn't difficult." He waited a long time before he asked, "Are you going to stay here at the ranch then, and not practice law?"

"I don't know what to do. I'm still trying to decide. That's another reason for the trip to town. I need to talk to Papa."

The way Seth looked at him made him wonder if Seth suspected the other reason he wanted to go to the Springs, but he only said, "Tell your father how it happened that the boy died."

Halfway to Two Dot, T. C. had another scary thought. "If Mrs. B. leaves, who will cook for the crew?"

On the train ride west from Two Dot, T. C. thought about the poor youngster who had died, but more often his mind turned to Felicity. It was peculiar that he hadn't thought of her in a romantic sense until the evening under the trees. Now he couldn't think of her in any other way. As he rode along, he finally realized that he wanted to propose marriage to her, but the realization that she might refuse his proposal made him hesitant. Her response to a proposal of marriage might be to laugh. He couldn't bear the thought of such an embarrassment. That very possibility made his stomach hurt. But she seemed to be fond of him. Perhaps she would accept. But perhaps not. Maybe she had a boyfriend in the east. So his thinking went, round and round, as the engine chugged along, pulling the cars westward over the tracks.

The train got to the Cottonwood Creek crossing only to find that a flash flood from a thunderstorm the day before had washed out the bridge. The engineer backed the train six miles to Martinsdale, where the passengers spent the night. In his bed in the dark, T. C. thought more about Felicity and his future occupation. Suppose she would marry him. Where would she like to live? Would she wish to be in town? Or would she be content to live on the ranch? Would Felicity want to do all of the hard work that Mrs. B. endured each day? She was a city girl who had never been faced with that kind of demand. T. C. finally slept, still without knowing what to do with his life.

July 31st

To T. C.'s surprise, his parents already knew of the young man's death. Word of the matter had been telegraphed to the Sheriff. He explained to them exactly how it all happened and how Seth handled the situation. After they discussed the matter thoroughly, they did not speak of it again. Such accidents were frequent, and though sad, were accepted as part of life.

He was relieved that neither of his parents asked about his plans for the future.

As soon as he could take his leave without seeming rude, T. C. hurried off to the store. He found Felicity in the back office, working on the books. She didn't hesitate to put her arms around his waist and tilt her head to be kissed. The kiss was long and warm. T. C. would have had it last longer, but she pulled away and breathed, "Well!" Felicity's eyes dropped to the floor as she ran her hands down along her skirt. She looked at his face again to whisper, "I've missed you." Turning toward her chair and without looking at T. C., she asked, "How long will you be in town?"

Although the back room had afforded enough privacy for the first kiss, T. C. wanted to get her out of the store and alone somewhere. He want to wrap her in his arms and hold her close. For a moment, he was not aware of her question. When he realized what she'd said, he stammered, "I'm not sure. I came to report to my father about the accident at the ranch."

Felicity hadn't heard of the death. When T. C. told her about it, she dropped to her chair, and tears filled her eyes. She pulled a handkerchief from her sleeve to wipe her cheeks and nose. Speaking softly, she remembered the young man, so young, handsome, and friendly. At last the conversation drifted away from the tragedy. The tears stopped flowing, and Felicity tucked the handkerchief away.

She brightened and said, "Well, you're here. Perhaps we can learn more about Miss Burke and who killed her. Everyone in town is wondering when you'll open your law office. They've even been asking me if I'll be your secretary." She blushed slightly, as though that possibility might embarrass him.

The thought of having a law office with her sitting close by had never occurred to him. That thought was tantalizing. T. C. pulled another chair near to hers and sat down, their knees almost touching. He had not intended to discuss his future with her quite this soon, but conversation with her was so easy that it just seemed natural to do so. He leaned forward as he spoke. "Seth is leaving the ranch and my father needs to know if I plan to stay there and look after things. If I'm not going to do it, Papa will need to find another man to manage the place." He squirmed in the chair, seeking more comfort. "But Mother has always wanted me to be a lawyer. I have the education and it seems a waste not to put it to work. What do you think I should do?"

When the question came out of his mouth, it was because he wanted her advice, but almost immediately, he understood that he was really asking what kind of life she would prefer for herself. He felt his face redden and hoped she didn't notice.

For Felicity, the question was of more consequence than T. C. imagined. It suddenly dawned on her that the kind of life that she might live depended upon the decision that he was now about to make. But, of course, she couldn't let him know that her answer reflected a personal concern. He might not have any intention of asking her to marry him. She asked. "What would you like to do?"

T. C. contemplated his answer for a long moment. "I don't really know what I want to do. I missed the cattle and the ranch work when I was in school. I'm sure that I wouldn't be content if I couldn't ride with the others while the cattle are being worked. I'm already looking forward to the fall roundup." He shifted in the chair again and rubbed his hand along his neck beneath his ear. "Still, it was interesting to be in court, and that's what I've been trained to do. I keep thinking that I could be of help to some people if I have a law office. It's the job of a lawyer to use the law to help folks resolve their differences. That part of it appeals to me."

"Can you do both? Would it be possible to live at the ranch and have a law practice out of the ranch house?"

"No, I don't think so. People would have to travel too far, and the courthouse is here in the Springs. I'd have to travel here too often for such an arrangement to be practical." He pounded his knees once with his hands. "No, I have to do one thing or the other." As T. C. said it he rose from his chair, stuffed his hands in his pockets and strode around the little room.

Felicity turned in her chair so that her eyes could follow him. If she knew what kind of life she wanted, she could point him in the proper direction. Did she want to live on the ranch as the wife of a cattleman? Or did she want to live in town as the wife of a lawyer? Since she didn't know, she ended the conversation by saying, "Well, I think you should do what you want, and you shouldn't think too much of your parents wishes." Then as her face grew sunny, she added, "Enough of this talk. Come, you can buy me an ice cream sundae." She clasped his hand as they walked out of the store together.

They wandered along the boardwalk without noticing those who passed by. When the sheriff approached, however, T. C. dropped Felicity's hand. After a tip of his hat and a nod to Felicity, Sheriff Shea told T. C. "Her father was in town… and so was Gordon Jordahl."

T. C. asked in an impatient voice, "Who was in town?"

"Penelope Burke's father." He looked from the young man to the young woman. "I talked to him while he was here. Penelope Burke was a widow. Her husband was killed after they had been married only two years. She was lonely when Gordon Jordahl appeared on the scene. He described Jordahl as a man older than Miss Burke and a smooth talker. He led her on and soon she found herself pregnant." He turned to Felicity and touched his hat again, "No offense, ma'am."

"Her father said that Jordahl took off as soon as she told him that a child was on the way. She had the baby and waited until the boy—the child was a boy—till he was a year old. Then Miss Burke," he paused to correct himself, "I guess she was really Mrs. Burke," he paused again, "she started to look for Jordahl and learned somehow that he was in

Montana. So, she left the child with her parents and came west. Her father didn't know why his daughter was in Two Dot. But evidently Jordahl learned where she was because he went to that town to visit her. She told her folks about it in a letter. Her father thinks that she got on the train that day to go to meet him again. That man is certain that Gordon Jordahl is the one who killed his daughter."

Looking at T. C. with a frown, he announced. "Now that I've learned all of this, I'm pretty certain that Gordon Jordahl was in the courtroom while the trial was going on. He had a seat in the rear near the doors. I happened to mention that name to the clerk at the hotel and he told me the man was registered there."

T. C. glanced toward Felicity who returned his gaze. Turning again to the sheriff, T. C. asked, "You mean the man who might have killed her was here in town during the trial?"

"It appears that's the case."

T. C. thought for a long moment and then asked, "How did her father learn that she was dead? Did you tell him?"

"No. He became concerned about her after he found out she'd seen Jordahl again. So he started for Two Dot. I guess he heard about her murder when he got off the train in Big Timber. That's why he came here to the Springs instead of going to Two Dot." The day was hot. The sheriff took a kerchief from his pocket, pushed his hat back and wiped his forehead. "Her father has an idea that Jordahl went to Bozeman. I don't know why he thinks so, but he left for Bozeman yesterday morning. That man's intent on finding Jordahl."

T. C. realized that the letter he wrote would get to the woman's home, and her mother would probably open it. He hoped that wasn't how she learned of her daughter's death. "What's her father's name? What's been done to locate the man who killed her?"

"We don't know that he killed her, do we counselor?" The sheriff's frown turned to a smile. "You argued the presumption of innocence very well in a trial recently, if I remember correctly."

The remark irritated T. C., but he let it go. "You're right, of course. I just want to see the murderer punished."

"We all do. I asked the Sheriff in Bozeman to look for Jordahl. Sheriff Mendenhall wired me yesterday that a man of his description stole money from a widow he'd been staying with. Then he lit out. He may be in Butte. We don't know for sure. Anyway, we don't have a thing to tie him to the murder." After a pause, he added. "Her father's name is Edward Crowley."

"Well, if her father catches up with him, Jordahl may decide that the best thing is to run to the authorities and confess." T. C.'s voice was grim. "A father's wrath could be worse."

"We'll see. Anyway, I'll let you know what comes up." With another tip of his hat to Felicity, the sheriff went on his way.

When T. C. began to stroll toward the ice cream parlor, Felicity pulled his hand and stopped him. "We have to find that man. We have to prove that he killed that poor woman."

August 1

When Mr. Morton handed her the letter, Sarah wondered who might have sent it. In her room, she opened it to find a note on a scrap of paper. There was no return address.

> *Dear Sarah,*
> *I have been busy with business matters but I will be at the Morton ranch to visit you in two weeks.*
> *Gordon*

After pondering long and hard, Sarah decided to refuse the position Mr. Jordahl offered. She wondered if she should write to him so he wouldn't make an unnecessary trip, but she decided it would be better to tell him in person. Not that she had much choice. The envelope was post-marked in Butte. She frowned at his impertinence in addressing her as Sarah, instead of Miss Kuntz. Let him travel. After all, she had gone to Bozeman at his request, and he hadn't even offered to pay any part of the cost.

The thought of the college in Bozeman had not left her mind. Mrs. Morton, who had been a school teacher, talked of the size of the library and the kinds of books that would be there. Sarah could take courses in any subject that she chose. She couldn't think of anything that the college had to offer that wouldn't interest her. Sarah Kuntz could do without Gordon Jordahl.

Ride the Jawbone

August 3rd

T. C. and Felicity were constant companions for three days. Mr. Spencer looked the other way when T. C. came to the store in the morning and took his niece away. Felicity helped Mrs. Bruce with the cooking in the evening and ate the evening meal with the Bruce family. During the days, they entertained themselves with buggy rides, long walks, and longer conversations. These conversations sometimes turned to the search that the sheriff was conducting for Gordon Jordahl, but more often it was very personal. They were sitting on the hill that overlooked the town from the north after eating a picnic lunch when they discussed the choice he had to make.

Felicity listened to T. C. recite the reasons for practicing law and the reasons for returning to the ranch that she had heard several times before. Finally she said, "Thad, you'll not be happy here in town. If you practice law you'll wish you were at the ranch. You should tell your father that you'll assume the ranch responsibility, and do it now so that he can let Seth know."

T. C. spoke again of his worries about his ability to manage men. He finished by saying, "And I'll need to find a cook."

There was exasperation in her voice when she said, "Thad, you'll need a wife!"

That's when he proposed.

August 6th

They told her aunt and uncle first, and then they told his parents. The four elders were pleased and not surprised that their conspiracy had worked. While the young couple wandered about in a fog, the older couples began to plan the wedding. Townsfolk soon learned of the engagement, and T. C. and Felicity found themselves the center of attention. Planning the wedding soon became a community project, much to the dismay of Mrs. Spencer and Mrs. Bruce.

Felicity's parents were notified, and they immediately made plans to travel to Montana. Her mother was shocked and frightened that her precious daughter would think of marrying a wild man of the west—some person they had never even met. In spite of much reassurance in letters from the Spencer family in White Sulphur Springs, her concerns were magnified by time. When Felicity's parents received a letter from Thaddeus C. Bruce, Jr. in which he expressed his devotion to their daughter and promised to care for her forever, her mother was relieved to learn that her future son-in-law at least had the ability to write.

One evening while the women were cleaning the kitchen, Mr. Bruce said to his son, "Your mother and I have been visiting. The work at the ranch is hard and Felicity needs time to adjust to ranch life. Mrs. Weston is a widow who needs work, and is willing to go the ranch and handle the cooking. She can live in the room in the house where you've been sleeping." He glanced at the door to the kitchen. "Your mother says that Mrs. Weston is a pleasant person, and that she and Felicity will get along. Before you leave for the ranch, you should hire her."

At that moment Mrs. Bruce stepped into the doorway with her hands on her hips, wearing an expression of disgust. "Thaddeus Bruce, listen to me! Felicity is the one who will work with Mrs. Weston. She's the one who will talk with her and hire her if she wishes. You and Thad stay out of it!" As she turned her back, T. C. heard her mutter, "Men!"

T. C. soon found that the groom is just in the way when a wedding is in the planning stage. He told his intended bride he should return to the ranch. She agreed immediately, but hugged him and whispered, "I'll miss you. But it won't be much longer before we'll be together and can really know each other." He almost trembled at the thought.

Before leaving town, T. C. spoke with the sheriff. The report from Bozeman stated that Gordon Jordahl was not in that town and Penelope Burke's father was still looking for him. T. C. and the sheriff ruminated over the fact that Jordahl had been in the courtroom during the trial. Was he there to see if they convicted Loco? What did he think when the jury acquitted that strange man? He must have wondered if they would then start to look for another suspect. The fact that he left town soon after the jury reached its verdict, seemed to indicate that he was worried. The sheriff allowed as how they might yet find Jordahl and have a chance to question him.

It was with that thought in mind that T. C. climbed into the stage to Dorsey.

Ride the Jawbone

At supper one evening, Seth told the men who worked at the ranch that he would be leaving in the fall and that T. C. would then be in charge. Not one of them said a word when the announcement was made, but T. C. noticed a subtle change in the way they acted toward him. Even though he harnessed up a team to a bull rake and worked the hay field with the others, he perceived a barrier between him and the crew. Chappy was the exception. Chappy accepted the fact that T. C. was the boss and began to treat him as he had always treated Seth. It was Chappy's job to care for the livestock, and that didn't change. He gathered the horses from the pasture north and west of the buildings each morning. During the day he rode the ranges looking for cattle that were lame or sick or needed care for some other reason. Each evening he reported his findings to Seth and, if there was a need for help with the cattle, asked for one or more of the men to ride with him the next day. He now started reporting to T. C. as well as Seth. After their discussions the three made decisions about the next day's operations.

Seth spent evenings showing T. C. how he kept his ledgers. He showed him a daily record that he kept of each day's work and accomplishment. He and T. C. reviewed the cattle tally book for several years past, and Seth talked of trends that could be ascertained from that review. The number of calves that they were branding had improved because the ranch was fully fenced and because of increased hay production, just as Mr. Bruce had predicted. The weight of the animals that were sold had increased as well. It all resulted in a greater net income to the operation. Seth shared his thoughts regarding the management of men. He believed that good food and good treatment secured more loyalty from his men than extra pay did. T. C. understood why men worked for Seth year after year. His philosophy made sense.

Mrs. B. tried to tell T. C. the things she felt he should know about her tasks but it was a wasted effort. She soon decided that she would spend her time more productively if she spoke with Felicity directly.

The days passed swiftly, but the nights were long for a young man in love.

August 16

The Mortons were not in the house when Gordon Jordahl arrived. Sarah answered the knock on the door and led him into the parlor. He wore the same clothes as before and his smile was as charming as she remembered. She pointed to one of the chairs as she seated herself in another. "Mr. Jordahl, I've decided that your offer is not one I should accept."

His smile stiffened but remained in place. "I'm terribly disappointed. Can I do anything to persuade you to change your mind?"

"No sir, I've made other plans."

"Sarah, I've traveled a long way. Surely you owe me an explanation. When you left Bozeman, I was under the impression that you would like to teach Gordy rather than teach at a country school. What changed your mind?"

"I needn't give any explanation to you, sir. My reasons are my own." Sarah rose to her feet to indicate that the discussion was at an end.

A sudden look of fury contorted Jordahl's face. He sprang from the chair, grabbed Sarah about the waist and pulled her body to him. Her eyes grew wide and her cry was sharp. "No! No!" The cry turned to a shriek. "Get your hands off of me!" She pushed on his chest but could not break free from his grasp.

With Sarah struggling to free herself, Jordahl used the fingers of one hand to tear open her dress where it was buttoned in the back. While he pulled at the fabric he snarled in her ear. "Give me the money. I know you have money in a belt." His voice became more fierce as he yanked at her clothing. "Give me the damn money before I have to hurt you." Jordahl held her tightly to his body while he jerked repeatedly the back of her dress with his free hand until buttons broke loose and flew across the room.

Sarah managed to rake the fingernails of one hand across and down the side of her attacker's face. "No! No! No! Let me go!" Her voice rose to a screech.

Then he hit her.

The blow was backhanded and struck her across her cheek below

200

her eye. As she staggered backward away from him, he pulled her dress off her right shoulder. She clutched with one hand to keep her clothing together and stretched her other hand out in front to ward off the next blow. Her eyes grew even wider as he crouched, reached beneath the back of his coat and pulled a large knife from a scabbard on his belt. Jordahl lunged with his left hand, grabbed the top front of her dress and jerked her toward him. The knife was in his right hand, pointed at her stomach. His voice was now a maniacal snarl. "I want the money. I want it right now."

Willard Morton heard the screech as he came through the door from the porch. He hobbled as fast as he could to the parlor just in time to see Jordahl pull the knife. The sight made the old man forget his gout and he ran across the room while gripping his cane in both hands. Jordahl released Sarah and whirled around at the sound of the footsteps. Before he could react, Morton rammed the end of the cane into Jordahl's midsection. Had not his large belt buckle received the blow, it would have put him on the floor. As it was, he doubled over, grunted, "Whoof" and let the knife fall at his feet. In an instant he straightened up with both hands pressed to his stomach and looked with wild eyes at Morton and then at Sarah. Jordahl lurched forward and shoved Morton aside as he rushed toward the door. As he passed by, Morton managed to swing at him with the cane and whacked him once between the shoulders. The blow didn't slow Sarah's attacker. He ducked out the door and ran to the rack where his horse was tied.

Willard Morton looked first at Sarah to see if she was seriously injured. Concluding she was not, he hobbled out onto the porch, calling loudly to his ranch hands for help. Two of the men were working in the barn and charged out the door in time to see Jordahl leap to his mount. He whipped the animal into a gallop and headed out of the barnyard toward the east. The ranch hands started back into the barn to get horses for the chase but were stopped by their employer who yelled. "Let him go. If he ever shows up here again, I'll shoot the bastard."

Morton was puffing so hard from his exertion that he had to lean heavily on his cane. His voice was a hoarse wheeze when he said, "Herman, saddle up and ride to Martinsdale as fast as you can. That man must have rented a horse in town. Tell the stable operator to hold him for the sheriff when he brings the animal in."

Sarah cowered next to the wall, white faced and gasping. She was trying to pull her clothing together when she looked down and saw Jordahl's hat and the knife lying near the middle of the room. She began to tremble, then her legs gave way and she crumpled to the floor with her arms clutched around her body. Sarah couldn't stop the shaking and soon dissolved into choking sobs. Mrs. Morton, running in from the garden, knelt beside her and wiped hastily at the blood that ran from Sarah's split lip with a small handkerchief. Then, grasping the emotional condition of her house guest, she dropped beside her and gathered the young woman tightly in her arms. Sarah buried her head in the old woman's bosom and wailed, both of them mindless of the blood that stained the front of Mrs. Morton's dress.

++++++++++

Gordon Jordahl flogged the horse to get all the speed the poor animal had to offer. From time to time he looked back over his shoulder as he rode and was surprised to see that no one followed him. His stomach burned with pain where the old man had rammed it with the cane. He wondered what to do? It was certain that Morton would send word of his behavior to Martinsdale, so he couldn't take the horse back there. Word that he'd assaulted Sarah would surely be telegraphed to Two Dot. His best bet was to hide for a time, perhaps in the brush along the river, and then head cross-country for Big Timber. When the horse began to falter, Jordahl slowed him to a walk. Engrossed in these thoughts, he rounded a hill to see Sheriff Shea and a deputy riding toward him, not one hundred yards away. The two law officers were traveling at a leisurely pace as they returned from investigating a rustling in the eastern part of the county. In a panic at the sight of the sheriff, Jordahl turned his horse and whipped the haggard animal into a gallop once again.

Observing Jordahl's behavior, the sheriff glanced at his deputy with raised eyebrows and said, "I don't know who that fellow is or what he's done, but he's running from something. I think we better gather him up and ask a few questions."

Their fresh horses had no trouble outrunning the one that Jordahl was riding. When Jordahl realized he couldn't outrun them, he pulled his horse to a stop and waited. The lawmen rode up, one on each side of their quarry, with Sheriff Shea watching carefully to be sure the man wasn't hiding a weapon. Seeing none, he sat with hands resting on his saddle horn and asked, "What's your hurry, mister? Who the hell are you, anyway?"

Jordahl looked first at the sheriff, then turned away to seemingly focus his attention on the Daisy Notch that scarred the ridge line of the Little Belt Mountains to the north. His face was pasty white, not the least bronzed by the sun. The smile that first attracted Sarah was gone and a sulky frown replaced it. Jordahl didn't answer the sheriff. Instead, he merely shrugged his shoulders and shook his head in a resigned manner. Asking again and getting no response, the sheriff said, "Well, since we're all going in the same direction, we'll just ride on into Martinsdale together. You can tell us about yourself, if you decide to talk, while we travel."

It seemed that everyone in Martinsdale already knew about the things that Jordahl had done to Sarah. And everyone seemed to know his name. The livery stable operator, looking at the man between the two law officers, confirmed it. "Yup, that's Jordahl, all right. I can see that he damn near killed my horse."

There was satisfaction in his voice when Sheriff Shea said to his deputy, "I think we've finally collared Penelope Burke's murderer."

+++++++++

Sarah paced slowly around her room, still clutching herself as though for protection. The side of her face was red from the blow she'd received and her eye was starting to swell. It would be black in the morning. She couldn't get the horrifying sight of Gordon Jordahl in a rage, with the knife pointed at her, out of her mind. Weary of the pacing, she collapsed on her bed and rocked back and forth as the tears ran down her face. Nothing that the Mortons had done could relieve her of her terror. Then her eyes widened as a sudden thought overran the terror. She stopped her rocking movement and whispered to herself, "Oliver." She put her fingers gently to her bruised cheekbone as she said it. "Oliver is a great big man." Her voice choked as she began to rock once more. "Oliver will never let this happen to me again." Finally she fell over on her side on the bed with her knees pulled up to her chest and let the tears pour out while her body shook in great, racking sobs.

August 17th

Morning arrived. Sarah found herself lying on the bed, still huddled with her knees to her chin. Slowly she stretched her legs and turned to lie on her back. She reached to touch the bruise on her face. Still painful. After a glance downward at the tatters that Jordahl had made of her dress, she pulled the ripped cloth together and held it in a clenched fist. For a long time she stared at the ceiling, her mind refusing to accept as reality the happenings of the day before. Then the memory of the attack by the enraged Jordahl, with all of its horror, came flooding back. But now, sleep having quieted her mind, Sarah found she could contemplate the attack in a more thoughtful, deliberate manner. Jordahl had committed serious crimes. Mr. Morton would provide testimony of them. The man would be captured and put in prison. She would not let fear of a man like Gordon Jordahl rule her life.

What should that life be?

One thing she knew. Mr. Bruce would marry that other woman. No need to think of him ever again. She didn't want to teach at the Flagstaff school. She must write to the Halls to tell them. There was no reason for Sarah to remain longer at the Morton ranch. But what to do if not teach at that school?

Her last thought the night before had been of Oliver—Oliver as her savior. Now a picture of the man he always would be came to her mind. Oliver standing slump shouldered, wearing bib overalls that had a red handkerchief hanging from the hip pocket. Oliver with a stem of grass dangling loosely from his lip. Oliver with the filth and stink from the hog pens clinging to his boots.

Then she saw herself standing by his side, clothed as she had been when complimented for her looks and demeanor by both the milliner and Joshua Farley. The contrast was just too stark. The two pictures were simply impossible to reconcile. No, she could never go back to Oliver.

Ride the Jawbone

Sarah raised her hands to rub at her eyes. She had seen the Montana Agricultural College and the library with all of its books. Why not go to Bozeman? There was enough money in the belt for a few months if she was careful and if she could find inexpensive living quarters. How much would it cost to attend classes at the college? What classes would she be allowed to take? Would there be employment opportunities for someone in her circumstances?

There was only one way to find out. She would go to Bozeman. She would get the education she had been denied until now. Sarah rolled to the side and dropped her legs over the edge of the bed to sit. First, write the Halls. Next, go downstairs and tell the Mortons of her plan.

Sarah Kuntz stood, allowed the damaged dress to drop in a heap to the floor and gave it a kick. She would never put it on her body again.

+++++++++++

Each evening the workhorses were turned out into a horse pasture northwest and over the ridge from the ranch buildings. A couple of mounts were kept in a small pasture near the barn for use in the morning to gather the others. Chappy arose from bed early to bring the work animals in so the others could catch their teams and harness them before eating breakfast.

About a half-hour before the morning meal, Chappy rode into the yard, tied up the wrangle horse and came to the house. Seth was helping Mrs. B. with the meal preparation. T. C. had just returned after carrying the slop to the hogs. Without preamble, Chappy announced, "The horses are gone. Something tore down the gate in the northwest corner of the pasture and the whole bunch went through. I followed their tracks for a ways, but they were on the run and it'll take time to find 'em. I thought you should know so you can put the boys to work doing other things."

Seth just nodded his acceptance. The unexpected didn't ruffle him. "Well, you better eat breakfast before you ride out again. The men can spend the time repairing machinery and fixing harness. The barn needs cleaning. There's plenty to do."

T. C. put the slop pail back where it belonged, then called back over his shoulder as he headed for the door, "I'll go with you. Give me time to catch the other horse and saddle up."

They rode north toward the river, visiting as they went. T. C. started to tell Chappy about his proposal to Felicity, but Chappy cut him off. So they talked of ranch matters and community happenings until the conversation finally turned to Jordahl. T. C. had already told Chappy and the others at the ranch that Penelope Burke's father was searching for Jordahl, whom he believed to be his daughter's murderer.

"How can they ever prove he's the killer?" Chappy asked. "It's not likely that anyone will know if he was on the train, and no one has figured out how her body ended up where Noseless Pete found it."

"I hope her father locates him. The sheriff thinks he may learn more by questioning him. He's still trying to find out where Jordahl is and what he's been doing. He's asking around about the man's activities while he was hanging out in this neck of the woods. Who knows, the sheriff may be able to tie him to the murder."

A high sandstone bluff, almost perpendicular and about one hundred feet high, overlooked the Musselshell River about five miles west of Two Dot. The railroad track carved its way around the base of the bluff where a large grove of cottonwood trees stood between the railroad and the river. As they approached the bluff, they could hear the sound of the train as it pulled out of Martinsdale, headed for Two Dot. T. C. and Chappy stopped at the top of the bluff to take advantage of its elevation in their effort to spot the lost horses. They dismounted and stretched.

While Chappy was getting a small telescope from his saddlebag, T. C. walked to the edge of the precipice and scanned the flats and ridges between the river and the mountains. A group of animals could be seen in the distance, far north of the river. T. C. couldn't tell if they were horses or cattle with his naked eye. Chappy joined him near the place where the land dropped off to the railroad track and focused his glass on the animals. After a moment, he announced, "That's them all right. The grey mare's in the lead." He pulled the glass away and asked, "How do you suppose they got through the fences to find their way over to the north side?"

T. C. was about to answer when he heard the faint sound of a voice coming from a coulee to the east; a depression that led away from the river bottom. The coulee was deep at the river end and became more shallow toward the hills. Whoever was making the noise was coming up the coulee and, as he got closer, the voice became more clear. He was singing a ditty that T. C. had never heard before, and it was hard to make out the words because the speech was slurred. They listened and watched as a hat appeared above the top of the coulee. Soon the rest of the man came walking into sight.

The newcomer saw them. He stopped his singing for a second, and then turned to walk in their direction. As he came toward them he continued to sing that strange song in a voice that sounded almost like a whine. The man was large and walked with a kind of lurching shuffle. He didn't come far before T. C. realized, with a start, that he was meeting Lawrence Silverman once again.

His erstwhile client recognized him at the same time. The singing stopped and the man's peculiar gait quickened as he hurried toward them. When he was about fifty yards away he began to talk. His voice had a higher pitch than T. C. remembered from the few words that he had spoken in the courtroom and a much higher pitch than the yowls that T. C. had listened to in the jail.

"There's the lawyer man that looked so fine in court. The fancy pants lawyer. Just another one of them people that's too good for old Loco." His voice rose in volume as he got closer to T. C. and Chappy. "You think you're so damned smart—talkin' to them jurors and tellin' 'em how Loco couldn't a killed her. You think you saved my life." His eyes shifted around, and it was impossible to know where they were focused. His beard and long hair were as filthy dirty as the first time T. C. had seen him. "Yeah, but they wouldn't a believed you if I hadn't put on my act—fallin' down the hill. It worked, even if that dumb bastard did shoot me." He stopped within ten feet of T. C. who almost gagged at the stench Loco carried with him. It was like a dead animal that had been soaked in alcohol.

Chappy put his telescope back in the saddlebag without taking his eye from Loco.

"Well, let me tell you, that woman insulted old Loco. She slapped me on the train, all right—up along side my head." His face contorted into a scowl. "But I let it go." One of Loco's eyes—the one that seemed to focus—shifted from T. C. to Chappy and back. "She had it comin', what happened to her. But I never set out to kill her like they said."

The filthy man took another step closer. If the overwhelming smell bothered Chappy, he didn't show it. "I kept on watchin' her. She got off the train at Summit, alright, but she didn't get off where everyone else did. She got off on the other side where no one would see her. A dandy man was waitin' there—a fancy lookin' sport, wearin' a fine suit." His look changed from angry to sly. "They walked off down the track together and he had 'is arm around her waist." The angry look returned. "She warn't about to let old Loco put a hand on her, you bet. But she let that dude grab her just like he owned her." Loco spat, shuffled his feet and kept moving closer to T. C.

Chappy, his face impassive, stood to one side with an eye on Loco.

"That train took me to Dorsey. The barkeep wouldn't let me in the saloon. Said I stunk too bad." He spat again. "Too hell with him!" The crude man wiped at his mouth with a filthy sleeve.

The sound of the whistle came from the west as the train approached a crossing. The noise didn't register with any of them.

T. C. managed to mutter, "How....?"

Loco's eyebrow rose. "You're wonderin' how I got to Summit?" He cackled. "I walked. It ain't so far, you know, when you cut across, stead of followin' the tracks or the road." The appearance of a grin moved his lips. "The saloonkeeper in Summit ain't so fussy. He'll always let me in, just so's I have money to pay." He was now standing right in front of T. C. "It was dark by the time I got to the edge of town. I came 'round the corner of the first building and that woman walked right into me." Loco's grin began to take on a weird appearance. One eye looked at T. C. while the other seemed to look at Chappy.

"Well, I wasn't expectin' anyone and I done what I do when an animal jumps me—I pulled my knife and used it."

T. C. could see the knife stuck in Loco's waistband where it could easily be reached. His mind was racing. Loco had killed her after all! He began to get red in the neck and the color crept up to his face while Loco kept on talking.

Chappy moved one step nearer to T. C. and stood quietly with his hands hanging at his sides.

Ride the Jawbone

Loco leaned toward the young lawyer and snarled, "I stuck her in the stomach. She started to open her mouth to scream, so I grabbed her and cut her throat 'fore she could make a sound." He cackled. "I begun to wonder what I was gonna to do with 'er. I couldn't leave her layin' in the street. They might figure out what happened and come after me. So I decided to get her out of there."

T. C. was horrified. As the story progressed, his horror turned to anger. His voice was deep and his eyes were wide as he growled, "Why, God damn you!"

Loco continued. "I picked 'er up—she warn't very heavy—and walked back along the tracks till I came to the coulee where that herder spotted her. I figured they wouldn't find 'er body for a while and then no one would have any reason to look for me. I just dropped 'er there." He continued to cackle as he talked. "When I started back, I found 'er hat had dropped off when I was toting' 'er along. I don't know why I did it, but I took it back and put it over 'er face." His laugh stopped. "I went back to the place where I'd knifed 'er to see how much blood was on the ground, and that's where I found the locket or whatever you fancy people call that thing. So I put it in my pocket and kept it."

T. C.'s face was now crimson with fury. "God damn you! You let me go through that, and all the time you were the one that did it. You bastard!" His voice was a bellow.

Chappy now stood within an arm's length of T. C., his hands still hanging loosely at his sides. Loco seemed to cast a glance in his direction.

The stinking man's eye focused on T. C. again. "There ain't nothin' you or anyone else can do about it now." His cackling laugh was louder. "Old Loco's been acquitted. You hear that?" He shouted. "Acquitted!" Then he resumed a more normal voice—at least as normal as he'd spoken till then. "As dumb as you think I am, I know what that means. It means I can walk up and down the street yellin' that I killed her, and nobody can do a damn thing about it. I might not be smart and you fancy people with all your ranches and all your schoolin' may not want a thing to do with me, but by God, I outfoxed every one of you this time."

T. C. couldn't control himself. He hit Loco in the chest with the palms of his hands and screamed, "God damn you! You killed her! God damn you to hell!"

T. C.'s hands were still in the air when the knife came out of Loco's waistband. His underhanded thrust was aimed at T. C.'s the midsection.

At the murderer's first movement, Chappy grabbed T. C., jerking him backward and to the side. Loco was quick, but Chappy's yank was quicker. The blade cut through the front of T. C.'s vest just as Chappy pulled him away. Loco had put all of his might into the thrust. When the knife met no resistance, the force of his swing carried him into a turning fall. He stepped out to keep his balance, but tripped on a rock and toppled over the ledge.

Loco slid headfirst a couple of feet, with his hands clawing at the ground in an attempt to slow his progress. Then he reached the first of several straight drops. He went into the drop headfirst but when he hit the next ledge below, his body bounced outward and fell down along the next drop, parallel to the cliff. When he hit the second ledge and bounced outward, his body was spinning. Up to that point he had not made a sound. When he spun off the last drop they heard the same yowl that had been Loco's only speech while he was in jail.

The final fall was about thirty feet. Loco's spinning body bounced outward from the last ledge and landed on the railroad bed with his head and one arm on the outside of the track and the rest of him lying between the rails. He didn't move.

The train was late by several hours and the engineer was determined to make up time. When he reached the Selkirk siding he was going down grade and using all the steam that the fireman could generate. Because the track curved around the bottom of the bluff he couldn't see more then three hundred feet ahead. The instant the engine rounded the curve, the engineer spotted Loco lying on the track just as the man struggled to raise himself up on an elbow. The engineer dynamited all of the brakes, but it was too late to keep the cowcatcher from snagging Loco.

From the top of the bluff, T. C. and Chappy stared as the train rounded the bend. They saw Loco start to move just as the train hit him. The base of the cowcatcher on the engine ran only a couple of inches above the track. It caught Loco's shoulder and neck and the engine dragged him along with his body under the cowcatcher and with his head and arm on the outside of the track. T. C. watched in horror as Loco's head bounced across the ties while the train screeched onward, all of its wheels locked. To the men watching from the ridge it seemed forever before the train slowly came to a stop. The engineer immediately threw the engine into reverse and backed away from the remains of Loco's mutilated body.

T. C. looked down at what was left of his one time client, fell to his hands and knees, and vomited.

Epilogue

They were married in the Episcopal Church. It was the finest social event of the year in White Sulphur Springs. Felicity's sister was the bridesmaid. Chappy wore a formal suit for the only time in his life and only because he was the best man. The newlyweds left in a buggy for Dorsey where they would get on the Jawbone to begin their honeymoon. All of the ranch hands, who had been celebrating the wedding with hard likker and lots of it, followed them on horseback for a mile or so out of town, whooping and yelling and firing their six-shooters into the air.

The wedding gift they cherished most was an oil painting from Pierre Bouteron that portrayed T. C. standing before the jury, gesturing as he spoke. Felicity's profile appeared in the foreground, eyes on her man. The signature in the lower corner simply read, "Noseless Pete."

Acknowledgments

But for the following people this book would never
have come into existence.

My sister, Kay Gleason, who went through a first draft
word by word and highlighted all of my
kindergarten mistakes.

Lauri Olsen who gave instruction, encouragement
and sage words of advice.

Jim and Rosemary Doyle, Joe and Peg Gary and
George and Thyrza Zebriskie, all of whom
assured me that the story had merit.

Florence Ore who offered constructive suggestions
for improvement in the writing.

And—especially—Janet Muirhead Hill
who believes that there are book lovers
out there who will enjoy
this yarn and has bet on it.

A Study and Discussion Guide
for Reading Groups and Classroom Use

1. The reader of Ride the Jawbone will notice a uniqueness in the way in which the book is divided into sections. What is the unique way the author determines section breaks in this book? Is there a significance to this technique in relation to the story? Why do you think the author chose this method? Over what time period does the story take place?

2. What descriptions near the beginning of the book give the reader a feeling for the setting and the historical time period?

3. A stagecoach ride may sound romantic to modern readers, but in this author's description of it, what might it have really been like? Is this description accurate? Can you think of any other things of the early 1900's which may be romanticized now in modern times?

4. Which characters grab your interest right away at the start of the book?

5. What does the reader learn early on in the book about T. C.'s family? What clues does the author give about them?

6. What did you learn about cattle ranching at the time during which this story took place? What were some of the changes that were going on? How was sheep ranching different from cattle ranching?

7. If you were a lawyer, would you take the case T. C. was offered? What factors played on his decision? What were some of his dilemmas? Why do you think he took the case?

8. Although the story takes place more than 30 years after the Civil War and is not set in the South, why do you think the author mentions Confederate and Union backgrounds as description?

Study/Discussion Guide

9. Do you agree with the point that T. C.'s father makes about the Civil War being about more than slavery? What is the analogy he makes between the Civil War and the Court System?

10. Are there any factors that bear upon the validity of the modern courts today that were the same or different in 1902? One group of citizens does not serve on the jury in this book. Who were they? Why is this?

11. What made T. C.'s mother change her mind about his taking the case?

12. T. C. wears several hats in this story – lawyer, ranch owner's son, cowboy…and a young man interested in young women. As the story moves along, he meets and becomes interested in two very different women. How would you describe their differences?

13. How does the author give a "first impression" of Sarah and Felicity? As the story moves along, what does the reader find out about their backgrounds? Do you find that they are different than your "first impressions?" What are clues to why each of them might act in the ways they do?
   In your experience are "first impressions" generally reliable?

14. What role does Noseless Pete play in the story? Does he have an importance beyond his role as provider of information about the dead victim? What, if any, is the significance of his being noseless? What more is revealed about him? Did you wonder about this as he appeared in the story?

15. During the trial preparation and the actual trial, the reader is exposed to a number of legal terms:
   M'Naughton Rule
   Burden of Proof
   Voir dire
   Beyond a reasonable doubt.
What did you learn about these terms and how they affect this case?

16. Do the descriptions of Lawrence Silverman convince you that he is truly crazy? Or guilty? Do you feel differently about this in different parts of the story – e.g. at the beginning, when T. C. meets with Loco in the jail, during the trail, when the court goes to the crime scene, etc.?

17. T. C.'s opening courtroom remarks frame the case he will make. How well do you think he did in accomplishing this task? Contrast T.C.'s opening remarks with Gallahan's remarks.

18. As the trial continued, did you think that T. C. was making his points effectively?

19. What effect would Gallahan's action of pulling down the bandana on Pierre Bouteron's face have had on you if you had been on the jury?

20. At one point, Pete asks T. C. why he defends Loco? What is T. C.'s answer? Had you wondered the same thing?

21. What is the fact that the jury judgment hinges on? Had you anticipated this? What would your vote have been if you had been on the jury?

22. When the trial is over, there is still about a quarter of the book remaining. Who first asks the question that carries the book forward at this point?

23. How does the author use the townspeople's reaction after the trial to comment on human behavior?

24. When do you first begin to get clues as to the real murderer? Do you think T. C. had a clue about the person in the courtroom? Who was this person?

25. In literature, there is a term "denouement" which means the unraveling or resolution of the intricacies of a play in a novel, drama,

or film. At what point in Ride the Jawbone does the denouement begin to appear?

26. The classic French definition of "Voir dire" is "to speak the truth." Does this book speak the truth to you? In what ways?

27. Many characters come and go in this book. Which characters carry the story through from beginning to end and impact upon its resolve?

28. This book weaves many topics in with the story. Did you learn any new things in the areas of ranching, law, geography, or Montana history from your reading of this book?

29. If you were T. C., would you have decided for the law office in town or for the ranch? Why do you think he decided as he did? What factors might have impacted his decision?

30. By the end of the story, did you rethink T. C.'s decision to take the case in the first part of the book?

31. What does this story say about justice?

32. What is the significance of the title, Ride the Jawbone?

Made in the USA
Las Vegas, NV
03 January 2021